To Hunt A Husband

To Hunt A Husband

Lowland Romance Book 6

Helen Susan Swift

Copyright (C) 2020 Helen Susan Swift
Layout design and Copyright (C) 2020 by Next Chapter
Published 2020 by Liaison – A Next Chapter Imprint
Edited by Elizabeth N. Love
Cover art by Cover Mint
This book is a work of fiction. Names, characters, places, and incidents are the product of the author's imagination or are used fictitiously. Any resemblance to actual events, locales, or persons, living or dead, is purely coincidental.
All rights reserved. No part of this book may be reproduced or transmitted in any form or by any means, electronic or mechanical, including photocopying, recording, or by any information storage and retrieval system, without the author's permission.

Chapter One

Midlothian, Scotland, September 1842

There is little more delightful than to rise in the early morning and watch the sun wake the world. It was my habit to do so, lifting the hem of my skirt clear of the dew-damp grass as I strode up Roman Camp Hill, or the Camp as we called it, with the laverocks sweetening the air with their calls. I loved the freedom of movement, the sense of being alone with nature, and the feel of autumn air against my face.

That morning started no differently. I rose, dressed hastily and left the house by the side door, breathing deeply of the crisp air. Winter Lodge stood on the flanks of the hill, with our grounds spread around us and the slope rising in a succession of small fields and patches of woodland. High above, stars faded in the abyss of the sky, little eyes of God watching over us. I wondered at the vastness of the cosmos and what may lie up there, stumbled over a tuft of grass and berated myself for not paying attention.

As I jammed my hat hard on my head, I heard voices floating towards me, looked up, saw two figures approaching, recognised the taller, and continued.

"Good morning, Miss Moffat," William Flockhart greeted me, while the man at his side gave a shy smile.

"Good morning, Will," I replied. We knew him as Wild Will, for he spent all of his life out of doors, either living rough on the local hills or on the tramp to see the world beyond the confines of Midlothian. Brown of face and rough of clothes, he was a local character who, rumour claimed, had never entered a building for 20 years.

"Good morning, Miss Moffat." The second man doffed his low-crowned hat as he spoke.

"Good morning," I replied. I did not know the fellow, although I had seen him in the streets of Dalkeith and among the colliers of Winterhill. He was an open-faced coal worker with steady eyes, one of my father's tenants.

As Will and his companion strode downhill, I continued my ascent of the Camp, enjoying the stretch and pull of my muscles until I reached my tree. My father had planted that horse-chestnut on the day of my birth, two-and-twenty years ago. Father had chosen the most splendid of situations, with a panoramic view that stretched from the eastern pyramid of North Berwick Law to the fertile fields of Fife across the Firth of Forth to the north and westward over the Midlothian plain to the Pentland Range. On a clear day, I could even see the distant triangle of Schiehallion, the sacred mountain of the Caledonians in far-off Perthshire. However, the day that my life altered was not clear in any way, with the sun struggling to dissipate the thin haar easing from the Forth.

The first sign that my life's ordinarily serene pattern was about to change sat astride his horse underneath my tree.

"Well met, my lady." The gentleman doffed his hat most gallantly. "I did not expect to meet anybody up here at this hour, particularly not such a handsome young lady as yourself."

"I come here most mornings, sir," I said, bobbing in a curtsey as I examined the stranger. He was handsome enough, in a rough-hewn way, with a weather-beaten face under his tall hat. His eyes held my attention as they laughed at me.

"Do you, indeed, ma'am?" he said. "You must be a local lady to make such an arduous climb."

"I don't find it arduous, sir," I said. "It is more of a pleasure than an imposition."

The man's nod was strangely unsatisfactory as he continued to survey me.

"And you, sir," I said. "You are not a local man, yet you also make the climb."

"Chetak made the climb," the man patted his horse's neck. "I merely sat astride her."

"I see." I was growing tired of this glib stranger's presence at my tree. "Did you come here merely to admire the view?"

"No, ma'am," the stranger said. "I came here to learn the lie of the land."

Well, that was honest. "You could not have come to a better viewpoint," I admitted grudgingly.

We stood in silence for a moment, watching dawn spread across Midlothian, or Edinburghshire, to give its other name. Some of the towns were already awake, with lights in Bonnyrigg, Lasswade and Penicuik, while the tiny collier communities seemed never to sleep as the men and women toiled long hours underground.

"This is a mining area," my handsome stranger said.

"Mining and farming," I found this man increasingly wearying. "With some manufacturing. Do you have business here, Sir?"

"I have business here. You must know a great deal about the place."

"I know a little," I replied, hoping he would leave soon so that I could enjoy my tree in peace. "Do you have a name, sir?" I was uncomfortable in his presence.

"I do," the man replied with a smile and a small bow from the saddle.

"In this part of the world," I said severely, "it is the custom for a gentleman to introduce himself to a lady."

"Indeed, ma'am?" My handsome man's eyebrows rose in pretended surprise.

"Indeed, sir," I countered.

"In that case, ma'am, I am Adam Carmichael." He bowed from the saddle again, with his eyes gently mocking.

"It is a pleasure to make your acquaintance, sir," I curtseyed in reply.

"In this part of the world, is it also the custom for ladies to respond with their name?" Adam Carmichael asked.

"It is," I said. "I am Robyn Moffat of Winter Lodge." I indicated our house, the roof of which could be seen as the light slowly strengthened.

"A pleasure to meet you, Miss Moffat. Or is that Mrs Moffat?"

"It is Miss Moffat," I told him.

Mr Carmichael bowed again, bending from the waist, so his face came momentarily closer to mine. "You will be Mr Thomas Moffat's daughter, I think?"

"I am," I said, slightly surprised that a stranger should know Father's name.

"Pray tell me," Mr Carmichael continued, all questions now, "as a local lady, have you noticed any unusual disturbances in the area of late?" Although the humour remained in Mr Carmichael's voice, his eyes were suddenly sharp.

"Disturbances?" I wondered at the question. "Nothing out of the ordinary."

"Even with the colliers?"

I thought before I replied. "The colliers have withdrawn their labour, but there have been no disturbances worthy of the name."

"The colliers have indeed withdrawn their labour." All the humour had vanished from Mr Carmichael's face. "Will that affect you?"

"I can't see why it should," I replied, slightly tartly. "I am not a collier."

"Do you know any such men?" Mr Carmichael was challenging in his questioning.

I decided I no longer wished to converse with Mr Carmichael. "My circle of acquaintances is hardly your concern, sir," I told him.

Mr Carmichael straightened in the saddle. "You are quite right, Miss Moffat." The humour was back, if a little less pronounced than before. "I should not have asked. And now I must leave you," he said. Only then did I see the long pistol he carried at his saddle, and I wondered what sort of man this Mr Carmichael was that he needed a gun to ride on Roman Camp Hill.

Erect in the saddle, he rode away, skirting the edges of the fields that led downhill, past Winter Lodge and onward in the direction of Stobhill and Gowkpen. I watched him for a while, wondering who he might be, then I leaned against the trunk of my tree, as was my practice. Nevertheless, my brief meeting with Adam Carmichael left me slightly unsettled, so it was with a bad grace that I returned downhill, following the trail I had made through the fields. For some reason, I could not get Mr Carmichael out of my head until I startled a lone hare that jinked across the ground at my side. I watched him for a long minute, which quite restored my good humour so I could return the gardener's greeting with a cheerful wave.

Winter Lodge was awake when I returned, with the servants all a-bustle and the aroma of breakfast greeting me when I opened the front door.

"Good morning, Robyn." Father looked up from the newspaper to greet me. "Did you enjoy your walk?"

"Not as much as usual this morning." I slid into my place at the table, helping myself to a slice of toast. "There was a strange man at my tree."

"Oh?" Father lowered his paper at once. "What sort of strange man?"

"A gentleman named Adam Carmichael who asked me about the colliers. He knew your name."

Father laid his paper aside. "Many men know my name. Perhaps you should refrain from taking your morning walk for a while, Robyn. These are troubled times, and I don't like the idea of strange men talking to you. What was he saying?"

"He asked about the colliers."

"What did he ask?"

I had seldom seen Father look so serious. "He asked me if there had been any disturbances and if I knew any colliers."

"I see." Father returned to his newspaper. "You'd do well to avoid gentlemen such as Mr Carmichael, Robyn." He spoke from behind the shelter of the printed pages. "If you insist on walking up Camp Hill, let me know, and I shall accompany you. Or one of the servants. Or perhaps Andrew Dewar or even Hugh Beaton." Lowering his paper again, Father fixed me with a steady look. "Andrew Dewar would be more respectable although I think Mr Beaton is the better man. He plays golf, and no man who plays golf can be all bad."

"Yes, Father," I agreed meekly, although I had no intention of giving up my solitary morning walks to accompany a hacking golfer. Although father had a set of clubs somewhere, I had never known him ever take them for a visit to a golf course.

"I am betrothed to Andrew Dewar," I reminded him, "not Hugh Beaton."

"Then walk with him, if the sedentary Mr Dewar decides to rise from his bed at that hour of the morning," Father replied from behind his paper.

I agreed. Andrew was notoriously lazy, so much so that I was not sure if he still liked me, or if he merely could not muster the effort to find somebody more to his taste.

"Someday Andrew Dewar will make his attachment to you official, Robyn," Father said, "so unless you find a better man before then, you can reconcile yourself with a lifetime with his peculiar practices."

I smiled, for Andrew and I had agreed to marry when we were still very young. "I told him once that I would only marry when he brought me a special ring from Paris," I said. "Although Edinburgh would do."

Father shook his head and returned to his newspaper. "There is little chance of that scoundrel venturing as far as Edinburgh unless somebody prods him with a pitchfork. You will have to settle for Dalkeith."

"I'd accept Dalkeith." I looked up as the door opened.

Mother walked into the room, half-dressed and with strands of hair hanging loose from her turban. "There you are Robyn!" She greeted me as if I had been exploring darkest Africa rather than merely walking on the hill behind Winter Lodge. "Are you seeing your young man today?"

"I rather thought I would accompany you to Dalkeith," I said. "I intended to help out at the ragged school, unless you had other plans, Mother."

"No," Father said at once. "You won't go to Dalkeith today."

"No? Why ever not?" Mother asked, vigorously towelling her hair with her turban. Lifting a knife, she looked at her reflection in the blade, sighed, and continued with her assault on her hair. "I look as if somebody's dragged me through a hedge backwards. Why shouldn't we go into Dalkeith today, Moffat?"

"There might be a disturbance," Father said.

"A disturbance?" Mother had a habit of repeating Father's words. "How strange that you should think that. What sort of disturbance?"

"Colliers," Father said.

Mother and I looked at each other in wonder. "Colliers," Mother repeated as if that answered all the questions that crowded into my head.

I nodded sagely. "Ah. That Carmichael fellow mentioned colliers."

"That is not surprising." Father did not lower his newspaper. "There is nothing wrong with your appearance, my dear, but I forbid you to go into Dalkeith today."

When Mother raised her eyebrows, I knew what she meant. I smiled in response and finished my breakfast, suddenly eager to join my mother in Dalkeith. A disturbance might break the monotony of rural life.

* * *

"Miss Moffat!" I had not expected to see Andrew that morning so looked up with a smile when he crunched across our gravel path towards me. As always, he looked supremely smart, with his low hat at a rakish angle and a look of curious disbelief on his face. "I had hoped to see you here."

"This is my home, Mr Dewar," I said, gently humorous. "I am often to be found here."

Andrew gave an uncertain smile. "I know, Miss Moffat. I meant you might be away."

I did not pursue that topic. "It is good to see you again, Mr Dewar."

"Thank you." Andrew hesitated, as if nervous, although we had known each other since childhood. "I am going to Dalkeith today."

"Oh?" When Andrew gave me no more information, I asked gently: "Why is that, pray?"

"I have something rather special to do there."

"Indeed?" I raised my eyebrows. "What sort of special is that, Mr Dewar?"

"You may learn by-and-by," Andrew told me, with what I think he hoped was a mysterious smile.

"I think I can guess," I said as my heart began to speed up, thinking of the ring I had mentioned to Father.

"You two!" Mother bustled out of the door, all orders and warmth. "How long have you known each other now?" She stood on the third top step, from where she could look down on us both.

"A long time," I said, trying not to smile at the expression on Andrew's face.

"A long time," Mother repeated, "yet you are still so formal! Call the poor boy by his Christian name at least, and you, Mr Dewar, my daughter's name is Robyn, as you know full well."

"Good morning, Andrew," I said, smiling as I dutifully obeyed Mother.

"Good morning," Andrew replied with a little bow, added "Robyn," turned away and marched down the path, kicking up so much gravel on to the lawn that our gardener would not be pleased.

"He is a strange fellow," Mother said, with a shake of her head.

I could not disagree. Andrew Dewar was a strange fellow with a unique way of doing things. I still liked him, however, although I could no longer find that extra spark that transformed liking into love.

"Come, Robyn," Mother said. "We have things to do."

Chapter Two

Dalkeith is the market town of Midlothian, a bustling place of inns, merchants and small businesses. It is a town where farmers buy and sell, innkeepers charge too-high prices for their goods, lodging houses cater for travelling shearers, curlers play their roaring game, cricketers cricket, and an annual games attracts thousands of spectators and competitors. At one time or other, all the people from the countryside will gather in Dalkeith, including the Moffat women from Winter Lodge. That late September day of 1842 Dalkeith was even busier than usual for it seemed that every collier in the world had congregated in the town.

"Your father was right," Mother said as she looked out of the window of our coach. "There are hundreds of colliers here. What in the world could have induced them to gather in such numbers?"

The colliers were indeed in large numbers. Everywhere I looked, colliers were standing in small groups, or marching purposefully this way and that, or talking in earnest knots at street corners. Although they were all dressed as respectable people, I knew they were miners by their appearance and demeanour. Muscular men with set, pale faces from working underground, many carried the blue scars of old injuries, while most wielded a walking stick. I recognised a few faces as men who worked in our pit at Winterhill, although I would be hard-pressed to put a name to them.

"Perhaps we should go home," I suggested.

"Nonsense!" Mother gave me a friendly poke in the ribs. "They're only men, and some are our tenants anyway. Come along, Robyn. We will do an hour or so teaching at the ragged school. After that, I wish to visit a shop or two, and no man alive will stop me, not your father and certainly not a group of miners."

Nothing loath, I obeyed. Although I must admit to a certain nervousness as I walked past the groups of colliers. However, none gave me so much as a second look – they were so engrossed with their own affairs. Indeed one or two lifted their hats with a polite, "Good morning, Mrs Moffat, good morning Miss Moffat," to which we responded in kind.

The ragged school was quiet that morning, with fewer children than usual, and the middle-aged teacher distracted by the crowds outside. Mother and I did our best, reading to the infants and trying to teach the basics of writing as the teacher continually turned to stare out the window.

"We'll finish early today," the teacher said at last. "I am a little concerned about the safety of the children with all these colliers in the streets."

"If I know colliers," Mother said, "they will pose no danger to little children."

"I am not so sure." The teacher had made up her mind, so we gentlewomen helpers had to comply. We ushered the pupils outside where they happily scattered among the colliers.

"More time for the shopping." Mother led me at a fast pace towards the centre of Dalkeith. As we entered the first of the milliner's shops, the colliers began to move, although I had not heard anybody give them an order.

"Where are they going?" Mother asked in a tone of wonder as if hundreds of grown men could not decide their own movements.

"Up that close," I pointed to a narrow lane that ran off the northwest side of the High Street.

"So they are," Mother said, and for some reason not unconnected with curiosity, we found ourselves walking up the same close in the wake of the colliers.

"Now they are entering that building." I pointed to the Freemasons' Hall, a building that hardly appeared 100 years old.

"Maybe they're all Freemasons," Mother said, and promptly lost interest as a length of purple linen in a window took her attention. "Now that would make a fine dress for your wedding if Andrew Dewar ever makes up his mind to ask properly."

We spent some time in the Dalkeith shops, for in truth living in Winter Lodge without distractions could be a mite tedious, and when we emerged, the town was like nothing I had ever seen before.

"Mother!" I stopped in some alarm. "Look at the army."

Opposite the closed doors of the Freemasons' Hall stood rank after rank of soldiers, with their scarlet uniforms bright in the autumn sun and their fists closed around long brown muskets. The officers stood in front, tall, erect men with long swords at their waists and the power of life and death in their command.

"Stay close, Robyn." Mother's hand gripped my arm. "We'd best be away from this place."

For one minute, I wondered if Adam Carmichael would be present to witness the disturbance, and then I heard the tramp of marching feet and dismissed him from my mind. With so much happening in Dalkeith that day, it was natural that a crowd should gather, with women and men clustering around the Freemasons' Hall, staring at the soldiers while keeping a wary eye on their muskets.

"What's happening?" The words rose to the grey skies above.

"What's to do?" a woman screeched. "Look at all the sojer-boys!"

"What the devil is the army doing here?"

Perhaps the only person who could fully answer that question was the Duke of Buccleuch, the principal local landowner, for he was a dominant figure, giving orders to the military and to the body of 20 or so special constables who also now poured into the centre of the town. In their long, blue, swallow-tail coats and glossy top hats, the specials looked quite efficient.

"Come away, Robyn." Mother's hand was firm on my arm.

"Not yet," I insisted. "I wish to see what's happening."

"It's not ladylike," Mother said, looked at me and nodded, vaguely smiling. "But I am also curious."

Squeezing into the entrance to a common close, we waited and watched. Luckily we were both fairly tall for women and, if we stood on tip-toe and stretched our necks, we could watch events over the heads of the equally curious crowd.

"I hope none of our neighbours can see us," Mother said.

"If they do," I reasoned, "then they must also be watching."

The duke, with his chamberlain, Mr Moncrieff, marched to the front door of the Freemasons' Hall to demand entrance. The buzz of the crowd eased as people waited to see what would happen, and the soldiers seemed to take a collective deep breath. I saw one of the officers, a lieutenant I believe, put an expectant hand to the hilt of his sword.

"Oh, please don't let there be any trouble," Mother said. "We should have left when we saw the army."

"It's too late now." I gestured to the crowd. "We'd never get through all those people."

The hammer of the duke's fist on the door echoed around the street. I saw one of the soldiers fidget, with his hands moving to the trigger of his musket, and then I noticed Adam Carmichael in the crowd. He was on the opposite side of the street from us, sitting on Chetak and equally interested in watching. There was no humour in his eyes, which were darkly reflective.

"Mother," I said. "There's the man I saw this morning."

Hush, Robyn." Mother's grip on my arm tightened. "Look what's happening."

After initially refusing access to the duke, the colliers inside the hall eventually opened the door. Immediately they did, the duke and his chamberlain hurried inside, followed by a rush of the blue-uniformed special constables, all seemingly eager to be first in and all carrying their long staffs of office.

Special constables have a dark reputation for violence and ill-discipline. Unlike the full-time, disciplined and trained policemen who walk the beat and deal with every-day crimes such as petty theft and drunkenness, the specials are civilians recruited for specific events such as riots or disorder. Mainly from the respectable strata of society, they are often heavy-handed in their eagerness to restore what they see as the natural order. Knowing such things, I was more than a little shocked when I saw my Andrew Dewar among the blue-coated ranks that stormed into the hall.

"Mr Dewar! Andrew!" I could not help myself. I shouted the name without thought and immediately hoped that the noise of the crowd drowned my voice. As bad luck would have it, the crowd had hushed at that moment, and my shout rang out, clear as a church bell on a sleepy Sunday, right across the centre of Dalkeith.

Happily, most people were too intent on the unfolding drama at the hall to pay much heed, but Adam Carmichael turned his head my way. Looking directly at me, he frowned, as if trying to remember where he had seen me before, lifted a hand in brief acknowledgement, and returned his attention to the hall.

"He heard you," Mother murmured.

"I know." I was torn between watching Mr Carmichael and the drama in which Andrew was playing his part.

"Andrew heard you bellowing like a fishwife." Mother was not referring to Mr Carmichael but Andrew. "Now he will wonder what sort of manners you have." She shook her head. "It's best to let men think you are eminently respectable if you wish them to marry you, Robyn. After the event, it is not so important."

"Yes, Mother." I knew the rules of the hunt. Men pursued women until the women caught them. I only wished that Andrew was more ardent in his pursuit.

While I had been thinking of personal matters, the drama before us had continued. With Andrew and the other specials at his back, Mr Moncrieff read out the names of three of the colliers and demanding they surrender themselves to the law. Not surprisingly, none of the miners stepped forward, so, after an awkward pause, the duke and his entourage left the hall and waited outside. With special constables on one side of the street, tapping their staffs in their palms, and the army standing at attention on the other, it seemed that there would indeed be trouble in Dalkeith.

Fighting my nerves, I caught Andrew's eye and smiled. Trying to look tough and capable with his colleagues, he ignored me as if I were not there, which awakened the devil within me.

"Should I go and talk to Mr Dewar?" I asked.

"No!" Mother said at once. "I think we should leave here." Despite her words, she made no effort to move. I knew that Mother liked a good drama as much as everybody else. Today's events would give her plenty of conversational material for the next few dull weeks in Winter Lodge.

Although Andrew did not glance in my direction, Adam Carmichael did far more. I could feel his eyes probing me as if wondering what on earth I was doing here. I looked up again, caught his gaze and smiled. Again he raised a hand in acknowledgement.

"That Carmichael fellow is watching me," I murmured, responding with a small nod.

"I am not surprised,"' Mother said. "And with you making such a spectacle of yourself. He must be wondering what sort of daughter your mother brought up."

I closed my mouth as the door to the hall opened, and the miners quietly emerged. The first man looked at the waiting specials, squared his shoulders, gripped his walking stick firmly and marched on, with others following behind.

"There won't be any trouble," I said, and then the specials pounced. I was surprised at the energy with which Andrew grabbed one of the miners, holding him firmly as another special snapped handcuffs on the unfortunate man's wrists.

"That was your Andrew," Mother said as if I could not see a man three yards in front of my face.

The specials arrested another of the colliers and lunged at a third. Rather than quietly submitting, this man eluded the clumsy grasp of the special, twisted away, cracked Andrew on the knuckles with his walking stick and ran. I blinked, for the escapee was the very man I had seen with Wild Will that very morning.

"Halloa! Catch that man!" Andrew raised the hue and cry.

"Stop, thief!" another Special shouted, and a dozen of the blue-uniformed men ran in pursuit of the fleeing collier.

"Come on, Robyn." Mother took hold of my arm once more. "Let's get home. We've wasted sufficient time here."

However, making our way back to the coach was not easy with what seemed like half of Midlothian either chasing the fugitive or obstructing those who were. We tried to negotiate a passage through the crowd, being buffeted by sundry people and saying, "Pray excuse me," as loudly as decorum permitted without any discernible effect.

"Oh, this is no use," Mother said. I could see that she was growing increasingly exasperated as the mob clustered around us. The cries of, "Stop thief!" "Murder!" "Help the unfortunate fellow escape!" or, "Catch that man!" resounded, with little boys running around in great glee and their mothers dealing out smacks and cuffs in frantic worry for their offspring.

"Are you all right, ladies?" Adam Carmichael reined Chetak in front of us, with that humorous gaze scanning us both. "Miss Robyn Moffat, we meet for the second time today."

"We do, sir," I even managed a curtsey amidst the chaos for Mr Carmichael's horse seemed to act as an island in the rush of people, creating a small oasis of relative peace.

"And you must be Miss Moffat's sister." My gallant Mr Carmichael bowed to Mother.

"I am nothing of the sort, sir, as you are well aware." Yet, despite Mother's hot words, her hand moved to straighten her hat, and I could see she was quite taken by Mr Carmichael. "I am Mrs Thomas Moffat, Robyn's mother."

"A good day to you, Mrs Moffat." Mr Carmichael lifted his hat. "If you stay close, ladies, Chetak and I will push through the crowd." Mr Carmichael said. "Where are you heading, Mrs Moffat?" He diplomatically addressed Mother rather than me.

"The White Hart Inn," Mother said. "We have left our carriage in the stable there."

"The very place I am going," Mr Carmichael said, touching his hat. "Pray, follow, ladies."

Glad of the escort, we obeyed, walking meekly behind the horse as Mr Carmichael created a channel through the roaring crowd. When one group of drunken carters tried to bar his passage, Mr Carmichael leaned sideways from his saddle and slashed the most impudent across the shoulders with his crop. 'Move aside there!'

"That's the stuff!" Mother cried in full approval.

I said nothing, wondering what level of steel lay beneath Mr Carmichael's jovial exterior.

The carter turned around, eyed Mr Carmichael, decided not to protest and moved aside for us. Mr Carmichael pushed on through the crowd.

"Here we are," Mr Carmichael guided us to the White Hart Inn. He stopped outside, dismounted with an effortless grace and lifted his hat first to mother and then to me. "I shall wait until you are safely away."

"Thank you, Mr Carmichael, but there is no need," Mother said. "We know the road from here."

"In that case," Mr Carmichael said, "I shall be on my way. I wish you both a pleasant trip home."

"Thank you, sir." Mother glanced at me. "I wish you a successful conclusion to your business, whatever it may be. You will have to visit us sometime in Winter Lodge, to allow me the opportunity to repay your kindness. I'm sure that Robyn would also be pleased to see you."

I nodded, although I was not so certain if I would be pleased or not. There was something vaguely unsettling about Mr Carmichael, some tension beneath the urbane exterior.

Waiting until Mr Carmichael walked his horse away, Mother smiled. "So that was your Mr Carmichael, was it?"

"He is not *my* Mr Carmichael, Mother."

"No, of course not." Mother's smile was so superior that I knew she was planning something. "He should certainly be *somebody's* Mr Carmichael."

Our driver was in the taproom of the White Hart, quaffing whisky and quite forgetting about his passengers until Mother reminded him of his position and sent him off with a flea in his ear.

"You have five minutes, George, to bring the coach to the front of the hotel."

"I thought you'd be another hour, Mrs Moffat, with all this confusion."

"We do not employ you to think, George, but to drive the carriage and do as you are told. Five minutes and not a second more."

It was only four minutes before George drove the coach to the front of the inn. Giving him a nod of approval, Mother boarded first, with me following. Hauling aside the curtains, I peered out of the window.

"Don't stare, Robyn," Mother said. "Simply tie open the curtains and sit back in your seat, as I do." She gave me a wink. "That way, you can look outside without anybody seeing your face."

"Yes, Mother." Settling back in the worn leather seat, I looked outside in time to see Mr Carmichael still there, sitting on Chetak and watching our coach emerge from the courtyard. I am unsure whether he saw me, despite my precautions, but when he lifted his hand in farewell, I was sure he gazed directly into the coach, with deep seriousness shading his mocking eyes.

* * *

I lay in bed that night, knowing that my life had changed, although I did not quite know how, or why. My mind whirled with images of Mr Carmichael beside my tree, Andrew in his smart blue uniform and the scarlet ranks of soldiers waiting outside the Freemasons' Hall, together with the face of that unfortunate collier as he fled from the police. Remembering that Andrew had mentioned he was going to Dalkeith for something special, I sighed. Rather than searching for a ring to seal our engagement, he had become a Special constable.

I sighed again. Unable to rest, I rose from the bed and paced my room until the creak of floorboards woke half the house.

"Get to sleep, Robyn," Father shouted. "You'll be tired and out of temper in the morning."

Knowing I could not sleep, I pulled on a pair of boots, slipped my winter greatcoat over my nightclothes, jammed a hat over my unruly hair and left the house. I did not intend to go far, merely to walk around the grounds until I eased the confusion inside my head. I was fortunate that the moon was nearly full, casting a friendly light over our smooth lawns with the splashing fountain, and casting shadows from the avenue of beech trees that lined our drive.

I paced up and down, soothing my mind as I tried to put order into the chaos within my head. I was so intent on my thoughts I barely heard the whistling owls or the barking of the deer from the woods a hundred yards to the east. Who was this Mr Carmichael, and what did I now feel for Andrew? I did not know. Mr Carmichael appeared the most courteous of gentlemen, yet he carried a long pistol at his saddle and had not hesitated to use force to part the crowd. I was not sure if he fascinated or repelled me.

As for Andrew? I continued to pace. Andrew and I had a long-standing arrangement that we would marry, with no date fixed. We were young when we made the pact, and my youthful ardour had cooled. Now I was unsure how I viewed him, or if I wished to spend the remainder of my life with a man I did not love, although I certainly did not dislike him. There were other men out there, Hugh Beaton for instance, or Derek Pringle.

With a breeze blowing clouds across the sky, the moonlight was fitful, sending shifting shadows over the ground. One moment there was darkness, the next light, so I was unsure if I had seen movement or not in the flicker of light at the head of the beech avenue. I watched, hoping for a deer or badger, for I do love to see the wild animals of the countryside. Instead, I saw the figure of a man darting across our lawn 100 yards in front of me.

"Oh!" I covered my mouth to stall my instinctive shout. My first thought had been to challenge the intruder, but I realised that action might be foolish. In the present disturbed state of the country, this fellow could be anybody, from a solitary poacher to a cracksman from Edinburgh looking to break into Winter Lodge. On the other hand, it might only be one of the servants returning home after some romantic liaison. I smiled at the latter thought, for the whole household knew that young James, the groom, was making sheep's eyes at one of the maids in Dalhousie Castle, a few miles down the road.

I stood still, prepared to run back to the house if need be and equally ready to say nothing if my nocturnal visitor was on some innocent pursuit. A stray poacher after a rabbit for the family pot did not concern me and, as for James, the best of luck to him, I say. We all need love in our lives, and that thought brought me back to my dilemma with Andrew.

What on earth induced him to join the Specials? I had never heard him express any interest in anything political. Indeed, I had never heard him express any interest in anything before, except maybe fishing. Andrew did not possess the most active of minds.

My thoughts were interrupted again by movement ahead of me. The man must have been lying prone in a patch of darkness and moved when the moonlight betrayed his position. This time I saw him distinctly as he shifted, bent double, across our lawn. I knew his face, if not his name, for he was the same fellow I had seen with Wild Will that very morning, and the same fellow the police had chased through the streets of Dalkeith.

At the same moment I recognised him, he also saw me. I had never seen such an expression of surprise cross a man's face as then.

"You," I hissed, pointing to him.

"Miss Moffat!" He whispered my name, placing a finger across his lips to compel me to silence. "Please! It is you I have come to see."

"Me? The police want you," I said, but not so loudly that my voice carried.

"It's all right," the man said, "I won't hurt you."

"What are you doing here?" I had the sense to keep my voice down.

"I need your help," the man said. "If the police find me, they'll throw me in jail."

Glancing back at the house, I saw it was still in darkness. "What have you done?" I was not sure if I should shout for help or allow this man to gang his ain gate, as we say. That means go his own way.

"I've done nothing harmful," he said, which was probably the answer any murderer or thief gave when first questioned about their activities.

Now, if he had been an ugly old man with warts and a bald head, I would probably have shouted, or run for help, for it is well known that the signs of depravity are visible on the physiognomy of any criminal. However, this man was, if not quite handsome, at least not unpleasing as to his countenance, and was about the same age as me or perhaps a few years older.

"If you've done nothing harmful," I said, "why do the police wish to arrest you?" I thought that rather a pertinent question, given the circumstances of this fellow roaming around our lawn at one in the morning.

The man began to look agitated, glancing at our house and behind him, as if he expected a score of policemen to erupt from our shrubbery. "People say I've done wrong," he said. "I'd be obliged if you did not tell anybody you've seen me."

"I won't if you are innocent," I said, rather enjoying the drama of the situation, and now feeling quite secure with this vulnerable and rather handsome young man.

"I am innocent of all crime. I swear it."

"I believe you," I said, nodding to add emphasis to my words. "Do you have a name?"

"I'm Matthew Juner," the man said, after a little hesitation that made me wonder if he was telling the truth. He looked up as a shift of wind uncovered the moon once more and light glossed across the lawn, so we stood as exposed as if it were full day. He was tall for a collier, too, which was in his favour. "Please, I must hide."

"Come with me," I said, making a sudden decision to help this unhappy man, although I could not say why. "I know the very place."

I led him off the lawn on to one of the narrow paths through the shrubbery, brushing past father's rhododendron bushes and down a steep, barely-marked track. "Where are you taking me, Miss Moffat?" Matthew asked.

"I grew up here," I said. "I know every nook, corner and secret spot. I'll take you to a place where I used to hide when we played childhood games. Nobody ever found me there." I favoured Matthew with a smile that was lost when a cloud concealed the moon. "It was my special place."

We slithered down the path, with the steep incline compelling us to use our hands as well as our feet. At the foot of the path, a gale of a decade ago had blasted down an ancient oak, which effectively blocked the path.

"You see?" I said, "Anybody would think that the road ends here."

Matthew nodded. "It looks like it."

I smiled, quite comfortable in this man's presence. "Follow me." Even in the dark, I could find my way through the small tunnel of branches that coiled around the oak to the near-overgrown path on the far side.

"Here we are," I said, smiling. "Nobody has come here in years."

"Thank you." Matthew touched my arm, which was very forward of him, I thought. "I can't thank you enough."

Even with September drawing to its close, the shrubbery at this corner of our policies was dense. After the mist of the previous day, it was also damp, so both Matthew and I were horribly wet before we reached our destination. It was an old folly, built by some long-dead ancestor a century or more ago, but still in a sound condition. Situated on the lip of a steep slope toward a small burn, the Winter Burn, the folly had a single arched door and three pointed windows, facing east, west and north respectively.

"You see?" I said proudly. "You are safe as houses here and can spy on anybody approaching."

"Thank you," Matthew sounded genuinely grateful. "Will told me you would help. He said you were always willing to support people in need."

"Did he indeed?" I said, resolving to have words with Master Will in the not-too-distant-future. I hesitated, unsure what I should do.

"I won't be here long," Matthew said. "I'll be off in the morning."

"All right then," I said. "I'll leave you alone now," and for some reason, I added, "Good luck, Matthew."

"Thank you." Matthew gave a shy smile. "There is one more thing," he said. "I don't like to ask."

"Ask," I said. "I don't like secrets."

"There may be a man looking for me," Matthew said.

"A policeman," I guessed.

"No. A essenger-at-rms."

I was familiar with the term but admitted I was unsure what a messenger-at-arms did.

"Have you heard of Sheriff Officers?"

"Servants of the court," I said. "They evict people on the orders of the sheriff."

"They do that and more than that," Matthew said. "Well, messengers-at-arms are officers of the Court of Session, which means they serve legal documents and enforce court orders across Scotland. They can arrest anybody, anywhere, at any time."

"Oh," I said. "Why is this messenger-at-arms looking for you?"

"There is a High Court order to arrest me."

Why?" I wondered if Matthew was a romantic highwayman or perhaps a murderer, this man who told me he had done nothing harmful.

"For encouraging the colliers to form a combination."

That was neither romantic nor exciting. "That's not illegal," I said.

"No, but the authorities frown upon it," Matthew gave a twisted smile. "They can alter facts to make me seem guilty of things I have not done."

I frowned, for we were a very respectable family, without any prejudice against the law.

"If I see a messenger-at-arms, I will tell you," I said, after a moment's thought. How will I recognise him?"

Matthew looked around his new abode. "I expect he will be a stranger to the area. He will be armed, probably with a gun, and will possess an air of authority and a hard jaw."

"I'll watch out for him," I promised.

I left Matthew at the folly, hurrying back home before anybody realised I was missing. Mother was awake, of course, and peered at the wet hem of the nightdress that peeped out from under my coat.

"Where in heaven's name have you been, miss?"

"I could not sleep," I said, "so I went for a walk."

"At this hour of night? Lord have mercy on us, girl! You'll catch your death! And you don't know what sort of people are out after dark. There could be sorners out there or gypsies."

"There haven't been any sorners this past 30 years or more," I said, truthfully, I think, for although bands of sorners, vagabonds who took over houses to steal and cause all sorts of trouble, had once been prevalent throughout Scotland, the breed seemed to have died out before I was born.

"There could be other people." Mother looked thoughtful as if she suspected I had been on an illicit assignation with a strange man.

"I doubt they'll come to Winter Lodge," I said.

"I certainly hope not," Mother closed the door firmly behind me. "I've never heard the like. You don't know what sort of gaun-aboot folk wander the night-time fields."

Mother's words were proven correct the following morning when there was a loud knock at the front door.

Sims, our butler, answered. I heard the conversation from my room, the door of which happened to be ajar just when I was conveniently sitting behind it.

"Is your master present?" The voice was educated but imperious.

That must be the messenger-at-arms, I thought.

"Do you have a card, sir?" Trust Sims to put an arrogant caller in his place.

"I do not. Pray tell your master that Inspector List of the County Police desires to speak to him."

"I shall tell him, sir. If you could kindly wait in the hall, I will see if Mr Moffat wishes to speak to you."

Sims always left unwanted guests standing in the hall, while the more welcome he ushered into the drawing-room. He had his own way of cutting the arrogant down to size without appearing anything except respectful.

A police inspector! I felt my heart begin to hammer twenty to the dozen. Thank goodness it was not the messenger-at-arms, but had the police found out about my encounter with Matthew already?

Chapter Three

Dressing hurriedly, I took a deep breath to control my nerves and tried to look unconcerned as I sauntered down the stairs to the breakfast-room, or rather the room in which we took breakfast, for we used the same place for all our meals.

"Did I hear the door?" I asked in my most innocent of voices.

"You did, Miss Moffat," Sims said. "A person from the police wished to speak to your father." Sims kept his expression neutral.

"Oh?" I tried to appear uninterested. "Probably something to do with poachers."

"I do not know," Sims said. "I am not privy to Mr Moffat's private conversations."

Like all the best servants, Sim could issue a rebuke with a straight face and an appearance of civility. Honestly, sometimes I wondered who ran our house, the family or the servants. I sighed. "Is the police person still with Father?"

"He is, Miss Moffat," Sims said. "You may be able to hear their conversation from the library." He paused for a significant moment. "I believe that is where you normally listen."

Refusing to rise to Sim's words, I merely nodded, grabbed a slice of toast from the plate on the breakfast table, and walked back upstairs as quickly as dignity allowed. In Winter Lodge, we had two small rooms on the upper floor of the east wing. In one room, Father had his study, with a splendid view over our policies toward the Pentland Hills and, right beside it, with an adjoining door, was a room we laughingly called the library. It was around half the size as Father's study, but shelves of books filled two walls, with a window occupying much of the third and a desk squeezed against the fourth. The desk had to squeeze, for it shared the wall with an inset door that led to Father's private domain.

Still munching my toast, I sneaked into the library, to see Mother already there. She hastily grabbed a book and looked up with an expression of innocence on her face. "Why, Robyn," Mother whispered. "I did not expect to see you here at this hour."

"No," I said. "What a coincidence that we should both decide to look for a book at the same time." I glanced at the volume Mother held. "I didn't know you were interested in European politics, Mother."

Mother smiled. "It's one of Mr Moffat's books. I wished to learn more about a subject that interests him." She raised her eyebrows, "and what brings you here, dropping crumbs from your toast all over the floor? Poor Agnes has to clean that, you know."

"What brings me here?" I cast a quick eye across the shelves. "Oh, I just wanted to hear what Father and the policeman were saying."

"Well, shoosh then, Robyn, and we can both hear." Ending any pretence at reading, Mother put down Father's intensely tedious book. Moving as close to the connecting door as we could, we strained to hear the conversation in the study.

"A fugitive, you say?" Father's voice was firm.

"That's what we believe, sir." Inspector List was not as authoritarian with Father as he had been with Sims. "He was reported as coming into the policies of your house."

"God damn it, man," Father did not sound pleased at all. "When was this?"

"Shortly after midnight, sir." List said firmly.

"Shortly after midnight," Father repeated. "Who was around to see such a thing in our policies shortly after midnight?"

I did not hear the inspector's somewhat mumbled reply, only Father's scornful snort. "I see. A poacher is hardly a reliable witness, Inspector. Our family has been in this area for centuries, List, and we have always been the most respectable of people. I assure you that we are not hiding any fugitives from justice on my lands or in my house. I would soon know, by God."

I tried to hide the sudden rush of colour to my face when Father said that. Instead, I bit into what remained of my toast, sending a stream of crumbs over Mother's arm as she leaned on my shoulder.

List mumbled something again, making me wonder why some men don't speak louder when I am trying to eavesdrop.

"I can do that." Father, at least, had the good grace to speak out like a man. "I will get it organised today, although I assure you there is no need. I know my own grounds."

Mother and I tried to hear List's mumble again, both of us leaning against the wooden panels of the door so I was surprised that it did not burst open and send us tumbling into the study. The thought of Father's face if we suddenly fell upon him made me giggle, which caused Mother to give me a dirty look and such a sharp dig in the ribs with her elbow that I nearly coughed.

"Hush!" Mother said, and I hushed.

"Thank you, sir," the inspector said, quite distinctly, "I will send you some men to help you search." A few seconds later, I heard the study door open and close.

Mother put two fingers across my lips in case I should giggle again, or perhaps burst into song or shout out hallelujah. Only when she judged it safe did she release me. "What was all that about?" she whispered.

"Blessed if I know," I said. "I think the policeman said something about a fugitive in the grounds."

"That's what I thought he said," Mother agreed. "I wonder why it's so important that a police inspector came to see Mr Moffat. It can't be only a poacher, surely."

"Oh, it'll be something and nothing," I did not mention my early morning visitor. Matthew Juner would be my secret.

We both started when the library door jerked open, and Father burst through. "I expect you both heard all that?"

We tried to adopt looks of innocence.

"That was Inspector List of the County Police, as you know." Our pretence did not fool Father in the slightest. "There is a fugitive on the run, and the police believe he's in our grounds. I want you both to keep inside while the male servants and I search for this man."

"Yes, Moffat," Mother said.

"Although I know well that neither of you will do as I tell you." There was a glint of humour in Father's eye. "So if you must go outside, keep together, don't stray far from the house and if you see a stranger, return indoors immediately."

"Who is the fugitive, Moffat?" Mother asked. "Is it another poacher?" She gave me a hard look. "Or one of these sorners that our Robyn does not believe exist."

"Neither," Father said. "You will both be aware of the colliers' meeting in Dalkeith yesterday. As you both went to Dalkeith, against my wishes, you'll know there was some trouble."

"Yes, Moffat." Mother gave her most bland smile.

"Well, the police wished to arrest three of the colliers. They captured two, and the other escaped. Inspector List informed me that he is a very desperate man, one of the organisers of their foolish combinations and an instigator of violence. The Duke of Buccleuch wants to interrogate him in person."

I thought of Matthew Juner with his open face. "Does he have a name, this desperate fellow?"

"Matthew Juner," Father said. "He's one of our tenants, God help us, from the pit at Winterhill."

"Oh," I said. To explain, although our family had settled in Midlothian around the time of the Creation, we were only small landowners, with about 100 acres. However, Midlothian is both prime farming country with fertile land, and high-quality seams of coal relatively near the surface. It was the practice to sink mines to exploit the coal and abandon them when they were no longer profitable. Small, often squalid settlements of miners' cottages sprang up around the pit-heads, and Winterhill was one such hamlet, only quarter of a mile or so from our home.

"What is the trouble about?" I had not paid much attention to such matters in the past.

"Money,'" Father said curtly. "The colliers want more wages than the mine owners can afford to pay."

"The colliers' strike affects most of the country." Mother was more detailed. "Miners' wages have been falling with the price of coal, and although your father is the most benevolent of landlords and charges the minimum of rents, the colliers still want more wages."

I thought of the village of Winterhill, with the poor-looking women, ragged children and exhausted men. "We are not poor," I said. "Can we not help these people?"

Father's look was as cold as I had ever seen. "Business is about supply and demand," he said. "Unless the price of coal increases, I'll not make sufficient money to keep us in a stable financial condition."

"But, Father..."

"There can be no buts,'" Father said. "At present, we are managing to remain on an even keel. If I paid more, then our accounts would slip into deficit, and I'd have to sell some land, or close the pit completely and put all the colliers out of work." He paused for a moment. "The alternative would be for your mother and you having to live without your little luxuries."

I opened my mouth to say something, saw Father's look and closed it again. I was venturing into areas beyond my knowledge. "Can I help search the grounds, Father?"

"Certainly not!"

I knew by the way he reacted that the thought of his family in possible danger from a fugitive collier stretched Father's nerves.

"We'll stay indoors, Moffat." Mother touched my shoulder. "Come on, Robyn, and let the men do their work."

Once more in the breakfast room, I surveyed the table with its array of foodstuffs, thought of the poverty of the people of Winterhill, thought of poor Matthew hiding in my draughty folly and hoped nobody would discover him. Standing at the window, as was my wont, I watched as Father marshalled the male servants outside the house, giving them orders and directions in a clear voice that left no doubt as to his intentions.

"I did not tell your father you were wandering outside last night," Mother said. "I think it best it remains like that or he will worry."

I nodded. "Yes, Mother."

"I know you will not venture out at night again until it is safe." Mother said.

I nodded again, wordless.

"Come, Robyn," Mother tried to divert my attention. "You can help me with my charity work. I am hoping to travel to Fisherrow in Musselburgh soon, to help the poor fisherfolk."

At that moment, I had no interest in fisherfolk, poor or otherwise, so gave Mother a short answer that did nothing to ease the tension within the household.

"Charity work is the Lord's work, Robyn," Mother replied mildly. "It is our duty, and should be our pleasure, to aid those less fortunate than ourselves."

"Yes, Mother," I said, watching the movement outside our window as a couple of our neighbours arrived to help, which was of far more interest to me.

"There is Derek Pringle." Mother was at my side, sipping a cup of tea that Agnes, our newest maid, had brought. "He is a handsome man now, Robyn, and free of any attachment."

I agreed, Mr Pringle was indeed handsome. A few years older than I, he had an excellent mansion near Dalkeith. Although the property was officially Beaumont House, everybody thought that name rather pretentious and called it the Pringle place, which seemed to annoy Mr Pringle.

"And there is Hugh Beaton." Mother replaced her cup in its saucer. "He is the younger son, I believe, and is making his career in law."

"So I hear," I said. I had known these men all my life, but now I was growing older, I viewed them through different eyes. Mr Beaton was taller than most men, slender and, I thought, slightly diffident. I could not regard him as husband material, so allowed my attention to drift away.

"You must decide soon, Robyn," Mother said. "Will it be Andrew Dewar or some other man?"

"I am not yet sure," I said, watching Mr Beaton listen to Father's instructions. He was slightly stooped, I noticed, unlike the very straight Mr Pringle.

The steady crunch of feet on gravel announced the arrival of List's promised police reinforcements, and my heart gave a lurch when I saw Andrew in the forefront, stiff in his brave blue uniform and carrying his staff in his right hand. I knew one of the other specials to be a small farmer, while the remaining two were shopkeepers from Dalkeith. I viewed Andrew again, allowing my eyes to slide from his highly polished boots to the tall hat perched on his head.

"He looks splendid in his uniform." Mother sipped at her tea again.

"He does," I allowed. "It quite suits him."

"And you have had an agreement for many years."

"We have," I said. "Mother, I think you will be content to see me married off to any man, just so long as I am married."

"I am merely trying to help, Robyn," Mother told me, severely.

Father did not look overjoyed to see the Specials.

"We don't need you," Father said, "but now you're here you may as well make yourselves useful."

"Yes, Mr Moffat." Andrew drew himself erect, with earnest duty evident in every line of him.

"And for God's sake don't get all military on me." Father was in a tetchy mood this morning.

"No, Mr Moffat." Andrew remained as he was.

"He is trying his best, poor lamb." Mother glanced at me. "You cannot fault him for that."

Father was less impressed. "Go and make yourself useful." He addressed Andrew and the three Specials who stood with him. "Go and search the stable block for this unfortunate man." He shook his head. "You'd think he tried to assassinate the queen rather than just organising a stoppage of work."

I felt an immediate surge of affection for Father after hearing his words. I watched Andrew lead the Specials away at a brisk trot, snapping at them to march in step as if they were soldiers on their way to fight Bonaparte rather than civilians in ill-fitting police uniforms.

"Come away from the window," Mother said when the Specials disappeared into the stables, presumably to question the horses. "You're blocking the light."

"I want to help," I said.

"Aye, there's no show without Punch." Mother shook her head. "What would you do if this Juner fellow jumped out from behind a bush?"

"Punch him on the nose," I said, "or invite him in for breakfast. Mother, he'll be trying to hide, not trying to attack anybody. Besides, I think I know him. He's that serious-faced man from Winterhill."

"You know him?"

"I believe I have seen him with Wild Will," I said, carefully.

"Oh." Mother's eyes narrowed. She knew Wild Will as well as I did, and I am sure she guessed I was only giving half the story. "I know a few families of that surname, but I can't think of a Matthew Juner."

"You'll know him if you see him," I said. "I can't believe he is dangerous." I looked out of the window again, watching Andrew leave the stables, having found nothing. One of his men trailed straw from the bottom of his trousers.

Mother smiled. "I see," she said. "You're still watching Andrew Dewar."

"He's still out there," I said.

Mother laughed. "That's my girl. Why don't you go and say good morning to him? Don't stray far from the house."

"He's busy," I said.

"He won't be too busy to say good morning to you." Mother gave me a gentle push towards the door. "Or if he is, he's not the man I hope him to be. Go on, be off with you."

Happy to get outside, I slipped out of the side door, lifted the hem of my skirt and hurried over to Andrew. I had thought he would have been preoccupied with his duty, but Mother was right. He stopped immediately he saw me.

"Halloa Robyn," he said, twirling his long baton. "I hoped I'd see you here."

"Did you?" I asked, for Andrew was not lavish in his words of affection.

"You're the only reason I volunteered for this job." His smile took me by surprise. He did look attractive when he smiled.

"You look very smart in your uniform." I told him the truth. I stood back to admire this man I had known all my life. "Whatever possessed you to join the Specials?"

Andrew hesitated before replying. "I thought it my duty, what with these miners causing trouble all over the country."

"I haven't heard of them causing any trouble here," I said.

"You were in Dalkeith yesterday," Andrew said. "You saw the riot."

"I saw the police chasing two or three colliers," I said, "and a curious crowd running to see what was happening."

"The worst of the colliers escaped," Andrew said. "He's a dangerous man, and we're searching for him now."

"Ah," I tried to look suitably impressed.

"You'd better return inside the house." Andrew hefted his baton, looking big, brave and bold, or so he imagined. "I'll make sure it's safe out here."

"Thank you, Andrew," I dropped in a curtsey, wondering if Andrew realised I was mocking him.

"That's all right," Andrew said. Preening himself, he stalked away, shouting orders to his companions.

I returned inside the house, asking myself if I still even liked him and how I had got entangled with such a man. But what were the alternatives? I once again considered all the eligible bachelors in the area. Some were so far above me on the social scale they would never entertain a woman of my rank. Others were from too different a way of life, however worthy they might be as people. That left a bare dozen men of roughly my age and station in life. Of that number, six were already spoken for, although they had not yet walked up the altar.

I listed the six who remained. Three were the sons of respectable tenant farmers. They were decent, solid men, marriage material, as my Mother charmingly put it, but I had no desire to spend my life listening to tales of fertilisers and drainage schemes, with the Dalkeith market my social highlight. That left three whom I might consider.

There was Hugh Beaton, the younger son of Beaton of Marchar Bridge or Derek Pringle of Beaumont House who was older than me by three years, a fine horseman and the heir, it was said, to a fortune of some unspecified magnitude. He might do. And then there was Andrew Dewar, who was at this minute trying to disentangle himself from the bramble bush into which he had led his men. All three were in our grounds at present.

"Poor Andrew," Mother said. "He tries so hard."

"He does," I agreed, as my worries for Matthew returned. "I think I'd better go and guide him through the policies before he falls in the ha-ha or drowns in the burn or something."

Mother winced as Andrew unravelled a long bramble tendril from high around his thigh, flinching as the thorns stuck in a tender spot. "I think you had better do so, Robyn. Stay close to Mr Dewar in case the unruly collier lad comes."

"If he's a friend of Wild Will he won't harm me," I said, running out of the door before Mother changed her mind.

"Andrew!"

Still hefting his staff, Andrew turned to face me. "You'd be safer indoors."

"And you'd be safer with a guide," I told him. "I know these grounds better than anybody else. I'll come with you if you promise to stay close in case that collier fellow attacks me." I smiled. "I know I'll be safe with you and your brave men to protect me."

I swear Andrew grew an inch higher when I said that. Honestly, some men are so susceptible to flattery that one can wrap them around one's little finger.

"Where did Father order you to search?" I asked.

"Over by the west side," Andrew said.

I nodded. That was where the folly stood, the Winter Burn ran, and Matthew lay hidden, no doubt alarmed by all this activity in the grounds. "Come this way, then," I said, as cheerfully as I knew how.

Grabbing hold of Andrew's sleeve, I pulled him away from another patch of brambles and on to the path. "We can walk this way," I said. "Nobody in his right mind would jump into a thorn bush."

The other Specials nodded their agreement. I could see they were already regretting their decision to hunt down the fugitive.

"Follow me, gentlemen," I said.

I led them a merry dance around the policies, taking care to avoid the area where the folly was situated. I chose the most winding paths, stopped at the most unlikely places and had them poke their staffs into dark corners and prod the pools of the Winter Burn in case poor Matthew had hidden under the water. Twice we came within yards of the folly, but because of its situation and screen of coniferous woodland, not even my keen policemen could see it. I took them as far as the fallen oak to prove the path was impassable and suggested we climb over the top.

"What's over there?" Andrew asked.

"The slope to the Winter Burn," I said, adding helpfully "It's a bit steep but not too far to fall."

"Nobody will be so foolish as to hide there," one of the other men said.

"No," I said, at last, pitching my voice so that Matthew could hear it. "There is nobody in this part of the grounds. You can tell Father than he is safe in his abode."

Dishevelled from the places where I had brought them, the Specials were glad to hear my words. Refraining from their pointless poking at the undergrowth and trampling over Father's precious plants, they turned towards the house.

Andrew stepped to my side, so close we were almost touching. "Thank you for your help," he said quietly. "I'd have got lost among all these trees."

"I'm sure you would have been fine." I much preferred this quiet Andrew to the bragging one. There was still potential in this man.

Mother must have been watching for she appeared at the front door. "Cook has hot soup ready, boys!"

"You officers go ahead," Andrew ordered. "See what Mrs Moffat's cook has ready for you."

We slowed down to allow the other Specials time to draw ahead.

"I hardly see you now," Andrew said, turning away from the house.

"You're such a busy man," I replied, "with your business interests and now joining the Special police as well."

"Even so," Andrew replied as he brushed loose leaves from his uniform, "we should see each other more often."

We slowed further when we reached a secluded part of the grounds, where Father's prize collection of imported trees soared skyward. "After all," Andrew said, "we are betrothed."

"We are," I agreed, although I was again lukewarm over the prospect of spending the remainder of my life with a man who lacked the sense to avoid a patch of brambles. Honestly, my emotions were as erratic as a March hare, leaping around inside me.

"We should agree on a date," Andrew said. "You're not getting any younger."

I looked at him. "No," I said, "and you're nearly in your dotage now. You must be 25 at least."

"I am 24," Andrew said severely. "I was thinking of you. It's not so important for a man."

"Oh?" The expression in my face should have warned Andrew off, but he blundered into a patch of verbal and emotional brambles, and after a nearly promising start, too. "What were you thinking about me?"

"I was thinking of your age," said my incredibly stupid fiancé.

"My age?" I stopped underneath the branches of a very expensive North American pine that my father had imported. For a man who expressed money worries, he had no qualms about spending vast sums on his botanical hobby. "What about my age?"

"Children." Andrew plunged deeper into the thicket. "You are already in your prime child-bearing age, so we'll have to marry quickly if I am to have heirs."

"Oh, I see." I did not slap him, although the temptation was strong, and who could have blamed me if I did? "I'm getting too old for you."

"Not yet," Andrew made a clumsy attempt to withdraw. "But you must want children."

"Must I?" I asked, as innocent as Eve's serpent.

"Yes, and your mother only managed one."

"She only managed one, did she?" I repeated Andrew's words.

"A good one." Andrew's hasty amendment did not help his cause one little bit.

"Is having heirs your reason for marrying?" I kept my voice as level as I could, although the temptation to scream at him was almost overwhelming.

"No, of course not." Andrew sounded genuinely surprised. "It will also merge our landholdings and make us a stronger family."

"Oh." I said nothing else as I walked on, long-striding, towards the house, leaving Andrew standing outside, looking bemused, I nearly pushed past Mother on my way to my bedroom.

"Robyn!" Mother called after me.

Ignoring her in my anger, I slammed shut the door and kicked the end of the bed, hurting my toe. Taking a deep breath, I walked up and down for a few moments until I calmed my nerves.

So then, I said to myself, staring out of the window, *Andrew wishes to marry me to get heirs and expand his family lands. He does not want me for my sake*. Oh, I was very aware of the pragmatism of his reasoning, but I would have liked some sort of show of affection. Love might have been too much to expect, perhaps, but a declaration of liking would have helped. I lifted my chin. Although I had few options, I did not wish to spend my life in a loveless marriage. Andrew had helped me make that decision with his heartless, soulless, careless words.

A flock of sparrows passed, chattering to each other like schoolboys let loose for the holidays. I watched them, suddenly nostalgic for my departed childhood. Once, when I was young, a plump robin had been a regular visitor at my window. I had always liked robins, and not only because they shared my name. I had fed that little bird until one day it decided not to return. I always thought it had taken a bit of my happiness with it. One day, I thought, my robin would return and bring happy days with it. One day, but not today.

Still staring out the window, I saw Father approach the newly-fed Specials with a shotgun under his arm and a pair of dogs at his feet. Easing open the window, I heard Father speak.

"You may go now, Dewar." Father sounded more curt than usual. "Thank you for your help."

Touching a hand to his tall hat, Andrew led his men away. I watched, wondering if he would look up at my window. He did not.

"Gather the servants." Father looked quite comfortable and entirely in control as he stood at the head of the steps leading to our front door. One by one and in small groups, the servants and tenants collected at the foot of the steps. Derek Pringle and Hugh Beaton strolled up, talking to each other like the old friends they were.

"Thank you, men," Father said. "I am now quite satisfied that Matthew Juner, the runaway collier, is not hiding in my lands."

The men looked at one another, nodding their agreement.

"All those tenants who wish, may repair to Somerville's Public House and ask the landlady to give them a quart of beer, on my account. All those servants who wish may repair to the kitchen, where Cook will provide the same, or a bowl of soup. Mr Pringle and Mr Beaton, you have my gratitude and you are welcome to join me in a morning glass of claret."

As the men cheered this munificence, Father returned inside. I continued to stare out the window at a future that contained nothing but darkness.

"Robyn!" Mother opened the door without her customary knock. "Hugh Beaton and Derek Pringle are in the drawing-room with your father."

Still thinking of Andrew's words, I am sure I only goggled at her, not comprehending her meaning.

"Go down there, Robyn." Mother gave me a less-than-gentle push. "Let them see you. Talk to them." Bending her face close to mine, Mother spoke quietly. "It's a serious matter, to hunt for a husband. You can't rely on Andrew Dewar, and you can't allow any opportunity to slip past."

Father looked up when I entered the drawing-room. "I saw you with Mr Dewar," he said.

"I was guiding him through the paths," I said. "Mother suggested I should."

"Stay away from danger." Father looked genuinely concerned.

"Yes, Father," I said.

The other two men watched without comment. I wondered which of the two was the more handsome.

"I'm sure you were of great assistance to Dewar. Hugh Beaton topped Mr Pringle by half a head, even with his pronounced stoop.

"I tried to be," I said.

Derek Pringle was undoubtedly the more athletic, with a determined chin and whiskers he had trimmed to points along his upper jaw. He looked at me with a smile. "Are you still taking your morning walks, Miss Moffat?"

"I am, Mr Pringle," I said.

"Good," Mr Pringle nodded his approval. "Women should endeavour to keep fit as much as men do. Outdoor exercise is a worthy pursuit for all, don't you think, Beaton?"

Poor Mr Beaton looked startled to be asked a question when a woman was present. Much more slender than Mr Pringle, he was also pale, showing the results of many hours of indoor study to pursue his career in the law. "I wish I could do so," he said.

"Are you a practising solicitor now?" Father asked the question.

"I have become an advocate." Mr Beaton spoke with his head down, as if ashamed of his achievement.

"Congratulations," I said. "Your family must be very proud of you."

Mr Beaton coloured. "I don't know," he said. "I would hope so."

"Well," I said. "I would be proud if you were my brother or any other relation." Let him take what he liked out of that, I thought.

"Oh." Mr Beaton glanced at me and away, while Mr Pringle turned away to pour himself a second drink.

"It's an impressive accomplishment," I said.

"Thank you, Miss Moffat." Mr Beaton favoured me with a quick bow. "Please excuse me." Placing his untouched drink on the cabinet, he left the room with more haste than dignity.

"Beaton is a little shy." Mr Pringle spoke over the rim of his glass. "Especially with women." He took another drink. "More especially with attractive young women."

I curtseyed to acknowledge the compliment, thinking that Mr Pringle was more amiable than Mr Beaton, if a little forward.

"I, however, am not shy," Mr Pringle said. "I have no need, you see."

"I see," I said.

Mr Pringle gave a little bow. "Especially not with attractive young women."

"I see," I said again.

"Such as yourself," Mr Pringle's gaze did not leave my face as he took another sip of his claret.

I curtseyed, wondering if I was also shy, as I was very uncomfortable with Mr Pringle's compliment. "Pray, excuse me." I said, thinking of one of Mother's sayings. "A boaster and a liar are near kin," Mother often said, and I rather thought that Mr Pringle was a bit of a boaster.

I could feel Mr Pringle's gaze following me as I withdrew from the drawing-room. Of one thing, I was certain – any man I married would not be as shy of me as Hugh Beaton, nor as arrogant as Derek Pringle. Unless I had no other choice. The man I would marry must care about others as well as himself – a man like Matthew Juner. At that moment, I was unsure if I even wanted a husband, I was so confused about men.

Chapter Four

"Matthew," I whispered the name into the dark. "Matthew, it's me."

"Miss Moffat?"

"That's right." Emerging from the shelter of a tree, I scurried to the folly. "I've brought you some food."

Matthew sat in the farthest corner of the draughty building. Huddled beneath one of the windows with his knees drawn up to his chest and his arms wrapped around his shins, he looked very vulnerable. "Thank you." When he stood up, I could see he was shivering with the cold. His eyes seemed too large in a face thin with lack of nourishment.

Glancing behind me, I unwrapped the bundle I had brought. "Look," I said. "Bread and cheese, with a portion of a pie Cook made. It's not much but better than nothing." I saw Matthew reach forward hungrily before he remembered his manners and thanked me again.

"There are some candles and a tinder box to make a spark," I said, "and a small flask of whisky." I was sure Father would not miss the whisky, which I suspected had been illicitly distilled in some secluded glen in the Pentland Hills.

"Thank you." Matthew's face twitched into a bleak smile. "I don't drink."

"Nonsense. It will help keep the cold out." I knew that all colliers liked their whisky – that was a generally accepted fact.

Matthew smiled again without touching the flask. I could see that he was shivering.

"You are cold, aren't you?" I could feel the chill spreading from him, like ripples in a pond when one dropped a stone. "Here," slipping off my greatcoat, I wrapped it around his shoulders. It was too small, naturally, for miners tend to have highly developed torsos, if weak legs.

"Thank you," Matthew pulled it close. "You are a kind lady."

"I am only doing what any Christian would do," I said.

When Matthew looked up at my words, his eyes were grey and remarkably clear. "You are doing more than that," he said. "Wild Will told me you were the best of ladies, and he was correct."

"I am sure William exaggerated," I said.

"I am sure he did not," Matthew said. "If anything, he understated the truth."

I frowned slightly, for I was not used to one of Father's tenants contradicting me, and only then did I wonder at Matthew's choice of words. "Understated?" I said.

"Yes."

I had not expected a miner to know such a word. If it was an accepted fact that they all drank too much, it was also generally believed that they were uneducated, illiterate men, little above the level of beasts. "How long do you expect to be here? The authorities are searching for you."

"I know," Matthew said. "I saw you misdirect the specials. That is another reason I have to be grateful to you."

Misdirect? This man had an extensive vocabulary.

"You have no reason to be grateful." I kept my tone cool. "As I said, it's only Christian charity."

"If you say so, Miss Moffat," Matthew gave a little bow. "To answer your question, I shall be away from your father's lands shortly."

"Where will you go?" I had a sudden desire to learn more about this articulate collier with the steady eyes. Fine eyes too, I decided, with a straightforward gaze and not a hint of the shiftiness that some men possessed.

Matthew hesitated. "I'd rather not say, Miss Moffat."

"Come now," I said, sounding more like a schoolteacher with a reluctant pupil than a 22-year-old woman talking to a recalcitrant tenant and fugitive. "You can trust me."

"I don't doubt that," Matthew said at once. "But it might be best for you not to know."

"Oh?" Naturally, that information only inflamed my curiosity. Sitting on the floor of the folly in a most unladylike manner, I smiled at Matthew. "Pray tell me more, Matthew Juner."

He shook his head, with a small smile playing at the side of his lips. "I would not wish to place you in danger, Miss Moffat."

I sighed. "You are the most obstinate of men, Mr Juner."

"If so, Miss Moffat, it is not from any feeling of ill-will towards you. Rather the reverse, I promise you."

I smiled, although with the cold from the ground already penetrating my rather thin night-dress, I wished I had not succumbed to the dramatic gesture of sitting down. "I shall not move until you do tell, Mr Juner, and then you will have the responsibility of my death through cold on your conscience."

"I would not wish that," Matthew removed my coat from his shoulders and replaced it where it belonged, although it was my nether parts that most needed covering at that moment. I wondered how Matthew would react if I told him that, stifled my smile at the thought and was shocked at myself.

"You must tell me, then," I said.

"It seems that I must." Matthew did not hide his smile as his beautiful eyes scrutinised me. "I am meeting a man very soon," he said, "and we are travelling to Edinburgh."

"Ah," I said. "I will say nothing. You have my word." Although I was quite comfortable in Matthew's company, I would be glad to see him leave, for I was concerned about working behind Father's back.

"I desire no more than that," Matthew said.

Somehow I felt that those six words contained more genuine praise than an entire paean to Apollo or any other Greek deity.

"I'll escort you back to the Big House," Matthew said.

"There is no need," I said. "I know the way."

All the same, I did not object when Matthew walked a few steps in front of me until we reached the lawn. The moon cast clear light to our front door, showing the rest of the house to be in darkness.

"I'll watch until you're safely home," Matthew gave another small smile. "There are some dangerous blackguards around, you see, colliers and the like."

"So I've heard," I said. Slipping off my coat, I replaced it on Matthew's shoulders. "Keep warm." I ran across the lawn to the door. On an impulse, I turned at the top of the stairs. Matthew stood where I had left him, holding my coat and with his face white in the moonlight. For some reason I could not fathom, I lifted my hand in farewell, smiled at his answering wave and entered the house.

After 22 humdrum years, my life had entered a period of intrigue and adventure. I nearly hugged myself as I slid into bed. Would my good friend Amy

Peacock not be beside herself with envy if she only knew the half of it? I must tell her and watch her face turn green.

Chapter Five

Amy leaned forward on her chair. "You met a mysterious man?" I swear if she had opened her eyes any wider, they would have popped from their sockets and rolled around the floor, which would not have pleased the unfortunate maid whose task it was to clean the room.

"I did," I said.

"Who was he?" Amy reached out and tapped my knee. "You can tell me your innermost confidences, Robyn. After all, I am your most particular friend."

Oh yes, I thought, *I can tell you my innermost confidences if I wish all of Midlothian to hear everything.* I smiled, knowing Amy would add sufficient additional salacious detail to write an entire volume that would make a marine blush scarlet from his toenails to his eyebrows.

"He told me his name was Adam Carmichael," I said, fully aware that the intelligence would reach Andrew as quickly as Amy could run, "and he is the most charming of gentlemen." *That should make you take notice of me, Andrew Dewar.*

"Adam Carmichael," Amy repeated, "what a romantic name." Amy would have used that phrase if the name had been John Smith or Ebenezer Zachariah. Truth mattered less to her than the drama she could create with her words.

"He is a most romantic man," I tried to mirror Amy's rounded eyes. "Most romantic."

"Where did you meet him?" Amy tapped my leg again in a manner just a little too familiar for my taste.

"On Roman Camp Hill," I said. "And again in Dalkeith."

"You met him twice?" Amy said. "You know the old saying that if you meet the same man three times near, wedding bells you soon will hear."

"No, I don't know that saying." I was sure that Amy made that little ditty up. "He saved my life the second time." I could elaborate any story as well as Amy could.

"No!" This time I was sure that Amy was genuinely surprised. "What happened?"

"Did you hear about the riot in Dalkeith?"

"These colliers?" Amy asked.

"That was the one. Mother and I were caught up in it with soldiers and policemen and colliers battling and fighting all over the town. We did not know where to run until Adam, I mean Mr Carmichael, appeared on his great white horse and rescued us."

"You called him Adam," Amy said.

"A slip of the tongue."

"You called him Adam," Amy repeated. "That means you already think of him by his Christian name." She smiled slyly. "You're a dark horse, Robyn Moffat, pretending innocence and piety and all the time you have men queueing up to propose to you."

I took a deep breath, hoping that Amy would mistake the resulting flush of blood to my face for embarrassment. "I have nothing of the kind."

"You have." Amy sounded delighted at having discovered my supposed secret. She leaned forward once more. "Don't you worry, Robyn. I won't tell a soul. I'll carry your secret to the grave before I divulge it to a single person."

I released my breath as circumspectly as I could. "Thank you, Amy," I said. "I know I can rely on your discretion. Now I think it is time for some refreshments." I did not wish to bother a maid, so I poured us both a glass of claret.

"How condescending you are," Amy sipped at her glass. "Tell me all about Adam, I mean Mr Carmichael."

So I did, of course. I told Amy precisely what I wished Andrew to know. I mentioned his gentlemanly appearance, his grace, charm and elegance, as well as the steel I had witnessed behind the polite urbanity. Amy lapped up every word, with her eyes shining at the pictures I drew in her mind.

"Your Mr Carmichael sounds every inch the gentleman," Amy said.

"Every inch," I said.

"Shall you see him again?" Amy asked the pertinent question.

"Perhaps." I teased her with a shrug.

"What do you mean, perhaps?"

"I mean, I do not know." I said. "I have no immediate plans to meet him again, but if he should arrive in my life, I will not turn a cold shoulder."

"I should think not, indeed," Amy said.

"Could I beg a favour of you?" I lowered my voice and poured more of father's claret into Amy's glass by way of a bribe.

"Anything," Amy nearly whispered.

"Could I prevail upon you to keep an eye out for Mr Carmichael?"

"With all my heart," Amy said.

"Thank you," I said. "And remember, not a word to anybody."

"Not a word," Amy said.

So that was how Andrew learned all about Adam Carmichael. Sometimes women have to be circuitous to reach a destination that is right in front of us.

Chapter Six

"I swear somebody's been at my kitchen," Cook complained.

"What do you mean?" Mother looked up from the table around which we sat.

"Stealing," Cook said. "I have lost bread, meal, bacon," she spread her arms wide. "Somebody has stolen them."

"Stolen them?" Mother repeated.

"I know what is in my kitchen," Cook said. "I know what I use and what I should have."

"Who would do such a thing?" Mother looked at me in genuine shock. "Surely not one of the servants."

I saw Agnes stiffen. She dropped her tray with an almighty clatter that seemed to echo around the room.

"You clumsy idiot!" Cook rounded on her right away. "Now look what you've done! You've made a right mess and broken one of Mrs Moffat's cups!"

"I never meant to!" Agnes, the maid, was new to our employ and a bit nervous. "Please don't send me away!"

"Send you away? For dropping a cup? What a ridiculous notion," Mother was on her hands and knees, helping Agnes clear up the mess. I joined in, of course, while Cook, far too dignified for such work, watched. We were a bizarre household, some thought, but it's what we were.

"Careful now, Agnes," Mother said. "Don't cut yourself."

"No, Mrs Moffat, I won't, Mrs Moffat," Agnes said. "I never stole anything."

"I didn't think you did for even one instant," Mother said. "Come now, and get about your business."

With the mess cleaned up and Agnes away, sniffing, I decided to join in the conversation.

"I don't think any of our servants would steal from us." I tried not to appear guilty.

"Nor do I," Mother said at once. "No; are you sure you checked thoroughly, Cook?"

"I am sure, Mrs Moffat." Cook looked hurt that Mother could doubt her efficiency.

"In that case, somebody must have sneaked into the house," Mother made the only logical decision.

"I'll ensure the doors and windows are securely locked." Father had listened to the conversation. "Maybe that collier, Juner, is prowling around, after all."

Mother tapped her fingers on the table. "Maybe he is, and maybe he's not. If somebody is stealing food, they must be hungry, or their family must be hungry. I think we should leave one window open, and have some bread, cheese and a small sack of meal available in a locked room."

"You mean we should tempt them in and catch them?" Father spoke without leaving the sanctuary of his newspaper.

"I mean I won't see anybody go hungry as long as we have food to spare," Mother said.

Father gave her a long, hard look. "You will be encouraging theft, Mrs Moffat."

"Theft is when people take things without permission," Mother said. "I will leave a note: 'For anybody who is hungry and needs food'."

"You'll have every beggar, tramp and blackguard in the area flocking to our house." Father said. "I won't permit it."

Mother smiled. "You could no more have children go hungry than you could dance on the moon, Moffat."

Father looked at Mother, then at me. "We can try it for a few days if it amuses you. If we are inundated with blackguards, I will call that man of Robyn's to lock them up."

"Which one of Robyn's men?" Mother asked sweetly. "There are so many. Why, only yesterday Mr Hugh Beaton and Mr Derek Pringle both approached her."

"I mean her betrothed, Dewar, as you know full well." Father liked to appear as a hard, ruthless landowner and businessman, but we knew he had a heart of rose petals.

"Ah," Mother said. "Thank you, Cook. Please leave aside some spare items of food, and I'll arrange a place to leave it."

"Yes, ma'am." Cook called Mother "ma'am" only when she disapproved of her words.

"That will be all," Mother said, and Cook bustled away.

Sitting at my place at the table, I tried to still the hammer of my heart. Helping people could lead to unforeseen consequences. I had stolen the food for Matthew without thinking that little Agnes might get the blame.

Mother looked out the window. "Here comes one of your men now, Robyn – Andrew Dewar, by the manner in which he sits his horse. You'd better go and receive him."

"Yes, Mother," I said. Although I was not looking forward to speaking to Andrew again, I would not shirk the meeting either.

* * *

"Robyn," Andrew spoke even before he dismounted at our front door. "What's this I have been hearing about you?"

"I'm sure I don't know what you've been hearing," I said, truthfully enough.

"Something about another man," Andrew was in his civilian clothes, with a tall hat perched on his head and a ridiculously bright check to his inexpressibles. Why do men wear such extravagant clothing, yet criticise women's dress?

"Andrew," I said patiently, "I speak with many men. Indeed, this very day, I shall no doubt, talk to a few."

"Who?" Andrew dismounted with what he might have considered a flourish, landing with a pronounced thump that must have rattled his teeth.

I explained that Mother and I were about to embark on a tour of our more elderly tenants. Mother liked to check on their well-being, handing out small parcels of food and warm clothing as a buffer against the oncoming winter. Although Father had set his cap against the striking miners, Mother decided that Christian charity was more important than politics and continued with her efforts. I always came along, for I was on Mother's side in this domestic disagreement.

"So as you see, I have met many men," I said, truthfully, "indeed, as I said, Mother and I will meet a few this very day."

"I don't mean your charity work with tenants," Andrew snapped, quite forcibly for him. "I mean you spoke to a gentleman!"

"Oh, a gentleman," I said. "And are they so very different?"

"You and I are betrothed," Andrew said.

"There is no need to remind me," I kept my voice gentle, surprised that Mother remained silent as she stepped up beside me.

"You have no right to speak to another man."

"Will you try to dictate who my friends are?" My anger was genuine. I felt, rather than saw, Mother looking at me.

"I will be your husband," Andrew said.

"That may be true." I put significant emphasis on the second word. "But I am not yet your wife and never will be your servant."

"I will be the master of the house," Andrew said.

"That may also be true," I said, "but I will not be a housemaid for you or anybody else."

I watched Andrew's mouth work as he thought what to say next. Saving him the trouble, I took hold of Mother's arm. "Come, Mother; we have work to do."

"You cannot walk away from me," Andrew shouted after me.

I said no more as I nearly force-marched Mother to the coach house, where George was crouching beside the front nearside wheel.

"Is the coach ready?" I asked.

"Yes, Miss Moffat," George sounded doubtful. "This wheel is a little loose."

"You can tighten it when we return," I said, "or drive to the wheelwright in Dalkeith while we are in Winterhill. Take us away, please."

George looked up in some surprise for I was not usually so forthright. "Yes, Miss Moffat," he said, looking at Mother for confirmation.

"Take us to Winterhill," Mother said quietly. "We will walk around the village while you ensure the wheel is safe."

"Hurry," I said, for I had no desire to speak further to Andrew. Already I felt myself shaking after my outburst.

With Charlie the horse between the traces and the coach door closed, we had lurched into motion before Mother began her inevitable interrogation.

"Are you and Andrew having a disagreement?"

"Yes, Mother," I said. "Andrew wants an heir and extensive lands rather than a marriage of love and devotion."

"I see." Mother was quiet for about 30 seconds, which was a long time for her. "What do you want in a marriage, Robyn?"

I opened my mouth, only to shut it again. What did I want? I was not sure. I stared out of the window as the coach rumbled from our drive on to the Winterhill road.

"It's a hard question, isn't it?" Mother's voice was surprisingly gentle. "We are not brought up to know what we want, are we? Girls are brought up to know only what is expected of us."

I looked at Mother, seeing the woman behind the matriarch for the first time. "What did you want when you married, Mother?"

"I wanted your father," Mother gave a small smile. "I didn't know anything else. I was happy to be a wife."

I dared the next question as the coach lurched over a hole in the road, making me fear for the insecure front wheel. "Are you happy as a wife?"

Mother's smile faded. "Your father is a good man. I don't agree with all he does or all he says, but he tries his best for us all, within his own limitations. You would do a lot worse than marrying a man in his image."

"You avoided the question."

"I am as happy as I could be."

I was silent after that until Mother asked her question again. "What do you want out of marriage?"

"You are forcing me to think," I said.

Leaning across to me, with her feet rustling in the straw on the floor and her eyes more intense than I had ever known them, Mother gripped my arm hard. "Then think, Robyn. Marriage is the most important decision of your life. Don't just drift into it, or accept the first man to come along. Make sure you pick a man who is right for you. I was fortunate with your father. Many women are not fortunate at all."

"There is little choice of men in this area." I could feel Mother's fingers pressing on my arm.

"It may be better to be a spinster than suffer from an unpleasant husband," Mother said. "Do you have any other men in mind? Derek Pringle, say?"

"There is Derek Pringle," I said, "and Hugh Beaton."

"Mr Pringle is a fine, handsome fellow with a good seat."

"Mother!" I was unsure whether to be shocked or pleased.

"A good seat on a horse," Mother corrected with a smile. "Although he also has a good seat. Don't look aghast, Robyn. Such things are important when you choose a man – you will have to live with him for many years, in bed and out of it. He is also wealthy, I believe, which is also important. Ten thousand a year, I heard."

I nodded. "I am not interested in money."

"You should be," Mother said seriously. "You would not enjoy poverty. You also know Hugh Beaton."

"He is shy of women," I said. "He ran away when I attempted a conversation."

"That may not be a bad thing," Mother said. "If he is shy of women, you need have no fear of his faithfulness."

I nodded. "Conversations around the breakfast table might be difficult," I said.

"You can do the talking," Mother said. "Prattle nonsense as I do. It is what men expect of us but we can guide them with golden nuggets among the dross. Is there anybody else?"

I shrugged and said, without thought: "Perhaps one other."

"Mr Carmichael, I would guess." Mother said at once. She leaned back in her seat, smugly satisfied that she had discovered my supposed secret.

Rather than admit my interest in Matthew Juner, I nodded. "Mr Carmichael could be an interesting man."

"I suspect he has inclinations towards you," Mother grabbed the leather strap within the door of the coach. "Hold on, Robyn; there is a jolt coming."

"I am not sure if I even like the man," I said and gasped as we swung around a corner as a sharp angle.

"Careful, George!" Mother shouted. "You'll tip us over next!"

"Sorry ma'am," George said. "This road is getting worse."

"So is George's driving," Mother said, softly. "Now, Robyn, think what you want in a man. When you know, tell me, and we can discuss this further." She leaned back again, smiling. "Now you are casting your net wider, be sure you know what type of fish you wish to catch."

I nodded. "Thank you. I wish I knew."

"Most women don't even think." Mother said seriously. "Allow your heart to guide you, but use your head as well. A gypsy may seem romantic, but can you adapt to the way he lives his life?"

"Winterhill," George shouted as the coach juddered to a halt.

When George opened the door and pulled out the step, we left the coach, gasping as a blast of cold air hit us. As always, I felt a sense of shame when I saw the conditions in which the colliers lived. It made me appreciate the luxuries of Winter Lodge.

As the name suggests, the village sat on the side of Roman Camp Hill, with the extensive views all around the only positive thing that could be said about it. With no sanitation, the houses were ramshackle, little more than shacks that hugged the ground. Damp was widespread throughout the miserable dwellings, while the interiors were most often shells with only a few sticks of furniture. Or sometimes less if the tenant had a fondness for the bottle. Only that year, an Act of Parliament had banned women and children from working underground, but women who had toiled in the pits since the age of five made poor wives and mothers. The results were slovenly homes and wild children.

Mother had resolved to do what she could to alleviate the situation, with my help of course, and her subtle hints led Father to pay higher wages than the average and help when accidents created widows and orphans.

I looked up as a skein of geese flew high overhead, dragging winter on the tips of their wings. I always loved to see the geese, although they often heralded cold weather.

"Come on, Robyn," Mother knocked on the first door. "This is Mrs Flucker."

The woman looked about 80 as she lay on the bundle of damp straw and rags that comprised her only bed.

"What do you want?" She did not rise as we entered.

"We've come to help you." Mother said brightly.

"I don't need your help," Mrs Flucker said. "Get out of my house."

"We've brought you some soup." Mother produced one of the canisters she carried.

"Get out!" Mrs Flucker repeated.

"We can leave it here," Mother said.

"Get out!"

We left Mrs Flucker's house. "As you see, although the colliers are poor, they are also proud." Mother smiled at the expression on my face. "Don't get upset, Robyn. We can't expect people to fall down with gratitude at getting a few crumbs from our table."

When I looked around the mean little houses clustered on the hillside, I desperately wanted to help the colliers.

"This house next," Mother took me to a cottage a few doors further along. "This is Mrs Juner."

The woman looked up as we entered. "Good morning," her voice was cracked with hardship.

"How are you, Mrs Juner?" Mother asked. "This is my daughter, Robyn."

Mrs Juner looked at me through wise grey eyes. "Good afternoon, Robyn."

"Good afternoon, Mrs Juner," I gave a brief curtsey, already aware that this woman was connected to Matthew Juner – the eyes gave it away. I could not ask with Mother present.

"We've come to make sure you are all right." Mother was all business as she bustled around the room. Unlike Mrs Flucker's house, Mrs Juner's was clean and tidy, with her floor swept and a clean linen cloth covering the deal table. There was even a small collection of books sitting on a shelf. Being a lover of books, I had to read the titles. Where I had expected popular novels, I was surprised to find volumes of theology, history and philosophy.

"You read books?" Mrs Juner had watched my movements.

"I do," I said.

"Our Robyn's always got her nose in a book," Mother said.

"So had my son Matthew," Mrs Juner's words confirmed my suspicions. "You'll know of him."

"I've heard the name," Mother said, as I looked around the house in which my fugitive collier had lived, trying to find out something about the man who had entered my life. "The police are searching for him."

"I know." Mrs Juner said.

"You keep a spotless house," Mother changed the uncomfortable subject. "How are you for food?"

"I'll survive," Mrs Juner said. "We pull together in Winterhill. The men look after the old folk."

"They can't if they're idle," Mother said.

"There are rabbits in the fields and fish in the Esk," Mrs Juner mentioned the possibility of poaching as casually as if she were talking about breathing.

"It must be hard for you with Mr Juner not working," I joined the conversation.

"It is hard even when the men are in work," Mrs Juner said. "Mr Juner, my man, died two years ago, underground. Now my son Matthew looks after me." She paused for a moment. "And everybody else he can."

"Is Matthew a good man?" Mother asked.

"He is a very good man." Mrs Juner seemed to be studying me, weighing me up. I wondered if Matthew had told her about me.

Pretending only the most casual interest, I tried to find out more about Matthew Juner. "I heard that the court had sent a messenger-at-arms in pursuit of him."

"Aye, I heard that as well." Mrs Juner struggled to sit up. "Fetch my stick, will you, Robyn? It's over by the wall."

When I brought it, Mrs Juner swung herself off the bed on which she had been lying. Only then did I see she had only one leg.

"Mrs Juner lost her leg in a pit accident." Mother had seen the direction of my eyes.

"I can't work any longer, Robyn," Mrs Juner said. "Your father paid for the doctor to amputate my leg. My son keeps me, or he did, until…"

"Until?" I prompted, sitting on the three-legged cutty stool, which was nearly the only other item of furniture in the room.

"Until he tried to help too many people and the mine-owners turned against him."

"I don't understand," I said. "Why would the mine-owners turn against your son because he tried to help people?"

Mrs Juner stood, balancing on one leg. "There is help and help, Robyn. Your mother helps people one by one. My Matthew tried to help all the miners and their families by forming a combination."

Since I first met Matthew, I had studied such organisations and knew they were a union of workers who banded together to ask for higher wages or some such. "What was the combination for?"

Leaning on her stick, Mrs Juner limped across the room and threw open the door. "Come here, Robyn."

I glanced at Mother, who gave a brief nod.

"Look at Winterhill."

I looked, not quite comprehending. It was the same collection of ramshackle cottages I had seen a few moments before and had seen a hundred times in my life.

"Down there is Mrs Flucker. She lost her man to the black spit, one of her sons to firedamp and her daughter when a piece of stone crushed her. Beside her are the Conningtons – man, wife and two daughters all work in the pit or on the surface. Then there are the Hoods. Three children under eight all working underground until this year. Now they are idle, earning nothing and the family goes hungry. Need I go on?"

"Why did they send the children to work and not to school?" I asked.

"To help pay the rent and keep them out of trouble."

"The school would keep them out of trouble," I said.

"Aye, if you can afford to pay the skelp-doup. Earning enough to eat is more important to most folk than learning to read and cypher, skills that are no good in the pits. Education is difficult for most." Mrs Juner gave a small smile. "Although in my opinion, and to quote the old saying, better unborn than untaught."

I began to get a better understanding of the lives of my father's tenants. "I'll speak to Father," I said.

Mrs Juner touched my shoulder. "Your mother has tried that, Robyn. Your father pays better than most, but his hands are tied, as well. No single mine owner can alter things. It will have to be done by all of them, which is why the colliers are creating combinations."

"So Mr Matthew Juner is trying to help everybody," I said.

"He is, but the majority of mine owners don't wish to pay higher wages and improve conditions, so they say combinations are hurtful to trade and the smooth running of the mines."

"They are not unlawful." I showed a little too much of my reading. "They have been legal for upwards of 20 years."

"That's correct." Mrs Juner seemed to approve of my knowledge, although Mother threw me a very queer look.

"Mrs Juner," I nodded to her bookshelf. "If there is no education, why do you have books?"

"I said education was difficult, not impossible. My father taught me, and I taught Matthew as best I could." When Mrs Juner looked at me through these intelligent grey eyes, I could sense her determination.

"I am sure he is a good man," I said.

"You know he is," Mrs Juner said, too softly for Mother to hear.

"What?" I looked up. Mrs Juner smiled and hobbled back inside her home. "And now, don't you ladies have other people to visit?"

Mother touched my shoulder as we left the cottage. "That was Mrs Juner. She is the best of women."

"I didn't know that collier women could be so articulate," I said.

"Mrs Juner is one of a kind," Mother said. "She may be a harbinger of a different future for the colliers. Her and her son."

I looked at Mother, wondering how much she knew.

"Right then, Robyn, on to the next."

By the time we left Winterhill, my mind was racing. I was now torn between two desires. One was to help alleviate the poverty of the colliers, and the other was to find myself a good man for a husband. Although Andrew remained my fiancé, the candle of love I had once lit for him had dimmed to only the faintest spark, while other men had edged into prominence. There was Derek Pringle, the bumptious sporting heir to a fortune. There was Hugh Beaton, tall, diffident and rising in the legal profession, and there was Matthew Juner, intelligent, concerned for others but from a different social background.

I pondered my choice as we returned in the carriage, and I continued to ponder as I paced the floor of my bedroom later that day. When I stepped downstairs to eat, there was a letter waiting for me. I glanced at my name on the front of the sealed packet.

"Who's that from?" Mother peered at the letter over my shoulder.

"Amy Peacock," I said. "Not one of my many followers, Mother."

As I expected, Mother immediately lost interest and drifted away, allowing me to open my letter in peace. Where I had hoped for juicy gossip about our mutual acquaintances, Amy had only scribbled a short note suggesting that we both attend the next hunt meeting. I replied in the affirmative, for one should never neglect one's social circle, particularly Amy Peacock as she had the most vicious tongue, and I had no desire to be the object of her vituperation.

* * *

I had quite a bundle for Matthew Juner that night when I slipped out of the side door. Although the moon was no longer full, it still carried sufficient light to make my passage through the policies clearer. An owl called to its mate, the sound reassuring, and I heard the faint rustle of a deer away to my left.

"Mr Juner!" I whispered. "Are you there?"

When there was no reply, I stepped forward, wondering if he had already left for whatever adventures he had in mind. I smelled the wood smoke at precisely the same time as I saw the flames winking through the autumn-desolate trees. "Mr Juner?"

Wondering what had happened, I stepped forward more cautiously. The folly was empty with the moon casting shifting shadows, elongating the pointed windows and creating monsters out of friendly trees. The fire was lower down, beside the rush of the Winter Burn.

"Mr Juner?"

I heard a splashing sound and moved closer, sliding down the muddy banking, wondering what Mother would say if she saw her darling daughter now. When I neared the burn, I stopped, grasping the trunk of an elder tree for support.

The fire was small, and smoky because of the damp twigs piled on top. After a single glance, I ignored it and paid more attention to the array of men's clothing that decorated the bushes on the far side, in the direction of the prevailing wind and away from the smoke it carried. The splashing caught my attention.

I turned around, to see Matthew emerging from the Trout Pool. It had been many years since there had been trout in that pool, but we retained the name in case they should miraculously return. Now, sheltered by the ragged elder tree, I watched Matthew. He must have been washing in the cold water of the burn for he was stark naked.

One cannot live in a house like Winter Lodge, complete with servants, without glimpsing the occasional bare body. It is part of life – one either averts one's eyes or pretends not to notice. Yet this was the first time I had ever had the time, or the inclination, to stand and look. I was quite aware how immoral my behaviour was but remained behind my tree.

Matthew's upper body was superbly muscled, wiry, rather than bulky, and embellished with the blue scars of old injuries. Wasp-waisted, he had slender hips, while his legs were not as sturdy as his upper torso, but there was certainly no reason for shame. Unable to prevent myself, I looked at Matthew's other parts. There was nothing to be ashamed of there, either, despite the cold water of the burn.

Matthew turned away, sparing my blushes until I realised I was staring at the curves of his rump as he walked towards his clothes. I had to take a deep breath to still the sudden increase in my heartbeat. What was happening to me? I was Robyn Moffat of Winter Lodge, and this man was a collier, a man hunted by the law. I was admiring, undoubtedly appreciating the naked body of a wanted fugitive. Yet, even knowing that, I was not ashamed of myself, allowing my eyes to roam where they would.

I only wished I could tell Amy of my experience, for that hussy would go green with envy. I closed my eyes, said a word I learned from the servants and opened them again for a final look.

Moving quietly so as not to alert Matthew, I withdrew a step or two, watching as Matthew dressed. It is a privilege to watch without being seen, to witness a man who does not know one is there. Matthew must have washed all his clothes, for he tested each item for dampness before sliding it on. Only when he was fully dressed did I move even further back and make my presence known.

"Matthew Juner! Mr Juner! Are you there?"

I heard a rustle from the fireside and smiled, imagining Matthew's confusion.

"Mr Juner! Are you there?" I stood within the folly as though as I had just arrived.

"Miss Moffat." Matthew looked pleased to see me. "I'm sorry, I've no razor." He touched his face, where three days' stubble proved his words.

"It doesn't matter." I wondered what Matthew would say if he knew what else I had seen. "If I had thought, I would have brought a razor." I hesitated for a moment. "I found a book for you. I know you like to read."

"Thank you." When Matthew smiled, he looked younger. I wondered if he had many opportunities for smiling, living the life he did. I had heard of the wild parties that colliers had at certain times of the year and tried to imagine Matthew roaring drunk among his colleagues.

"Would you like me to bring you something to drink next time? Our cellars hold bottles of Father's claret."

Matthew shook his head. "Don't you turn into a thief for me,' he said. "You are already doing too much."

I hesitated. "I spoke to your mother yesterday. She told me what you are trying to do."

"She would do that." Matthew said. "I wish there was some way I could pay you back."

"You already have," I said, remembering the glorious view I had of Matthew emerging from the trout pool.

"I don't understand," Matthew frowned. "I have not done anything for you."

"I mean, you are trying to help other people."

"Not very successfully, I fear." Matthew's frown cleared at once. I could not help but meet his gaze, with those wonderfully clear grey eyes. I think that eyes and mouths define a man. The eyes are said to be mirrors of the soul, while a man's life creates his mouth. Matthew's eyes were the brightest and most steady I had ever seen, as if he had summed up the meaning of life and understood how to help his comrades. His mouth, however, told of the hardships he had endured. Although Matthew could not have been much older than I was, his mouth was compressed, with a firm line that told of great determination.

"Are you all right, Miss Moffat?" Matthew asked gently.

I realised that I had been staring into his eyes for some time. "Yes, yes, of course. I do apologise, Mr Juner. That was unforgivably impolite of me."

"You are a very amiable lady," Matthew said. "I hope you are not taking risks on my behalf. I would not wish you to get into trouble."

"I won't get into trouble," I said. "I am glad to help."

Matthew's bow was awkward as if he had little opportunity to practise a skill he had only read about in books. "I wish there were more women like you."

"I wish there were more men like you," I countered, unsure what to say. Although I was reasonably comfortable with men in my own social circle, I had little experience with colliers. After all, they were my father's tenants, not men with whom I could normally converse. I was only beginning to realise that social class was only a front and the hearts and souls of people were far more important than their economic background or whether they held their knives and forks correctly.

"The world makes us who we could be." Matthew motioned me to sit within the folly. "But some of us have the ability to make ourselves what we should be." He eyed me.

"I think you have that ability, Miss Moffat."

I was not sure what he meant. "Robyn," I said. "My name is Robyn."

"Robyn," Matthew gave a small nod of acknowledgement. "I am Matthew."

We smiled at each other across the width of the folly, with moonshine creating an ethereal glow around us. Although it was deep autumn, I did not feel cold – it was as though Mathew's personality was sufficient warmth.

"What do you plan to do now?" I asked.

"Continue the struggle," Matthew said.

"Even although the authorities have sent a messenger-at-arms after you?"

"Even so," Matthew said. "I cannot let my personal position interfere with my work."

"I see." I wondered how long I could shelter Matthew for, and how Mother would react if I brought him into the house. Although Mother had a soft heart for waifs, strays and the afflicted, I could not see her welcoming a fugitive into Winter Lodge.

"Here's Matthew Juner," I would say. "The man for whom I am developing feelings."

Was I? Was I developing feelings of genuine affection for this collier?

I took a sudden deep breath, knowing that I was. As I looked at Matthew across the bare stones of the folly, I had an impulse to lean over and kiss that hard mouth. I wondered what he would do, how he would react.

Oh, dear Lord, I must not think such things, especially not after seeing him emerge all naked from the Trout Pool.

"And now," Matthew said, "you had better get home. You should not be wandering around at this time of night."

"I'm not as fragile as you think," I said. "Why, until this year, children of five years old worked long hours underground, and women younger than me hauled great weights of coal, half-naked."

I wondered if I had said too much when a dark shadow crossed Matthew's face. "That is true," he spoke slowly, "and it is abominations such as that I hope to end by ensuring that men earn sufficient to keep a family without assistance from wives and children."

"You are a good man." I spoke without thought.

"There are better," Matthew said, rising to his feet. "Come on, Robyn. I'll get you back to your home."

We walked in Indian file along the path, with Matthew a few paces in front and the trees an autumn bower around us. He helped me cross the tangled boughs of the fallen oak with as much aplomb as any gentleman born, and not once did he cross the bounds of decorum.

"I'll wait here until you are safely inside the house," Matthew stood just within the fringe of trees.

"Thank you." I responded with a polite curtsey.

"Aye, there are some queer men going around this season," Matthew repeated what he had said on the last occasion we parted. "Escaped colliers, messengers-at-arms and the like."

"I have heard of them."

"You do not need to bring me any more food," Matthew said. "I will be leaving very shortly." Reaching forward, he touched my arm. "God bless you, Robyn Moffat."

"And you." I said. It was an impulse that made me dark forward and plant a single kiss on Matthew's forehead, before turning, taking hold of the hem of my skirt and running to the side door. When I turned around, he stood there still, with one hand to the spot I had kissed. I slipped into the house and closed the door, wondering if I had made a major mistake. I did not doubt that Matthew was a good man with a sincere desire to help others, but was that reason enough to try to deepen my friendship with him?

I did not know. Already regretting my imprudent kiss, I resolved to be more circumspect in future. Yet the last thing I remembered before I slept was not my view of Matthew emerging from the Trout Pool, but the expression of surprise on his face as I kissed him.

Chapter Seven

"Who's that coming up the drive?" The position of Mother's chair enabled her to peer out of the window without doing more than crane her neck. "It's a man." She glanced at me. "Probably one of your followers, Robyn."

"I don't believe I have any followers," I said. "Except for Andrew Dewar."

"The Special Policeman who falls into the bushes." Father spoke from behind his newspaper. "He'll have to do better next time. That collier fellow is still loose, so Dewar is not a very effective guardian of the law."

"Is Juner still at large?" I tried to inject supreme indifference into my voice.

"It's not Mr Dewar," Mother said. "It's another man. It's that fellow who helped us in Dalkeith, Robyn, Mr Carlisle or Cambuskenneth or some such name."

"Carmichael," I said. "His name was Carmichael, as you know full well, Mother." I felt my heart give a great lurch. Had Mr Carmichael discovered Matthew? If that was the case, I thought I had better be first to confront him to try and find out more. Rising from the table, I took a sip of my tea to clear the toast crumbs from my mouth.

"I'll let him in," I said.

"That's Sim's job," Father did not move his newspaper.

"There's no need to bother Sims," I could feel Mother watching me. "No, Mother," I said. "I don't even like the man."

"Of course not, Robyn," Mother said comfortably.

"Mr Carmichael!" I curtseyed politely as he entered our house.

Mr Carmichael doffed his hat and gave a little bow. "Good morning Miss Moffat."

"Did Mother invite you?" I asked, hopefully.

"She did not," Mr Carmichael said, with his gently mocking eyes smiling at me. "I am here at your father's invitation."

"Oh." That was slightly upsetting. Was Father taking an active interest in hunting poor Matthew? "I'll take you to his study." I dismissed Sims, who had appeared in the hall. "Pray come this way, Mr Carmichael. Father is having breakfast at present, but I am sure he won't keep you waiting long."

Mr Carmichael glided up the stairs, so light that I hardly heard his feet on the stone steps. "Straight ahead," I said and opened the door of Father's study. It was neat and business-like, with a small pile of documents on the desk and an estate map pinned to the wall. The room smelled of tobacco smoke and leather seats, homely, masculine and secure. "Please sit down, sir, and I'll fetch Father."

"Thank you, Miss Moffat."

"There's no need to fetch me, Robyn. I am here." Father's heavy tread contrasted with Mr Carmichael's nearly dance-light feet.

"That's Mr Carmichael to see you, Father," I said.

"So I heard." Father stepped into his study, hand extended in welcome, "Carmichael, come in. You are the messenger, I believe."

"Thank you, Moffat. Yes, I am." Carmichael stepped into Father's study, then turned to face me. "Thank you, Miss Moffat."

I curtseyed politely, agog with curiosity. Why on earth was Mr Carmichael visiting Father? Now I had proof that he was the messenger that Matthew had warned me about, I undoubtedly had to discover more.

The second that the study door closed, I hurried to our library and the connecting door. Walking as quietly as I could, I squeezed against the door, in time to hear Father's voice.

"I have a problem with my colliers."

"So I believe," Carmichael replied. "I may be able to help you there."

My interest increased even as my heart plunged. Mr Carmichael must be trying to capture Matthew to end the strike. That must be why he asked me about the miners. I shivered slightly, remembering the steel behind the mocking eyes, and the pistol at his saddle. I hoped that Father knew how dangerous the smiling Mr Carmichael really was.

"Pray, continue," Father said and after a brief pause, "My apologies, Carmichael; I trust you will excuse me."

I was waiting to hear more when the connecting door thumped open, and Father put his hand on my shoulder. "Not this time, Robyn. Carmichael and I are engaged in a private business discussion."

I could feel Mr Carmichael's eyes laughing at me as Father ejected me, quite gently, from the library. "Out you go, Robyn."

Mother was waiting in the drawing-room, pretending to attend to her sewing. "Well?" She asked, raising her eyes. "Did you learn anything?"

"Not a thing." I slumped into the chair at her side.

"I wonder if your Mr Carmichael came here to see your father," Mother said, "or if he hoped to see you."

"Me?"

"You." Mother returned to her sewing as if the conversation was completed.

"Why would he wish to see me?"

Sighing, Mother looked up again. "Look in a mirror for the answer, Robyn."

"He knows nothing about me," I said.

Mother smiled. "He is talking to your father, who knows a great deal about you."

"They were talking about the colliers," I said.

"They were talking about the colliers when Moffat knew you were listening," Mother said. "You do not know the subject of their conversation when you are not there."

"I would love to be a fly on the study wall."

"You'll hear by and by," Mother said. "Or you'll hear as much as Father, or your Mr Carmichael, chooses to tell you."

"He is *not* my Mr Carmichael," I said.

"If you insist, Robyn." Mother did not try to hide her smile.

I snorted in a most unladylike manner to hide my emotions, for how did I feel about Adam Carmichael? I knew he was hunting my poor Matthew Juner, and perhaps for that reason, I tried to ignore the sudden hammer of my heart when I heard male feet coming down the stairs.

"Steady the Buffs," Mother said. "That's Moffat."

I knew Father's tread, but I also recalled that Mr Carmichael was butterfly-light on his feet. For that reason, I was less surprised than Mother was when both men entered the room.

"Mrs Moffat," Father began very formally, "I believe you have met Mr Carmichael."

"I have," Mother responded to Mr Carmichael's bow with a slight nod. "Mr Carmichael was good enough to escort us through a most disturbing crowd in Dalkeith."

"And this is my daughter, Robyn," Father said, 'whom I believe you have also already met."

Mr Carmichael's bow to me was lower than to my mother. "We have met on three occasions," he said. "Including today."

Father nodded without requesting more information. "Mr Carmichael and I are to combine in a business venture," he told us. "It is likely he will be a frequent visitor to Winter Lodge."

When I looked at Mr Carmichael's laughing eyes, I could not help but remember the gun he carried at his saddle and the efficient manner in which he escorted us through the Dalkeith crowd. I had no desire to be friendly to the messenger-at-arms whose arrival Matthew dreaded.

"Indeed?" I kept any emotion from my voice.

"I hope that we all become firm friends," Mr Carmichael said, "as Mr Moffat and I become staunch business partners."

"Oh," Mother said. "That is also our desire. Is that not so, Robyn?"

I thought of poor Matthew, a hunted fugitive in his own country, and the colliers' poverty that he was attempting to alleviate, and could not bring myself to agree. I felt my Mother's disapproval at my silence.

"Is that not so, Robyn," Mother hardened her tone. "She is shy, poor thing."

"I have that effect on attractive women," Mr Carmichael said, bowing in my direction.

"I am not shy," I denied, perhaps with more heat than decorum.

"You have found your tongue," Mother said, as Father gave me a most uncharacteristic glower.

"Perhaps Miss Moffat is merely out of sorts." Mr Carmichael pretended to be charitable.

"Miss Moffat is…" I wondered how to react. Swallowing my pride, I stood up. "Miss Moffat would like to apologise for her behaviour," I said, curtseying towards Mr Carmichael. "And I would be more than delighted if our family became fast friends with Mr Carmichael."

"That's better." Mother was instant forgiveness.

So was Mr Carmichael, drat him, as he bowed, smiling. "I am glad to hear it," he said, with his eyes half-mocking, half appraising me.

I forced a smile.

"Good," Father said. "Now Mr Carmichael and I must depart. I'll be back before dark, Mrs Moffat."

"Be careful out there," Mother said. "I have not heard if the police have caught the fugitive collier yet."

"We'll be careful," Father said.

"Why the Friday face?" Mother asked as soon as the two men left the room. "That was very impolite to a man who has shown us nothing but kindness."

Unable to tell the whole truth without bringing Matthew into the conversation, I said, "I am not sure I wholly trust Mr Carmichael."

"When we spoke about your betrothal to Andrew Dewar," Mother sounded very severe. "You told me you had only a limited choice of eligible bachelors."

I nodded.

"Well, Mr Carmichael is not burdened by a wife."

"How do you know that?"

"I asked your father."

"Mother!" I was angry at Mother's interfering on my behalf.

Mother gave a faint smile. "It's best to know these things before one sets one's cap at a man. Finding out later about a hidden wife can be so inconvenient and may lead to unwished-for complications."

"I am not setting my cap at Mr Carmichael," I said.

"You told me you found him interesting," Mother smiled at my confusion. "I am glad you apologised to the man, Robyn. That was well done."

I looked away. I had not apologised from any sense of guilt, or because I wished to become close to Mr Carmichael. On the contrary, I hoped to find out his movements to ensure that poor Matthew was safe. I was the most devious of women.

"I am not setting my cap at Mr Carmichael," I repeated.

"So you say." Mother returned to her sewing. "It is of no interest to me, of course. I am only your mother. There is no need to tell me anything."

"It's all right, Mother." I touched her shoulder. "I will tell you everything just as soon as I have anything of interest to tell."

Mother smiled over her sewing. "Make sure that you do," she said, "or I will find out from others."

* * *

The note was waiting on the table in the breakfast-room, carefully folded and tied with a red ribbon.

"That was left for you," trust Mother to hover as I lifted the note. "Sims said a young man handed it in at the side door."

"At the side door? I wonder why?"

Even with Mother watching, I could not contain my curiosity any further and unfastened the neat bow. I did not recognise the writing.

Miss Robyn Moffat
Winter Lodge
Midlothian.

"Unfold it, then," Mother urged.

The message was short.

'I cannot thank you enough for your help. If it were not for you, I could be in prison, so God bless you, Miss Moffat.'

It was not signed.

"Well?" Mother was trying to peer over my shoulder. "Who is it from, and what does it say?"

I managed what I hoped was a coy smile. "It's from a man, and it's for me." Refolding the letter, I thrust it up my sleeve.

"Which man?" Mother asked.

"It is not signed," I said, "and that's all I am telling you."

"Andrew, then," Mother immediately decided, thought for a moment, and smiled. "Or is it Mr Adam Carmichael?"

"It was not signed," I said. "Either one of those gentlemen could have sent it, or even somebody else."

"I won't ask for details," Mother said.

You won't get any, I thought, even as I said: "Thank you, Mother."

"You look as if you need time to yourself." Mother said no more as I fled the room to think.

That letter was from Matthew. He was safe somewhere and remembered me, which was good. Now I could put him from my mind and concentrate on other things, such as Andrew Dewar. My thoughts of the previous evening had been foolish. I liked Matthew, even admired him, but I could never develop a meaningful attachment with him. I could now also forget about Mr Carmichael, or so I reasoned. Now that I knew for sure that he was a messenger-at-arms, a servant of the court, I had lost all interest in the man. The little I knew about such people was all unpleasant – they were a heartless breed.

That left a choice between Andrew Dewar, who wanted me to breed his children and enlarge his land holdings, Derek Pringle and Hugh Beaton.

As I often did, I stared out the window at the distant ridge of the Pentland Hills while I tried to make sense of my life. I lifted my chin as I came to a decision I should have made a long time ago. Whatever else happened, I no longer wished to marry Andrew Dewar.

I was surprised how calmly Mother took the news when I told her.

"Will you hold to your decision?" She looked up from her sewing.

"I will," I said.

Mother nodded. "You'll have to tell Mr Dewar," she said. "Talk to him, honestly and openly. You may alter your opinion. Remember the old saying that a winter's night, a laird's purpose and a woman's mind often change."

"Yes. I am quite settled in my decision."

"Talk to him anyway, Robyn. No man is perfect, and he may not be as bad as you think." Mother bit her thread, holding one end between her teeth. "It would be unkind to keep him in ignorance of your decision."

I sighed. "I'll talk to Andrew, Mother." I knew that it would not be easy.

Mother returned to her sewing. "Do you want me to come with you?"

"No, thank you." I sat opposite her beside the fire. "I'll see him alone."

* * *

Andrew lived in Dewar House, an establishment much more extensive than ours, set within pristine parkland on the southern flank of Roman Camp Hill. I visited in person, rather than sending a note, and curtseyed politely to Mr Dewar, Andrew's father.

"Miss Peacock, isn't it?" Mr Dewar had answered the door in person.

"No, Mr Dewar," I said. "I am Miss Robyn Moffat."

"Oh, of course," Mr Dewar was a small, plump man with an obsidian stare. "That one." He stepped away. "We had Miss Peacock here yesterday. Andrew is in the gun room." Turning, Mr Dewar walked away, swaying like a sailor after a long voyage. "That way." He gestured vaguely down an unlit passage.

The first thing I noticed in the gun room was the sweet perfume of gun-oil. The second was the muzzle of a shotgun that Andrew pointed at me.

"Robyn? What the devil are you doing here?"

"I've come to talk to you," I said. "If you could kindly put that gun down."

"It's not loaded," Andrew said.

I pushed the barrel to one side. "I wish to speak to you," I said.

"I'm a little busy at present," Andrew said.

Glancing at the array of weapons in the room, I nodded. "I can see that," I said, "but what I have to say is important."

Andrew sighed as if nothing that I had to say was as important as his guns. "What is it, Robyn? Be quick as I am joining Pringle and Peacock on a shoot in half an hour."

Peacock was Alistair Peacock, Amy's brother, an eager young man of 20 who was as sporting as Derek Pringle without his bumptiousness or skill.

"I wanted to discuss our engagement." I perched myself on the table beside two of his guns.

Andrew frowned. "What is there to discuss?"

"Our future." I said.

"We know our future." Andrew checked the lock of his shotgun and began to oil the mechanism. "We will marry and move into my house. We'll have three or four boys, and when my father dies, I'll inherit the estate. When your father dies, I'll inherit Winter Lodge and merge the lands." He looked at me. "That's been settled for years."

"That's not the future I see," I felt my heartbeat increase, but whether it was through anger or nervousness, I was not sure.

Andrew barely paused in his examination of the shotgun. "We need at least three sons in case one or two die." He shrugged. "Babies often die."

"Sons are not merely there to maintain the blood-line," I kept my temper with difficulty. "And we might also have a daughter."

"I hope not," Andrew opened the shotgun and peered down the barrel. "Girls are too much trouble."

"Does that include me?" I asked sweetly.

"You're hardly a girl any more," Andrew said.

"I'm glad you noticed." I took hold of Andrew's shotgun. "Put that thing away, Andrew, and talk to me. You might think my words even more important than killing small birds."

"I haven't the time," Andrew jerked the gun free. "Pringle and Peacock will be here soon, and I can't keep them waiting."

"Do they matter more than I do?"

For the first time, Andrew looked directly at me. "We've had this shoot arranged for a week, Robyn."

"Talk to me, Andrew." I urged.

"Perhaps later," Andrew said. "After the shoot."

"Do I matter less than a shoot?"

Andrew looked at me as if I had uttered blasphemy in the church. "I cannot let my friends down."

"Andrew," I slid off the table in a flurry of skirts and petticoats. "We are getting nowhere here, and neither is our engagement." Catching his attention in the only way I could, I swept my hand across the table, knocking two of his precious guns to the floor. "If my company matters less to you than your friends, and my words are less important than killing birds, then we are not suited, Andrew Dewar!"

Andrew was on his knees, picking up his guns. "Look what you've done!"

"Do you understand me, Andrew?" Bending over him, I shouted in his face. "I no longer wish to be engaged to you! As from this minute, our arrangement is finished, our partnership dissolved, our agreement in disagreement."

As Andrew's attention strayed from his guns to me and back, I wondered if he understood what I had said. "We are no longer engaged to be married," I said, more gently. "You'll have to seek another woman to bear your children."

"Yes." Andrew remained engrossed with his guns, and that was how I left him. I walked out of Dewar House with as much dignity as I could muster and only then did I wonder why Mr Dewar had thought I was Amy.

Chapter Eight

Now that I was without a fiancé, I faced a solitary future, unless I managed to snare a marriageable man. I was only 22, still relatively young, and although Father spoke about his perilous financial position, he remained a man of some standing. As his only relative, I stood to inherit his property when he died. Looking out of my window at the Pentland Ridge, I planned my next move, for I had no intention of allowing fate to decide my life for me. I would organise, scheme and manoeuvre myself into the most advantageous position for a favourable marriage with the best possible man I could find.

Unfortunately, the choice was limited, and some men might view me with wariness now I had removed myself from the trap of engagement to an unsuitable suitor.

Although the prospect was nerve-racking, I was excited at hunting for a husband, being the hunter rather than the quarry, the hound rather than the fox. That analogy was rather fitting, I thought, as my first move would be at the next meet of the Midlothian Hunt.

* * *

"You look happy," Mother said when I came down to breakfast.

"I am," I said.

Father folded back the upper half of his newspaper. "Why is that, pray? I'd have thought you were unhappy, having lost your betrothed."

"He was not worth keeping," I said. "He was a selfish blackguard."

Father raised his eyebrows. "Strong words for a man you were engaged to for years. He might be a blackguard, Robyn, but he was a blackguard who could have kept you in comfortable circumstances. There are few such men around."

"I can think of a couple," I said.

"Perhaps," Mother said, "but a dear ship lies long in the harbour."

"What on earth does that mean?"

"It means that if you are very exacting in your choice of husband, dear Robyn, you may have a long wait, or perhaps a fruitless one."

"I do not intend to wait at all, Mother," I said. "As men hunt for foxes, I intend to hunt for a man."

"Oh?" Father lowered his newspaper, grimly humorous. "Hunters have a pack of hounds to help. How do you intend to find your quarry?"

"I may use these same hounds." I was aware of Mother's gaze on me as I smiled to Father.

"What do you want, Robyn?" Father asked at once. "I know that smile."

"I want to ride in the Midlothian Hunt," I said.

Father folded his paper, placed it beside him, sighed, and looked at me. "Why?" He asked. "You've taken no interest in hunting before."

"It could be entertaining," I said.

"You may not like the hunting set." Father understood at once.

"I may not," I agreed.

"Who will be there to entertain you?" Mother knew me well.

"Amy Peacock," I said, truthfully.

"And for whom are you hunting?" Mother asked.

"Derek Pringle."

"As far as I am aware, there is no need for an invitation or a formal introduction," Father said. "You only need a horse, hard-wearing clothing, and strong nerves for the chase."

"May I borrow Maida, Father?" I asked. Maida was the favourite of Father's three horses, a strong bay stallion with an iron jaw and the heart of a lion. Father had named him after the dog of Walter Scott, a writer he admired.

"You may," Father said. "Do you have the stomach for the kill? I believe it can be a bloody experience."

I had thought of that. "I might not stay for the kill," I said.

Father nodded. "That might be best. Don't take any unnecessary risks," he said. "I don't want you to break your leg or your proud neck."

"Nor do I," I agreed.

Father lifted his newspaper again. "You may find Derek Pringle less amiable than Andrew Dewar if you succeed in catching him."

"I may," I said. "But I have few choices."

So that was why I was awake well before dawn on the following Friday, taking a cup of coffee to break my fast and trying to control my desire to chatter on about nothing in particular.

"You do like to talk in the mornings, don't you?" Mother had left her bed to ensure I was safe. She stood with a coat thrown over her night-dress, a loose turban on her head and her feet bare on the floor. Honestly, if men saw women in the morning before they prettied up, they might lose many of the foolish romantic notions they have of us. Marriage, of course, dispels all illusions. Mother always termed dressed-up women as "Sunday wives", women who looked their best to catch a man. Amy was one such. So far, I had not been so inclined, but I knew I might have to follow that path if I failed to interest Mr Pringle.

"If words formed a net, you could catch a whole boatload of men," Mother said, "and throw those you did not like back into the sea."

I smiled, swallowing coffee as I listened to the wind hammering for admittance at the door.

"Save some of your energy for the hunting," Mother said, smiling with sleep-heavy eyes. "Is it only Mr Pringle that you are after?"

"He is my hope." I put the empty cup down.

"Aye, as I said, he has a good seat so you'll have to ride hard to keep up with him."

"I'll do my best."

"Take care," Mother put her hand on my arm. "I'd prefer a daughter with no husband to a daughter with a broken neck."

"I'll take care."

I knew little about fox-hunting save the maxim that the best horse for hunting had the head of a duchess and the bottom of a cook. With that slender advice in mind, I examined Maida before mounting. He had long, intelligent ears, which was always a good thing in a horse, and wide-open eyes, which I thought beneficial. Strong-boned, with powerful hindquarters, he looked like a hunter to me. I knew that Maida was a spirited horse, and at 16 hands was a little large for comfort, but I had ridden him on a few occasions, so he knew my touch. He seemed happy to be out of the stable, whinnying at the bite of the wind as I led him on to the path. Mother helped me into the side-saddle, patting my thigh as I sat there.

"I'd be happier if somebody was going with you."

"I'm 22," I said. "I can cope."

"Ride safely," Mother said and slapped Maida's rump. Although I did not look back, I knew she was watching me.

Using a long rein, I walked Maida out of the grounds and downhill, with the shrewd breeze of autumn biting at my ears and the smell of damp earth a pleasant introduction to the day.

The meet started at Newtonloan Toll-house at the bottom of the hill, with a round score of riders milling around, some drinking a glass of claret or port, others chatting or laughing, and one or two attending to the horses. I looked around the gathering, running my gaze over all the men present, assessing each for potential marriage material.

Walter Elliot – married, James Smith – too old, Emmanuel Slater – too ugly, the Duke of Buccleuch – married and far above me in the social scale, Adam Carmichael – what the devil is the messenger doing here?

Shifting my horse, I resolved to avoid the messenger-at-arms, while still wondering if he carried his gun. Was he practising hunting down poor colliers? I wondered, imagining him setting a pack of hounds on some unfortunate man and chasing him up a tree? For all his undoubted charm, his presence unsettled me.

"Robyn!" The voice cut through the deep babble of male conversation.

"Amy!" I smiled to her as she sipped at a stirrup-cup. "I am glad to see you here. I thought you had forgotten our arrangement!"

"Oh no," Amy said. "You are my most particular friend. I'd never forget you." Her smile was every bit as sincere as her words.

I walked Maida up to her. "What a splendid idea to come here? When did you become interested in the hunt?"

Amy sipped daintily at whatever she was drinking. "Oh, Robyn, I've always watched them ride past, and I've attended the last two hunts. It's such fun and so stimulating."

I had to admit that she looked the part, with her full hunting attire on and her boots so glossy one could nearly see one's face in them.

"And Robyn," Amy leaned across to put her gloved hand on my arm. "One meets the most interesting people. Did you know that Mr Carmichael also rides to hounds?"

I admitted that I had seen him with the others. "Although," I said, "I was not aware you knew the gentleman."

"He's such a charming fellow. And the duke is so condescending when he speaks to me." Amy looked away, as coyly as a reptile. "I do wish the duke were not a married man."

"He is a bit old for you, don't you think?" I said. "I know you are a leetle older than me, but the duke is old enough to be your father." I hoped my words stung Amy, who was much more concerned with her years and spinster status than I was.

"Perhaps," Amy brushed away my words. "But not so with Derek Pringle. He might think you a leetle young, while I am more his age."

The witch had her eye on my target and had used my own words against me. At that moment, I hated Amy with the passion that only a woman can have for her most particular friend.

"Derek Pringle?" I pretended unconcern. "Is he here? I must confess I had not noticed."

Amy saw through my pretence and pounced. "Oh, Mr Pringle is such a handsome man, and the best rider of the hunt."

"I'm sure you have more than sufficient experience of such matters," I said, turning Maida's head away.

Amy smiled, knowing she had scored a significant point. "Oh, there's Derek now," she emphasised the use of his Christian name before she raised her voice. "Mr Pringle!"

I watched as Amy rode up to Derek Pringle, fighting the wave of jealousy that came over me. One balances on a horse by sticking out one's chest and Amy was adept at that art, as the direction of Mr Pringle's gaze adequately proved. With Amy's light-grey riding skirt allowing freedom of movement to her legs, these shapely appendages of hers were also on display, much to Mr Pringle's entertainment. I had joined this hunt mainly to see Mr Pringle, and now Amy was attempting to steal my thunder. I could not allow that, so walked Maida close to them with the intention of catching Mr Pringle's attention.

"Miss Moffat!" Adam Carmichael intercepted me before I reached my intended destination. "I did not know you followed the hounds." Splendid in tight trousers and a short jacket, he walked Chetak through a yapping pack of hounds.

Knowing that I was in the public eye, I put on my most charming smile. "Mr Carmichael! How good to see you here! I've long been a supporter of the hunt,"

I said, "but this is the first time I have participated. Father was saying that there are too many foxes around Winter Lodge."

"Master Reynard can be a pest." Mr Carmichael reined up beside me, quite blocking my view of Derek Pringle, "although they do have benefits as well, reducing the numbers of rats, mice and other vermin."

"Including runaway colliers, perhaps?" I said, smiling.

Mr Carmichael frowned, shaking his head. "I would not classify any person as vermin."

"Nor would I." I said. "With the possible exception of those who hunt down the unfortunate."

"Quite," Mr Carmichael said, trying to look confused.

A blast of the huntsman's horn signalled that we were to rally around Buccleuch. About 40 years old, Buccleuch boasted an elegant set of whiskers that framed his handsome face. He gave crisp instructions.

"We will head towards Carrington," the duke told us, "and see what the hounds find. I believe the farm of Aitkendean has been bothered by a dog fox and a vixen."

Some of the hunters cheered the news, with much excitement. I saw Amy glance towards Derek Pringle, then guide her horse, a lean brown mare, to his side. I tried to edge in the same direction, only for the insufferable messenger once again to block my path. Honestly, I was plagued by the most unsuitable of men while the eligible seemed to look at the Amys of this world.

"This is your first hunt, you said?" Mr Carmichael enquired politely.

"Yes." I again tried to walk Maida towards Mr Pringle.

"Stay with me then." Mr Carmichael's Chetak matched Maida, step for step. "I'll see you right."

The last thing I wanted was for Mr Carmichael to see me right, but what could I do? "Thank you," I said, promising myself that I would lose this persistent man at the first opportunity. With a horse such as Maida under me, I should have the legs on Chetak, who looked a decent enough mount for every day but hardly a hunter.

I did not see the master of foxhounds arrive. One minute he was not there, the next he was beside Buccleuch, with the whole pack of hounds yapping and barking around us as Buccleuch led the way and we dutifully followed. Pringle was in the group immediately behind the duke, with Amy riding nearly level with him, aping his every movement and laughing at his words, which he appeared to adore. From my position, far to the rear, I could only see the pair of them jogging along together, with Pringle proving that Mother was correct – he did have a fine seat in every sense of the word.

"If this is your first hunt," Mr Carmichael told me. "It's best if you keep behind the leaders until you understand what to do."

It was probably sound advice, but frustrating as I tried to push forward to Mr Pringle's side, only for others, more experienced in this endeavour, to block my path.

From Newtonloan Toll, Buccleuch rode across the Galashiels Road and headed down a steep slope towards the village of Carrington, with the hounds yapping at his heels. We crossed the South Esk River at Shank Bridge with Pringle fording the river in a spectacular display that I would have emulated if Amy had not beaten me to it. She cantered beside Mr Pringle, throwing me a look of triumph over her shoulder and her horse nearly hidden behind a curtain of spray.

"Well done, Miss Peacock," Mr Pringle's voice sounded above the general hubbub.

"Yes, well done," I echoed, but not quite softly enough, for Mr Carmichael cocked an eyebrow at me.

"I suspect you know that lady," he said.

"That is Amy Peacock," I told him.

"And is the man her particular friend?"

"It appears that she would like him to be," I could not disguise the bitterness in my voice.

We were trotting across prime farmland now, with the horses' hooves churning up the rich soil as the farm servants watched from the open doors of their cottages and the barking of their dogs challenged the baying of our hounds. Over to the west, dark clouds blew up over the Pentland Hills, an ominous warning of wild weather to come.

"You'd be better wearing a heavier riding cape," Mr Carmichael said to me.

I thought of Matthew and my greatcoat. "I'll be all right," I said. "You're only wearing a jacket yourself."

Mr Carmichael smiled. "Touché."

Passing the substantial farm of Carrington Barns, we thundered into the hamlet of Carrington with its 18th-century church echoing to our hoof-beat and the inhabitants wondering at this invasion of their village.

"Gather round." Buccleuch ignored the staring villagers.

"Stay with me," Carmichael said. "I suspect things are about to get interesting."

Amy, the hussy, was so close to Mr Pringle that they were virtually stirrup-to-stirrup. I had one glance at her laughing face and looked away, unable to hide my disappointment. Between that man-hungry woman and this man-hunting messenger, my plans lay in red-coated tatters. Buccleuch was talking, his voice rich and fruity.

"The farmers around here tell me that master Reynard has been getting rather bold of late. Let us solve that problem."

Again there was much cheering and shouting. Amy shouted as loud as anybody else, leaning over in her saddle until she was nearly touching Mr Pringle as she said something that made him laugh out loud. I watched, knowing I lacked the skill to make men laugh.

"Your Miss Peacock seems to be very attached to that gentleman," Mr Carmichael said.

"I fear so," I watched with increasing jealousy, for Amy was acting in precisely the manner I would have, and with more success.

"If she is not careful, she will tip off the saddle," Mr Carmichael continued, "and end up with her face in the mud." He looked at me. "Somehow, although Miss Peacock is your friend, I think you would like to see that."

"I would not!" I denied hotly, although I had an immediate mental picture of Amy toppling from her saddle to land in a sea of liquid mud with her oh-so-elegant bottom sticking up in the air.

Mr Carmichael smiled. "Would you not? I rather think I'd like to see it myself. She seems a rather forward miss." I did not expect his wink or my inadvertent smile. "That's better, Miss Moffat. Hark! We're off!"

The hounds must have picked up a scent and, with Buccleuch in front, the hunt trotted behind the pack. Once again Pringle was with the leading riders, with Amy still riding so close that their stirrups were nearly touching, and once again Mr Carmichael and I were with the backmost pack, riding through the descending clumps of mud thrown up by the horses in front. My view was of the bouncing rumps and flicking tails of horses, rather than of Mr Pringle's smile.

"Come on," I shouted to Mr Carmichael. "Let's get further forward."

Kicking in my spurs, I urged Maida to greater effort, although Mr Carmichael kept pace with me with more ease than I had expected. Overtaking the less able riders, we were soon with the second pack as the hunt streamed out across the fields, with the sun rising behind us and the serrated Pentland range now black against a heavily bruised sky.

Although I had no desire to watch the death of a fox, I could not deny the excitement of the hunt. I felt part of something unique as men, women, horses and dogs stretched across the fields, leaping over the low hedges, laughing to the sound of the huntsman's horn, scattering geese and seagulls from the fields, hearing the drumbeat of hooves on the ground, feeling the wind in our faces. Life was good at that moment. I forgot all about my hunt for a husband as I strove to catch up with Amy and Mr Pringle, determined to prove myself a better horsewoman than my hated friend.

Unfortunately, I was not.

"Come on, Mr Carmichael," I shouted, even as I applied the whip and spur in my attempt to leave him behind.

One of the fields had a low hawthorn hedge that Buccleuch took at a gallop, leaping high in the air to cross and thunder on. Mr Pringle was next, soaring across the thorn, with Amy, laughing with the joy of life, hard at his heels, and jumping well, rot her. By that time, I was well up the field and, using Maida's strength, shouldered aside a thin-faced merchant from Dalkeith, put my horse to the jump.

"Be careful, Miss Moffat!" I heard Mr Carmichael's warning shout an instant too late, for Maida was already in the air when the deer burst out of cover. I saw them clearly, two female roe deer, both with huge eyes and the distinctive white rump as they exploded from the hawthorn where they had been hiding. While one leapt left, along the length of the hedge, the other ran into the field, jinking left and right so Maida could not see where to land.

Maida panicked at the shock, rearing up and twisting to the side at the same time. I shouted, sawing at the reins, but Maida was more used to Father's touch than mine. Landing with a thump, he bucked, kicking wildly. I held on as best I could until Maida leapt and twisted and I flew into the air. I had learned to ride sitting sideways on a conventional saddle, but since the invention of the two-pommel side-saddle a few years ago, I had mastered this novel method. It is safer than a traditional saddle because your right leg is anchored, while your hips are beneath your shoulders, as they should be. However, not even the best of side-saddles can protect one from a madly bucking horse, and I was propelled into the air.

For a moment, I seemed to be floating, with the ground drifting towards me, and every tuft and blade of grass clearly defined, and then I landed heavily. The impact drove every ounce of breath from my body, so I lay there, wheezing as the other riders galloped past, more intent of keeping up with the duke than with ensuring I was unhurt.

I lay still, gasping, with my head in a whirl, unable to move or even to think where I was or how I got there. It felt strangely safe down there.

Chapter Nine

"Miss Moffat!"

I heard the voice as from a long distance away.

"Miss Moffat!"

Somebody was calling me, although I did not know who, or why. I lay still, wishing whoever it was would leave me in peace. I was quite comfortable lying still, watching through the green curtain of grass as the hunt galloped away. A spider scurried through the grass, its legs lifting daintily.

"Miss Moffat! Robyn!"

I took a gasping breath, feeling the air burning my lungs. "Who's that?" I was unsure if I was in my bed, or flying to the moon.

"It's me, Adam Carmichael. Let me help you up." I felt Mr Carmichael's strong hands on my arms. "Can you stand? Is anything broken?"

I did not know yet. Allowing Mr Carmichael to support me, I tested each foot, gasping when I placed my left ankle on the ground. 'That hurts,' I said, lifting my foot.

"What hurts?" Mr Carmichael sounded concerned.

"My left ankle," I tried to put my weight on it, winced and nearly fell against Mr Carmichael. "You go on," I said. "I'll be all right. Don't miss the hunt on my account."

Mr Carmichael gradually relaxed his grip. "It's too late for that," he said. "The hunt's well away, and so are our horses."

"What?" I looked around. I had been so intent on trying to keep up with Amy and Mr Pringle that I had taken no notice where we were. I had never been in this part of the world before. "Maida is Father's horse. He'll be angry if I lose him."

"Maida will probably make his way home," Mr Carmichael said. "Horses are intelligent animals."

"Where is your horse?"' I asked.

Mr Carmichael shrugged. "Chetak followed your stallion. Can you walk?"

"I think so." I tried a step, winced and found Mr Carmichael's arm around my back. "I can, but my ankle can't."

"You may have sprained it, or perhaps even broken it," Mr Carmichael said. "Is there a village near here?"

"Carrington is the nearest," I said, "or Temple, somewhere over that way," I nodded forward, past the line of trees that screened the far side of the field.

Mr Carmichael glanced upward as a spot of rain splashed on his head. He grunted, picked up his tall hat which had fallen off, and jammed it on his head. "Which is closer? It's going to get wet."

I considered for a moment. "Temple, I think."

"Then to Temple we will go," Mr Carmichael decided for us both. "If you lean on me we'll get there quicker."

Although I did not desire Mr Carmichael's company, I knew I would not make it to Temple alone with my injured ankle. Swallowing my pride, I took hold of Mr Carmichael's arm and allowed him to support me.

The rain increased steadily from a drizzle to a downpour that quickly turned the ground to a quagmire.

"Here," Mr Carmichael removed his hat and placed it on my head, for my own hat had disappeared in my tumble. He stepped back, smiling. "That suits you." He said. "You should wear a topper more often."

I tried to smile through my misery for, having given my greatcoat away, I found that my light summer coat was no protection against autumn weather. The rain had already soaked me to my skin, adding to the mud that caked me from my feet to my knees. Even such a ridiculous item as a top hat was welcome protection.

"It's getting heavier," Mr Carmichael said, with the rain sleeking down his dark hair and dripping down the length of his nose. "We'll have to find shelter soon."

I agreed. My plan to meet Derek Pringle had not worked. My first hunt had turned into a disaster, and now I was stuck with this most abominable man whose occupation was hounding the poor and unfortunate.

"Arniston House is nearby," I suggested.

"I doubt Lord Dundas would approve of us arriving in such a state," Mr Carmichael said. "Unless he is a particular friend of yours."

"He is not," I said. "I've never spoken to the man."

We moved on, with me limping and Mr Carmichael supporting me. After another few hundred wet yards, we stumbled into an area of dense woodland.

"At least there is shelter under the trees," Mr Carmichael was supporting more of my weight now, as my ankle weakened every time I placed my foot on the ground.

"Yes," I felt my hat grow heavy under the burden of rain. Ducking under a low branch, I stumbled, to feel Mr Carmichael's arm tighten around my back.

"We'll find somewhere soon," Mr Carmichael murmured in my ear. "Or I can carry you."

"No," I said, alarmed at the thought of Mr Carmichael picking me up. I had no intention of subjecting myself to that indignity.

We slogged through the trees, sliding down a steep slope that had me gasping as my right ankle protested under the strain of supporting much of my weight. "Mr Carmichael!" My appeal for help was a trifle too late as my ankle gave way and I slid to the ground to land with a heavy thump in a sitting position.

The sudden pull on Mr Carmichael's arm brought him down as well so, after slithering for a few yards, we sat side by side on a muddy slope. Although Mr Carmichael laughed, I failed to see anything funny in our situation.

"Come on, Miss Moffat," Mr Carmichael rose to his feet. "There's no profit in sitting here in the wet."

I tried to stand, failed and slid further down the slope.

"Oh, well," Mr Carmichael said. "I suppose there's no help for it." Stooping, he lifted me bodily in both arms. "If you can't walk, Miss Moffat, then we must continue this way."

Strangely, despite my feelings of only a few minutes before, I did not object. There was something comforting in Mr Carmichael carrying me through the rain. I felt like a child again, although with stirrings of emotions that were anything but child-like as I felt the strength of Mr Carmichael's arms and the hardness of his chest as he held me close.

No, I told myself. *This man is the messenger-at-arms. In all probability, he is using me to catch Matthew. I can't trust him.*

We moved faster now, descending the wooded slope, and marching, or rather stumbling, onwards. "There's a building ahead," Mr Carmichael shook water droplets from his face.

Twisting my head to look, I nodded. "That's the old Balantrodoch Church," I said. "It's been a ruin for years since they built a new one."

"That'll do until the rain eases off," Mr Carmichael said. "I need to get you under shelter."

"I don't mind the rain," I said.

"You'll catch pneumonia," Mr Carmichael told me severely, as if it was a fact that everybody who stood in the rain went down with that sickness. "And then what would your father say?" He deepened his voice in an imitation of Father's growl. "You allowed my daughter to catch pneumonia, Carmichael, so how can I trust you with a business deal?"

Despite my misery, I smiled. Mr Carmichael sounded very much like Father pretending to be angry. "Which business deal?" I asked, remembering who and what Mr Carmichael was, and why he was here.

"Does your father discuss his business with you?"

"No," I said. "Father has a strict rule that business matters should remain in his study."

"Then I shall abide by his rule." Mr Carmichael waded across a very muddy field to reach the walled enclosure in which Balantrodoch Church stood. He stopped for a moment, surveying the ruins. "There's not much left, is there?"

"Not much," I agreed. "I know about the colliers' combination," I said, hoping to draw information from Mr Carmichael. "I know you and Father are discussing such things."

Mr Carmichael walked on slowly, still carrying me. He did not respond to my words.

Whoever had destroyed Balantrodoch Church had done a thorough job. The walls still stood, with the gable ends pointing skyward, but only a small vestige of the roof remained in one corner. It was to this corner that Mr Carmichael hurried, carrying me as if I were a baby in his arms. I felt slightly bereft when he deposited me, very gently, on the stone-flagged floor, where the walls and roof afforded some shelter from the rain. He stood there for a moment, looking at me as the rain dripped from his face and his sodden clothes clung close to his muddied body.

"You stay here. I'll be back as soon as I can."

"Where are you going?" I asked.

"To search for dry wood," Mr Carmichael said. "We need a fire in this weather." With that, he turned and strode away. I watched, unable to prevent myself from smiling at the sight of the mud that caked the back of his trousers. I do not know why that should amuse me at such a time, but it did.

Shuffling backwards, I leaned against the cold stone wall and shivered. Although I was used to walking outdoors in all weather, I was unhappy sitting in the ruined church, watching the rain hammer down. After getting rid of Andrew, my plan for finding out more about Mr Pringle had resulted in a spectacular failure.

After a few moments pointless wondering, I pulled myself up on to my uninjured foot, then tried to stand on both. I might as well have tried to dance the Highland Fling. My ankle gave such a protest of pain that I immediately gave up the attempt and sank back down, to slump in sodden misery on the green-slimed slabs. I watched the rain teem down for a while, with big drips forming on what was left of the roof before they fell with a splash on the ancient floor. I felt – and must have appeared – the very epitome of misery.

As the minutes ticked away, I wondered if Mr Carmichael would return, or if he would leave me here. I knew that sheriff officers were notoriously flint-hearted so their superiors in authority, messengers-at-arms, would be devils incarnate. Despite Mr Carmichael's outward kindness and apparent good humour, I suspected he had an ulterior motive in depositing me in this desolate place while he wandered off on his own. Perhaps he had heard about me helping Matthew and wished to punish me.

All sorts of thoughts and fears ran through my head as I sat there in the dank cold. The rain did not cease, hissing down around my little shelter, bouncing from the ground and forming puddles that spread and merged to form a rippling pond on the ground.

"He's abandoned me here," I decided. "I'll have to find a farm and get help."

"Are you talking to yourself?" Mr Carmichael stood in front of me, mockery in his eyes and a bundle of sticks over his shoulder.

"I am." I had not been aware that I voiced my thoughts aloud.

Mr Carmichael grinned. "I do that all the time," he walked into my shelter and placed his bundle on the ground. "I can sometimes hold a long conversation as I work out a problem." Kneeling beside the sticks, he searched for the driest.

"My apologies for the time I took; it was not easy finding dry wood in this downpour."

When Mr Carmichael looked up, there was no mockery at all in his eyes. "Were you also working out a problem?"

"No." I shook my head, causing Mr Carmichael's top hat to slip over my eyes, while my wet hair splashed uncomfortably around my ears.

Mr Carmichael smiled as he adjusted the hat, so it balanced on top of my head. "Just talking, then. Here we are." He brought out a flint and tried to scrape a spark on to the small pyramid of sticks he had built. "Now it's time to pray for a flame, Miss Moffat." He looked at me with the mockery back. "At least we're in the right place for prayer. The Lord might look more favourably on us approaching him from one of his houses, even an abandoned one."

"It's not good to take the Lord's name in vain," I was not willing to allow this messenger any latitude.

"Quite right." Mr Carmichael was down on all fours now, trying to encourage his reluctant fire to life. I watched him move crab-wise around the pyramid until I had a splendid view of the patch of mud on his unmentionables. I shook my head, smiled despite myself, and looked away.

"Let there be light!" Mr Carmichael said in a tone of triumph. "We have the first spark, the forerunner of many more." Twisting to face me, the pleasure in his face was heartening. "Such small things please me," he said as I saw a faint curl of blue smoke rise from the sticks.

"I did not think you could do it," I said.

"Have faith, oh lady of the wet hat," Mr Carmichael said. "Look!" He pointed to the dark orange flame that licked around the side of his pyramid. "Soon, this fire will be ablaze, and you will be toasting, with dry clothes and a smile on your face." He paused for a moment. "And it is a face that deserves a smile or two."

"Oh." I was not sure what to say to that.

Mr Carmichael was correct about the fire. Under his care, the flames steadily spread and rose, sending welcome heat towards me. The ancient walls of the church multiplied the warmth, so my clothes soon started to steam. I pointed out that fact to Mr Carmichael.

"There, I told you so," Mr Carmichael said, grinning across the flames to me. "How is your ankle?"

I tested it and winced. "Sore," I said.

"Do you wish me to look at it?"

I blushed. "That would not be very respectable," I said.

"Perhaps not," Mr Carmichael agreed, "but if it is not cared for, it could swell and cause you considerably more discomfort and inconvenience." He stepped back, with his gaze never leaving my face. "I give you my word that I will take no advantage, Miss Moffat, and I have seen a lady's ankle before."

I considered for a moment. If shy Hugh Beaton had suggested such a thing or the exemplary Matthew Juner, would I have hesitated? No, I would not. But this man was a messenger-at-arms, a man-hunter, an ogre. "I am sure I shall be perfectly all right," I said, standing to prove my words. I yelped at the shooting pain, and only Mr Carmichael's arms prevented me from taking a nasty tumble on to the slabs.

Mr Carmichael raised his eyebrows. "Should I look at your ankle?"

I knew that men should not look at any part of a woman's leg. I also knew that my ankle was growing more painful and, if I wished to get home before dark, I needed all the assistance possible. "Yes, please, Mr Carmichael," I said in a small voice.

I expected a gloating remark from Mr Carmichael. He did not oblige me. Pulling over a large piece of masonry from the many within the church, Mr Carmichael bade me sit on it with a gesture of his hand. "I'm afraid it's a bit damp," he said.

"So am I," I replied.

Crouching in front of me, Mr Carmichael eased off my boot very gently, helped me remove my stocking and rolled up my skirt to mid-shin. Although I nibbled my lower lip and tried to ease the rapid patter of my heart, Mr Carmichael neither said nor did anything untoward, and all the while he spoke soothingly to me.

"It's all right, Miss Moffat – I won't cause you any pain." His hands were tender on my foot.

"There we are. What a pretty ankle to be hurt."

I said nothing but winced a lot as Mr Carmichael tested my ankle. Although his fingers were strong, they were also surprisingly gentle. I had expected to feel very uncomfortable with a strange man holding my leg. Instead, once my initial apprehension passed, I was quite relaxed.

"You have nothing broken, as far as I can see," Mr Carmichael said. "It is swollen, though, so either sprained or twisted. I am no doctor to tell which."

It was strange to have a man examining my leg in such detail. "Thank you, Mr Carmichael. You may release my leg now, thank you."

"Would you permit me to bind it?" Mr Carmichael ignored my request. "It might ease the pain or at least control the swelling."

"You don't have a bandage," I said.

"No, but I do have a shirt."

"What?" I said and then, "no, no Mr Carmichael, I will not permit it."

I was too late. Turning his back, Mr Carmichael divested himself of his jacket and waistcoat and pulled off his white shirt. Ignoring my protests, and he tore it into broad strips as I watched in horror.

"Mr Carmichael!" I protested.

Slipping his dripping waistcoat and jacket back on, Mr Carmichael knelt at my feet, his face a picture of concentration.

"Now you sit still, Miss Moffat. I'll try to make this as painless as possible."

"Really, Mr Carmichael," I said. "You cannot destroy your clothing merely for me."

"I cannot think of a better cause," Mr Carmichael said gallantly, winding the first strip around my ankle. Still warm from Mr Carmichael's body, the makeshift bandage was indeed comforting as he wrapped it around me.

"Can you wriggle your toes?" Mr Carmichael asked. "Go on, try."

I could.

"Good. It's not too tight, then." Mr Carmichael smiled again. "I don't wish to squeeze your foot so that it drops off. How could I explain that to your father?"

"He would be most displeased," I said solemnly.

"And with reason," Mr Carmichael was still working on my ankle, tying another strip from his shirt under my foot and high up to my lower calf. "There now; how does that feel?"

"Much better, but your poor shirt!"

"It did not feel a thing," Mr Carmichael assured me with his smile still in place.

"Will its owner not get a chill?" I asked.

"Not a bit of it." Mr Carmichael stood up. "There, that should help." He replaced the top hat which had fallen off my head. "Rest it for a day or two, and you should be right as rain."

"Was that intended to be amusing?" I indicated the rain that continued to pelt from the heavens.

"It was not." Mr Carmichael glanced at the clothes that clung damply to my person.

"Do you wish to dry your clothes?"

"Dry them?" I shook my head. "They'll dry on me."

"That is hardly the most comfortable method of drying clothes," Mr Carmichael said. "If I go away for half an hour or so, you could take them off and dry them properly."

I looked up at him in shock. "I can't do that!"

"Why not? There's nobody else here, and it's unlikely that anybody will visit in this weather."

"But," I looked at him. With my clothes clinging to me, the idea of peeling them off and drying them was very appealing.

"It's all right." When Mr Carmichael leaned closer, his lips nearly brushed the top of my head. "I promise not to return for at least half an hour, and I'll shout out when I am close." He barked a short laugh. "You are wondering if you can trust me, Miss Moffat. Yes, you can – I would not insult a woman such as you by spying on her, or anything else."

I started. Was that another compliment? "I cannot do what you suggest, sir," I tried to sound formal and dignified.

"It was only an idea," Mr Carmichael said gently. He sat beside me for a few moments in pleasant companionship. "I assure you, Miss Moffat, I will not abuse your trust."

I looked at him with his battered, sun-browned face. "I believe you would not." I said.

"Besides," Mr Carmichael was looking into the fire rather than at me. "Your intended would not approve. Andrew Dewar is it not?"

"It is," I said, "or rather it was."

"Was?" Mr Carmichael looked at me, with smoke from the fire slightly hazing his face.

"We are no longer have an arrangement." I did not go into details.

"Why is that, may I ask?" Mr Carmichael stirred the fire with a stick and added more fuel, stepping back from the resulting sparks.

I wondered how much I could safely tell him. "We drifted apart," I said. "We were friendly when we were children but less so now." I smiled and tried to lift the suddenly sombre atmosphere. "Besides, Mr Carmichael, he did not supply me with the ring I desired."

"That is a horrendous crime! A sin! No wonder you rid yourself of him!" Mr Carmichael smiled across to me. "For not supplying you with a ring, he should be hanged, drawn and quartered!"

"And worse!" I said. "If I could think of anything worse."

Mr Carmichael pulled back from the now roaring fire. "So what was this ring that caused so much distress?"

"I wanted a ring from Edinburgh, or Dalkeith, or Paris," I said. "Just a sign he held some affection for me."

"Oh, Paris," Mr Carmichael said. "Undoubtedly Paris, although Edinburgh has its place, Paris is much the more romantic."

I smiled.

"What was the ring like?"

I tried to think of the fanciest ring I could imagine, although I had no real interest in such things. It was the idea that was important, not the object. "A central ruby with sapphires set around in a heart shape," I said, guessing wildly.

"Sapphires," Mr Carmichael said. "A stone that symbolises wisdom, kindness and sound judgement." He looked at me. "While rubies are nobility, purity," he paused, "and passion. Are you a passionate lady, Miss Moffat?"

I thought it was time to change the subject. "Well, Andrew will never know, since we drifted apart."

"No ring, then."

"No ring," I said.

We sat in companionable silence except for the friendly crackle of the fire and the steady hiss of the rain. A sheep called, the sound plaintive in that ancient place, and I shivered, wondering at the people who had been there before me, who they had been and what they had done. I did not need to speak – we shared the silence without any awkwardness.

When Mr Carmichael spoke, it was almost an intrusion in that holy place.

"You must be hungry."

"Hungry?" I had not thought about food until Mr Carmichael mentioned the subject. Now I knew he was correct. "I might be."

"I've nothing much with me," Mr Carmichael said, "and what I have is a bit soggy."

I smiled. "So am I," I said.

"Try this." Reaching inside his jacket, Mr Carmichael produced a small packet of hard biscuits, such as seamen use.

"Thank you," I accepted the biscuit with hands so cold I nearly dropped it.

"If you value your teeth, you will allow the biscuit to lie in your mouth before you try to chew." Although Mr Carmichael was smiling, I sensed some anxiety in his words.

Crouching in a most unladylike fashion, I tried to break the biscuit. Mr Carmichael leaned across, "pray permit me," he said and broke off a corner. "Forgive me. I should have done that before I handed it over."

"Thank you," I said again, wondering what else this remarkable man could produce apart from fire, bandages and food. I felt that if I asked him, he could pluck a rabbit from the tall hat I still wore, or pull a string of ribbons from his mouth. Instead, he slid a silver watch from the front of his jacket. "The rain won't do this thing much good," he said. "Which is a great shame as my father gave it to me just last Christmas. Now, Miss Moffat, it is a quarter shy of two o'clock, so it will be dark in three hours. There is sufficient wood to keep the fire alive for a couple of hours, and I am going for a walk."

"In the rain?"

"In the rain. Water has not melted me and never shall." Mr Carmichael gave his characteristic smile. "Why, if I were a fish, I would even thrive on it."

"Indeed, sir," I said, gravely.

"I will return in one hour, that is, shortly before three, which gives you time to dry your clothes, if you wish to."

"I do not wish to," I said.

"That is your choice," Mr Carmichael told me. "You may change your mind. I will give you due warning before I return." He stepped back, giving a brief bow. "I promise that I shall never intentionally do anything to discomfort you."

"Thank you, Mr Carmichael," I replied gravely, with a small nod. I believed him. Despite his dreadful occupation, Mr Carmichael seemed an honourable man.

"One hour then," Mr Carmichael repeated. He left then, striding long-legged and back erect into the rain. I waited for a few moments, as the fire crackled in front of me, and made my decision. It was supremely uncomfortable sitting in wet clothes, so I nervously peeled off my thin summer coat and held it in front of the fire. When the steam rose, I realised that it was my inner clothing that caused me most discomfort, so, after a quick look around in case any passing ploughman should be looking, I began to undress.

I cannot describe my emotions as I gradually removed my clothes. I was undoubtedly nervous, apprehensive in case somebody should see me, yet, somewhere within me, was a small, secret hope that Mr Carmichael should return without warning, or perhaps Matthew Juner. I shook my head. No, not Matthew. I had observed him in similar circumstances and had no desire for him to return the compliment. I did not think of Andrew Dewar. That man barely entered my thoughts at all.

With my heart pounding, I removed the final limp scrap of my clothing and stood as nature intended. I was afraid. I was undoubtedly afraid, although I also enjoyed the sensation of freedom; it was unlike anything I had felt before.

It was then, when I was at my most vulnerable, that I heard the voice.

"Take it down," I did not hear the words distinctly. Instead, they seemed to form inside my head, before drifting away.

"Take it down."

"Mr Carmichael! You said you'd warn me!"

I stepped behind the fire, wrapping my still-damp coat around me and looked around frantically. I heard the voice again, masculine and rough, although this time I could not make out the words.

"Who's there?" Now I was alarmed. That was not Mr Carmichael's voice.

The voice sounded again, joined by another, growling around the deserted church.

"Take it down."

The words made no sense. I peeped cautiously from my side of the fire and saw nobody. Was it a trick of the wind, or my nerves getting the better of my senses? I do not know. I cannot explain that any further, so I shall not try. I was sure I heard voices and equally confident that nobody was there, and that is all there is to it.

When my confidence returned, I returned to my clothes-drying, although with many glances around me to ensure I was alone. Crouching behind the fire, I dried my underthings first and hauled them on, savouring the warmth against my chilled skin. Gradually, I pulled on the remainder, until I was fully dressed except for my coat, which steamed at the fire.

I heard the shout as if from far away.

"Halloa! Miss Moffat! Are you there?"

"I'm here!" I shouted back, strangely relieved to hear Mr Carmichael's voice. "In the old church."

"Are you respectable?"

Yes!" I hastily pulled on my coat. A few moments later, Mr Carmichael appeared, carrying a fresh bundle of sticks and leading Maida by the reins.

"Look who I found grazing by the river," Mr Carmichael said.

"You are indeed a remarkable man," I said. I spread my arms. "As you see, I am now dry."

"Good," Mr Carmichael said.

Maida nuzzled me as if to apologise for running away without me. I patted her, blew in her nostrils and fondled her ears. "I'm glad you're back," I said, slightly reluctantly. "Did you not find Chetak? Did you find your own horse?"

"No," Mr Carmichael shook his head. "She'll turn up. She knows her way to the Sun Inn."

"Is that where you are staying?" I knew the coaching inn between Winter Lodge and Penicuik.

"It is." Mr Carmichael said.

I nodded. "Mr Carmichael," I said, "when you were hunting for firewood and horses, did you see anybody else?"

"Not a soul." Mr Carmichael was busily adding wood to the fire.

"I heard somebody," I said.

Mr Carmichael's smile dropped. "Where?" The word was sharp.

"Here," I said. "Inside the church."

"Did you see anybody?" The messenger emerged from behind Mr Carmichael's polite mask, and I stepped back. I would not wish to be the man Mr Carmichael hunted.

"No," I shook my head.

"I'll scout around," Mr Carmichael said. "I certainly saw nobody." I watched as he moved swiftly away, looking at the ground as much as at his surroundings. He moved like a cat, fast and purposeful, and I imagined him hunting down men for the court. He was back in 10 minutes, shaking his head.

"Nobody," he said. "The only footprints are ours." He smiled. "It must have been the wind in the trees, or perhaps the ghosts."

"What ghosts?"

"Did you not know?" Mr Carmichael sat at my side, half in jest, whole in earnest, as we say. "This old church is said to be haunted."

Wondering if Mr Carmichael were pulling the longbow, I shook my head. "I find that hard to believe." All the same, I dragged my coat tighter around me, as if for protection against the supernatural.

Mr Carmichael slid down the wall until he sat in front of the fire. "You do know what this church was used for, don't you?"

"Religious services?" I hazarded.

"Who used it?" Mr Carmichael questioned me as if I were one of his suspects.

I admitted that I did not know.

"This is Balantrodoch, as you know." When Mr Carmichael turned away, he seemed to be addressing the fire, rather than me. "It was the church of the Knights Templar, once."

"Who are the Knights Templar?" I was not afraid to reveal my ignorance to this man.

"They were a military order back in the middle ages," Mr Carmichael said. "They guarded the Crusaders' routes to Jerusalem, I believe. This area," he gestured to the church and surrounding countryside, "was one of their Scottish bases."

"I had no idea it was such an important place," I said.

Mr Carmichael wafted more life into the fire. "The Templars were an interesting organisation, part religious, part military. I believe that Hugues de Payens himself, the Templar founder, was here. Even now, centuries after their order ended, there are legends about them, about their mysterious practices and their treasure."

I suddenly became interested in the Templars. "Treasure?" I said.

"So the stories go," Mr Carmichael stood back from the fire. "They were a major international order, so I expect they had great wealth once. It's all gone now, of course."

"Of course," I said.

"You sound disappointed." Mr Carmichael smiled across to me. "I expect that the various kings, queens, nobles and other blackguards grabbed all they could of the Templar treasure many centuries ago."

I gave a rueful smile. "So there are no pots of gold buried here."

"Not even a single gold doubloon, or whatever currency they used back then." Mr Carmichael said. He reached over to stroke Maida, his strong hands gentle, even sensual as they smoothed down the horse's fetlocks. "They did leave something behind, though."

"What was that?" I was not sure if he was teasing me or educating me. Perhaps it was a mixture of both.

"Their spirits," Mr Carmichael said. "The spirits of the Templars are said to appear to people who believe, or to people whose ancestors were associated with them."

"I don't believe," I said. "And I doubt I have Templar ancestors."

"It could not have been the ghosts then," Mr Carmichael said solemnly. When he looked up, the laughter was back in his eyes. "I hope you were decent when the ghosts did not appear. I noticed you had dried your clothes." The laughing eyes denied his sudden frown. "You were decent, weren't you?"

I said nothing as the blood rushed to my face.

"You weren't, were you?" Mr Carmichael was smiling. "You were drying your clothes at the time."

I still said nothing.

Mr Carmichael shook his head reassuringly "Ghosts can't see, Miss Moffat. They saw nothing."

"I would rather not discuss my state of dress or undress," I said.

"I apologise," Mr Carmichael stopped smiling at once. He reached out his hand without touching me. "I have no desire to make you feel uncomfortable."

I looked away. In a way, Mr Carmichael was correct – I did feel uncomfortable, but I was glad he did not know the other sensations I experienced.

"If you are ready," Mr Carmichael said, "we shall leave now. The rain has eased a little. I'll take you home and you can have your ankle properly attended to."

"Yes, Mr Carmichael." I said. "I do wish you had found Chetak though."

"It is a small matter," Mr Carmichael said. "If she doesn't return home, I'll post an advertisement in the press and offer a reward for her"

"I feel responsible," I said.

"There is no need for that," Mr Carmichael said. "You did not place the deer in the hawthorn hedge, nor did you force me to abandon Chetak in the field." He held out his hand. "Come now, and we'll get you home."

I admit that I exaggerated my infirmity, with the result that Mr Carmichael had to help me on to the saddle. I can be as devious a minx as Amy, it seems. I adjusted my seat as he removed his hand and smiled up to me. "It's a bit of a distance home," he said. "We'll have to go slowly as you can hardly jump over hedges with your damaged ankle, but we'll still get there before dark."

As I looked back at the ruins of Balantrodoch Church, I felt as if I were leaving somewhere significant in my life. I did not understand it. In trying to hunt down a man to whom I had barely spoken, and was not sure I liked, I found I was falling in love with a man I knew I should despise. I glanced down at Mr Carmichael as he walked beside me, dripping wet and no doubt cold.

"Mr Carmichael," I said. "Thank you." I did not say that no man, except my father, had ever gone out of his way to help me before. Certainly not Andrew Dewar. Nor did I say that I had no urgent desire to return home. For all its discomforts, I did not wish this day to end.

"Miss Moffat." Mr Carmichael spoke without facing me. "It was my pleasure."

As we walked away, a saw a robin, my favourite bird, circle the ruins, land on the slabs next to the still-glowing remains of the fire and peck at the biscuit crumbs I had left. It was the first robin I had seen in months. As I watched, a heron passed by, landed briefly and flew on.

"That's unusual," I said. "I didn't expect to see a heron here."

"That's good luck," Mr Carmichael said. "Our family crest is a heron." He looked at me over his shoulder. "Let's get you home."

I did not wish Mr Carmichael to get me home. I wished him to remain with me, despite his awful occupation.

Chapter Ten

"Robyn!" Mother must have been watching from the drawing-room window for she nearly ran out of the front door to greet me. "You're soaking wet! Are you all right? What happened to your foot?"

"Mr Carmichael has been taking care of me," I said. "You'll have to help me down from the horse."

"What in heaven's name happened?" Mother asked. "And, Mr Carmichael, where is your shirt?"

"Mr Carmichael's shirt is wrapped around my ankle." Rather than Mother helping me, it was Mr Carmichael who lifted me down from Maida and supported me as I balanced on one leg, holding on to Maida's saddle. There was no need for me to play-act, for my ankle had stiffened on the journey and now ached most abominably.

"Come inside, Mr Carmichael." Mother looked momentarily nonplussed.

Mr Carmichael wrapped an arm around me as I limped up the stairs and into the drawing-room, where he deposited me on a seat while Mother called Father down from his study. Within minutes the house was in an uproar as servants scurried hither and yon, spreading all sorts of rumours, chattering at the top of their voices and generally causing mayhem.

"Miss Robyn has broken her leg!"

"That gentleman found Miss Robyn on the ground and brought her home."

"Miss Robyn's horse threw her and Mr Carmichael had to save her life."

"A man found Miss Robyn lying in the ditch, dying."

Father thundered down the steps. "Silence!" He seldom resorted to shouting, so when he did, the household was shocked. "Thank you," he said when quiet descended. "Now, I want all of you to go about your business as efficiently as you always do. Miss Robyn fell off her horse and twisted her ankle. Mr Carmichael brought her home. That is all."

Father's words had the required effect. Calm returned to Winter Lodge.

"Sit you down and listen, Mrs Moffat. Now, miss," Father addressed me, "tell me what happened." He sat on his chair. "You too, Carmichael."

"It's all right, Father," I said. "Mr Carmichael was the perfect gentleman."

"That had better be the case," Father said. I had never seen him so intense. "Explain, Robyn."

With Father's gaze fixed on me, I recounted the day's events, missing out only my interest in Derek Pringle, the strange voices, and my stripping to dry my clothes by the fire.

Father nodded when I completed my tale. "Now tell me your version, Carmichael," Father said. Mr Carmichael did so, with some humour that I had lacked.

Only then did Father leave his chair to kneel at my feet and inspect my ankle. It was years since he had paid me such intimate attention.

"It's all right, Father," I said. "It's not broken."

"You'll live," my loving Mother said.

"Yes." Father twisted my foot this way and that. "I'll have Doctor Mercer have a look at it, but I think Carmichael's diagnosis was correct. You're a foolish girl, Robyn, but you know that already."

"Yes, Father." I had long learned that agreeing with Father was easier than arguing with him.

Placing a low stool under my foot, Father stood up, lifted the tails of his jacket and stood toasting his rump at the fire. "It seems that we owe you a debt, Carmichael," Father said, adding dryly, "and a new shirt."

"There is no debt, Moffat," Mr Carmichael said. "It was my duty as a gentleman to help a lady, especially your daughter."

It was my duty? For some reason, I felt a sharp disappointment. Was it only duty that had compelled Mr Carmichael to help me? I had thought there was something else. After hearing his compliments, I had hoped that Mr Carmichael had some feeling of attachment towards me.

"Even so, Carmichael, I shall not forget what you have done. I always say that a man who is honourable in his private life can be trusted in business."

"I did no more for Miss Robyn than I would have done for any young lady in need of assistance," Mr Carmichael said.

I felt as though Mr Carmichael had slapped me across the face. Only half an hour previously, I had felt a strong affection for Mr Carmichael. Now my feelings for him returned to what they had been as I thought of him hunting down poor Matthew, pistol in hand. I stared at him, knowing he had hurt me far more deeply than Andrew Dewar could ever have, for I had trusted this man.

Mother sensed my discomposure. "I think the excitement of the day has overcome you, Robyn," she said. "An early night in bed is the best cure for you. The doctor will come tomorrow."

"Yes." Hardly able to contain my emotion, I forced a smile. "Thank you again, Mr Carmichael. I'll leave you two alone to discuss duty and business. Mother is correct. I think I'll get to bed." I rose with some difficulty until Mother took hold of my arm.

"You seem upset," Mother said as we negotiated the stairs.

"No," I denied. "I'm just tired."

"You can tell me the whole story later," Mother said as she pushed open my bedroom door. "Including the bits you left out."

With my ankle throbbing, I lay in bed, thinking over the day's events. The morning meeting at Newtonloan Toll seemed a very long time ago. When I closed my eyes, I experienced my fall again, floating in the air with the ground rising towards me and the knowledge of a painful landing to come. Opening my eyes, I felt the ache in my ankle and remembered the two voices I had heard in the church, yet my final vision was of Amy with Derek Pringle, who was wearing a shirt cut into strips as he made a fire on the wall of Balantrodoch church.

* * *

"You thought you heard voices?" Mother spoke to me across the width of the breakfast table. Doctor Mercer had confirmed Mr Carmichael's diagnosis that I had only twisted and not broken my ankle. Patting my knee, the doctor told me that a few days' rest would suffice, so I sat at table with my ankle swathed in bandages and enjoying little sympathy from any member of the family. Honestly, one had to die in Winter Lodge before my mother would spare any tenderness.

"What sort of voices?" Father did not lower his newspaper, which signified he was only slightly interested in the subject.

"I can't describe them," I wished I had not mentioned the subject. "Men's voices."

"That was in Balantrodoch Church?" Father asked.

"Yes," I said.

"What did they say?" Mother leaned half across the table, with the trailing edge of her turban sliding across a plate of toast-and-marmalade.

"I am not sure. It sounded like 'take it down'."

"Take it down," Mother repeated. "How queer. What on earth can it mean?"

"I do not know," I said.

"Did you see anybody?" Father still did not lower his newspaper.

"No," I said. "Neither did Mr Carmichael."

"He's a sound man, Carmichael," Father said.

"It must have been your nerves," Mother decided. "Or the wind."

"Or the spirits of the knights." Father lowered his paper sufficiently for the top of his head to be visible.

That was probably the last thing I expected to hear from my taciturn and pragmatic father. I must have been silent for a good 30 seconds before I replied. "That was what Mr Carmichael said."

"Moffat?" Mother pushed down Father's newspaper until his face was fully visible. "What do you mean?"

"Balantrodoch Church is haunted," Father said as casually as if he were talking of the weather or the price of eggs. "When I was a small boy, we used to sit there looking for the ghosts."

"Did you see any?" I asked while Mother looked unsettled.

"Never," Father shook his head. "Not even once. You were extremely fortunate, Robyn, to hear such a thing."

"Moffat!" Mother found her voice. "We do not believe in ghosts, witches and such things."

"You're right, Mrs Moffat." Father said. "We don't. Very few people have the privilege of experiencing what you experienced, Robyn. I don't know if we can call it a ghost; perhaps it is a memory of the past that certain people can share."

I had never heard Father talk of such matters before, so listened intently.

"Which people, Father," I asked, "and why me?"

Father had completely discarded his newspaper now as he faced me. "Only people directly descended from the Knights Templar who lived in Balantrodoch," he said, "and only when they are undergoing a significant ordeal."

"I'm not descended from the Knights Templar," I said. "And twisting my ankle is hardly a significant ordeal."

"You are a direct descendant from Alexander de Moffat," Father said. "He was one of the last of the knights. Our family has held this property for time immemorial, if not longer."

"I didn't know we were so significant," I said.

Father lifted his tea-cup. "We're possibly the oldest family in the area, except perhaps Ramsay of Dalhousie Castle."

Mother sat quiet, with her eyes darting from side to side as she listened.

"As for the significant ordeal," Father said, "I'd think that choosing a husband is the most significant ordeal any woman can undergo."

"I was not choosing a husband in Balantrodoch Church," I said.

Mother tapped a finger on the table. "Perhaps you should have been. Your Mr Carmichael is a fine gentleman."

"He may be a fine gentleman," I said cautiously. "Or he may not. Either way, he is not *my* Mr Carmichael."

"He is a better man than your Andrew Dewar," Father said. "And you were attached to that fellow for long enough."

"I have no interest in Mr Carmichael," I said. "Nor has he any interest in me."

Father glanced at Mother, who raised her eyebrows, saying nothing.

"We have strayed a long way from the spirits of Balantrodoch," I said.

Father smiled, nodded and returned to his newspaper. "When you eventually choose your man," he said, "remember what happened in the old church at Balantrodoch. According to the old legends, the old spirits guide their descendants."

"That's total moonshine," I said, "I could not understand a word or what they meant."

I heard Father's low chuckle from behind the newspaper. "There are more than words in Balantrodoch."

"What does that mean, Father?" I asked.

"I've said all I'm going to say on the subject," Father said. "You will understand when the time is right, or when you have the right man."

Chapter Eleven

"Are you ready for church, Robyn? It's the Harvest Festival, remember."

I looked up. "I'm coming." Even nine days after the fall, my ankle was still delicate. "I'm ready." Lifting my walking stick, I hobbled after Mother, too proud to accept the servants' offers of help.

As was the tradition, we carried baskets of fruit from the kitchen garden for the harvest festival, so the earthy scent of carrots, potatoes and the sharp tang of onions filled the coach. This month was one of my favourite times of the year, when the soil yielded its bounty, the larder filled, Cook was temporarily contented, and the farmers began to plough their fields. I always found it deeply satisfying to watch the ploughs with their attendant flocks of screaming seagulls.

"Remember, Robyn," Mother held out her hand to help me into the coach, "this is also the anniversary of the Colliers' Loft."

I nodded, although, in truth, I had entirely forgotten. "I suspect the church will be full," I said. It was a full 100 years since the church consented to allow the colliers to worship with the rest of the people, after previously trying to ignore their existence. A century ago, busy hands had built a special place in the church, known as the Colliers' Loft. Each anniversary of that event, the colliers gathered to remember the day the church accepted them as members of the congregation. This year the anniversary coincided with the Harvest Festival, with the new Gowkpen Church honouring the tradition.

"The colliers were serfs then," Mother reminded me. "Slaves that were bought and sold with the pits."

"I have heard that," I said. "We were ayeways hard on the coal workers."

Knocking on the roof as a signal to George, Mother nodded. "I like to see everybody gathered together to worship. It's a reminder that we are all Jock Tamson's bairns, equal in the sight of God, whatever our status in life."

"Father would not agree with that," I said. "Or Mr Carmichael."

"Your father is a man of many complexities," Mother gave me a sideways look. "As for Mr Carmichael, I am sure you know him better than I do. I have not seen him since he brought you home from the hunt."

"Neither have I." I gripped my walking stick firmly, fighting a surge of anger, or was it disappointment? That day at Balantrodoch Church, I had experienced the strangest feelings for Mr Carmichael – I had thought I was falling in love with the man. His words that only duty had compelled him to help me had hurt more than I would ever admit. Now I hoped never to see him again, under any circumstances.

"Moffat told me that business called Mr Carmichael back to Edinburgh." Mother's gaze did not stray from my face.

"I am sure his duty was urgent," I said.

"I am sure it was," Mother said. "Just look at the crowds!"

I glanced out of the window. It was a beautiful autumn Sunday, with the sun peering behind shining bands of pink and silver to the east and the air crisply refreshing. Perhaps it was the glorious day that drew the people from their houses or the insistent clamour of the church bells. Whatever the reason, collier families filled the road between the little mining communities and the church. Some willingly stepped aside when our coach grumbled up, others were more reluctant to give way, so George had to crack his whip.

"George!" Mother shouted. "It's the Sabbath. Be gentle! These good people have as much right to the road as we have."

"You're a kindly woman, Mother," I said.

Mother pulled back her chin as she looked at me. "That is a queer thing to say, Robyn."

"It is true," I said. "You care for other people more than anyone I have ever met."

"Nonsense!" Mother turned away my compliment. "You could have worn a better coat today, Robyn. That one has never recovered from the soaking it got."

"I lost my better coat, remember?" I knew Mother was only deflecting attention from my praise. "Father said he wouldn't release money for another until I learn to appreciate what I have."

"Your father is quite right,"' Mother said. "We have so much while others have nothing, and they still attend church to give praise to the Lord."

I could not stop my words. "And some men spend their lives hunting and prosecuting those who try to alleviate that poverty."

"There are some such," Mother agreed while studying my face. "You can tell me what you mean by that later, lady. Here we are at the church, so I want nothing but charitable thoughts and words."

"Yes, Mother."

Although built on ancient foundations, Gowkpen Church was only a few years old, with a tall tower pleading mercy from the Lord. Around the building, even the stones in the far-older graveyard seemed to be looking upward in anticipation of the Harvest Festival. The people crowded into the church; gentlemen and ladies in sober clothes, farmers with broadcloth and broad shoulders and farm servants and cottars in their Sunday best. Walking awkwardly in unaccustomed boots, the children tried to behave while many colliers, ignored by all, carried produce from their patches of garden.

I started as I saw Amy there, making sheep's eyes at Derek Pringle, who returned the compliment with a gallant bow. I hoped that his hat would fall off, but it didn't, blast it. Amy gave a very elegant curtsey, noticed me looking and smiled in utter triumph at having captured a man I had hoped to snare. I put all my accumulated malice into my most charming smile.

"There's Mr Beaton," Mother said. "Straighten your face, Robyn – you look as if you lost a crown and found a farthing."

Hugh Beaton was taller than anybody else in the crowd, with his topper making him taller still. He walked with a long, awkward stride, touched the brim of his hat to Mrs Juner and a group of colliers' wives, and made way to allow them into the church before him.

"He is a true gentleman," I said thoughtfully.

"I have always believed so," Mother said. "Do you wish me to make a formal introduction?"

"Perhaps," I said. "It is only a pity that Mr Beaton is such a shy creature, and so graceless."

"Is he so shy?" Mother looked at me, not hiding her smile. "I have not noticed. As for the lack of grace, tall men are often embarrassed at their height."

I said no more as I watched Mr Beaton take his place in church with great dignity, if no style, removing his hat as he entered the building and sweeping up the tails of his coat before he sat down.

"Shall I ask him to Winter Lodge?" Mother asked.

"Not yet," I said. I had known of Mr Beaton most of my life, although until recently, we had only met by chance in the streets of Dalkeith. Save for formal balls, there were few occasions when young women and men could meet, and I was never inclined to dancing. I wished it were otherwise when I heard of many of my peers pairing off at such events.

"Time is passing," Mother reminded, responding to a curtsey from the wife of a tenant farmer. "You are not growing younger, and the list of potentials is shrinking. Why there is your particular friend Amy looking as if she's set her cap at Mr Pringle." Mother ushered me to our pews. "Were you not interested in Mr Pringle only a week or so ago?"

"I dismissed him from my mind," I said. "He ignored my predicament at the Hunt, which is not the mark of any gentleman I would have as a husband."

"If I recall from what you told me, he was well in front with Amy Peacock and would not see you." Mother pointed out. "Look, Mr Beaton is looking at you. Sit up straight."

I did, of course, for one must always do one's mother's bidding. Besides, Mr Beaton was more handsome than I remembered, or perhaps I was becoming desperate as my pool of potential husbands dried up. When I passed my gaze over the men in that church, Mr Beaton's shyness did not seem such a terrible thing.

As the church filled, the mumble of conversation increased to a roar, with women and men competing with each other to be heard inside the echoing building. I saw Andrew enter, but his gaze passed over me with as little interest as I had in him. He sat on the pew amid the Dewar clan, exchanged a pleasantry with that minx Amy and turned a cold shoulder in my direction. Only when the minister arrived did the noise gradually die away, and the worship begin.

While I sang our hymns as demurely as possible, I hoped that Mr Beaton was still watching me. During the prayers, I eased one eye open to peer around the church. The first thing I saw was that brazen hussy Amy Peacock poking out her tongue in the direction of Mr Pringle. His response was similar, the immoral blaggard. Mr Beaton was standing with his eyes firmly closed, not even thinking of looking in my direction. Somebody was though, I was sure of it.

I have to admit that despite my scepticism, ever since my visit to Balantrodoch Church, I had thought my senses sharpened in some way. I knew, or thought I knew, what Mother was going to say an instant before she said it, and I knew when the maids were about to enter a room. Now I could almost feel somebody's eyes on me.

A second check told me that Mr Beaton remained devoutly praying, while Mr Pringle and Amy continued to make foolish gestures to each other. Andrew Dewar was not interested in anybody except Andrew Dewar, wearing clothes too tight for his expanding body and an expression of intense righteousness on his face. As far as I could see, all the other gentlemen present were either married or too old to be interesting. Sighing, I was about to return to my worship when I happened to glance at the Colliers Loft, the area reserved for those colliers whom we had seen crowding the road. Right in the centre, standing among a group of his peers, Matthew Juner was staring right at me.

I swear that I gasped with the shock, for I had thought that Matthew was far away in safety by now. What was he thinking of, nearly thumbing his nose at authority by returning to the very parish where they were most diligently searching for him?

As soon as he saw me looking, Matthew raised a hand in acknowledgement, touching the lapels of his coat. No doubt he intended the gesture as a message, but it meant nothing to me. I shrugged, quickly looking away as the minister closed his prayer with a resounding Amen and called for another hymn.

As my heart beat a rapid tattoo within my breast, I sang lustily, wondering what fresh trouble Matthew was bringing on his head. Why had he returned? Did he expect me to help him again? Despite my fears, I could not deny that I was glad to see him, and even gladder that the charmingly obnoxious Mr Carmichael was away on business. No doubt Mr Carmichael was chasing some other poor fellow who was doing his best for his fellow beings.

As the service drew on, I found that I was glancing towards the colliers more and more, and every time I did, I met Matthew's eye. Sometimes he smiled to me. More often, he tapped the lapel of his coat and raised his eyebrows, evidently trying to convey some secret message. I frowned and looked away, hoping that Mother did not see the direction of my attention. Even if she did, she would not comment while we were in church. A great one for the proprieties, was my mother, as long as it suited her.

Eventually, the service came to an end, and we filed into the still-bright sunshine. "I noticed you were watching that collier man," Mother said the second, we stepped outside.

"That was Matthew Juner." I stopped Mother's questioning before it began. "Mrs Juner's fugitive son."

Mother took a deep breath. "He seemed to know you."

"We have met." I was always reluctant to tell a lie, and never on a Sunday.

Mother nodded. "He's rather foolish coming here," she said. "Anybody might report his presence to the police."

"I know," I said. "Please excuse me, Mother. I wish to speak to him."

"That may not be the best of ideas," Mother said.

"I know," I said. "It may even be the worst."

Leaving Mother standing, shaking her head, I limped towards Matthew, hoping to ask him what his gestures meant and what he meant by venturing into the lion's mouth, the anniversary of the collier's loft or not.

"Robyn!"

I tried to ignore Amy as she shouted my name, waving her hand in a most unladylike manner. "Robyn!" I might as well have copied King Canute and tried to stop the tide. Flapping her arms like a windmill in a gale, she stopped in front of me. "Robyn, I must speak to you."

"Amy, control yourself," I said, trying to look over her shoulder at Matthew. "People are looking."

Amy was nearly jumping with excitement. "I heard about your accident. I hope you are feeling better now."

I tapped my stick on the ground. "I still need this." I had not forgiven Amy for stealing Mr Pringle from me.

"Never mind that," Amy dismissed my injury with a lift of her hand. "I want to find out if Derek Pringle is the right man for me."

"I am sure the two of you can work that out between you." I tried to step around Amy as I saw a knot of colliers bearing Matthew away in their midst.

"I need your help, Robyn." Amy blocked my passage with ease.

"Why?" I asked. "Surely your arrangement with Mr Pringle is not my concern."

"I would like you to make it so," Amy said.

I did not reply to Amy's words. I could not think of what to say. The colliers were already hurrying Matthew out of the churchyard, with one man holding a hat to conceal Matthew's face.

"Good morning, Miss Peacock." Mother arrived to delay my progress towards Matthew even further.

"Good morning, Mrs Moffat," Amy dropped in an elaborate curtsey.

"Pray let me into the secret, Miss Peacock," Mother said. "What is so important that you must leap around like a monkey?"

Amy's smile could have charmed the birds from the trees as she curtseyed again. "I wish Robyn's help in a matter of the heart, Mrs Moffat."

"Oh? How interesting. In what way could Robyn help?" Taking hold of Amy's arm, Mother steered her away from me as I stared helplessly at the gate, where a great crowd blocked any possibility I had of catching Matthew. Amy spoke for a few moments. Then, I heard Mother's laugh.

"Robyn." Mother was trying hard to suppress her laughter on the Sabbath. "Miss Peacock wishes you to help find her perfect husband."

"Is that so?"

"I think you should agree," Mother said. "You have my full permission." She smiled again. "As Moffat is in Edinburgh on business with Mr Carmichael, there is no need to consult him, or even for him to know."

"That's a queer thing to say." Mother's interference had slowed me further. I could no longer see the colliers or Matthew.

"It's a queer method of finding a husband," Mother said. "You may even find it of interest in your own endeavours."

I sighed. Matthew was out of sight and out of reach. "What do you wish me to do, Amy?"

* * *

We stood by a bend in the River South Esk, hard by Trotter's Bridge, with a small cliff before us and a gravelly beach under our feet. The last leaves of autumn drifted down from the overhanging trees, to join their brown companions on the surface of the water.

"Is this the first time you have done this, Robyn?" Amy asked.

"It is," I said. "I honestly don't believe in such superstitions."

"Neither do I," Amy said. "It was my grandmother's idea. She has some queer beliefs."

"Old people often do," I looked around at the surrounding trees. Some rustled in the decay of autumn. Others stretched stark branches to the uncaring sky. All seemed to be watching me.

"Grandmother told me that in her day, girls came to this bend in the river to see their future husbands."

I shivered. "It's rather a strange place to come," I said. "It's lonely."

"That's the idea," Amy said. "Nobody will disturb us. Grandmother said that when the new moon appears, we have to ask its help, and we'll see the reflection of our future husband in the water."

For some reason, I shivered at the thought. The memory of these voices at Balantrodoch Church was suddenly very vivid. "That sounds like witchcraft to me."

"It probably was witchcraft, knowing my grandmother," Amy said. "She was the most witch-like person you could possibly conceive."

Looking through the naked branches, I saw the faintest glint of light through a shroud of cloud. "The moon will appear soon. We'd best get ourselves ready."

"Grandmother said we have to stand on that rock in the middle of the river." Amy shone her lantern towards a flat slab of stone about three yards into the dark water.

"You go first," I said. "I've been wet enough for one autumn."

"All right." Sitting on a fallen tree to pull off her boots and stockings, Amy lifted her skirt to her knees and stepped into the water. "It's freezing,'" she said.

"Go on," I encouraged, struggling with my laces. By the time I had my boots and stockings off, Amy stood on the slab with the river surging on either side of her.

"Come along, Robyn, or the moon will rise before you get here."

Closing the shutter of the lantern so we could see the moonlight better, and using my stick as an aid, I joined Amy. We stared upwards, waiting for the moon to appear through the ragged clouds. We must have shivered there a good 10 minutes before the moon deigned to shine on us.

"What now?" I already regretted coming out with Amy. It was dark, cold and miserable.

"Now we say a rhyme," Amy told me, "and our future husband will appear in that pool." She pointed to a deep pool that had formed downstream of our slab. "My grandmother calls that the Lover's Pool."

"Can we say any rhyme we choose?" I asked.

"No, silly, just this one," Amy chided me, chanting the first verse.

> *"New moon, true moon*
> *Tell unto me,*
> *If my ane true love*
> *He will marry me."*

I listened, wondering at my foolishness in letting Amy talk me into coming here.

"Come on, Robyn," Amy said. "You have to say the words as well, or it doesn't work.

Feeling very self-conscious, I followed Amy's lead, repeating the verses after her.

> *"If he marry me in haste*
> *Let me see his bonny face*
> *If he marry me betide,*
> *Let me see his bonnie side*
> *Gin he marry na me ava*
> *Turn his back and gae awa."*

When our voices trailed into silence, we peered together into the dark pool of water behind the slab. I saw only ripples and the splash of a single tiny fish, while Amy gasped and grabbed my arm.

"There!" she said. "Did you see that?"

"No." I was cold, tired and in no mood to play Amy's silly games.

"I saw a face in the water." Amy said.

"I didn't see anything," I said, grumpily.

"Good," Amy said. "That's because it was my true love and not yours. I saw Derek Pringle, clear as the nose on your face.

I grunted in a most unladylike manner. "This is a game for small children. You and Derek Pringle are well-suited," I said. I was about to add some very uncomplimentary remarks about leaving me to lie on the ground during the hunt when Amy took hold of my arm.

"Thank you," Amy said. "Do you honestly believe so?"

Amy looked so eager that I could not find the heart to hurt her. "Yes," I said. "Yes, I think he is a wonderful man, and I do hope the two of you find happiness together." I did not have to force my smile.

"Do you?" Amy's grip on my arm could hardly have been tighter. "You don't mind that he and I got together? I rather thought you liked him yourself."

"I've hardly spoken to the man," I said truthfully.

"Good." Amy hugged me, which was unwise while I was balancing one-legged on a small stone in the middle of a dark river. I yelped, dug my stick into the river bed and nearly toppled into the water. Amy yelled in my ear, and we ended up hugging and giggling together like schoolgirls as the moon gleamed down upon us.

"I'm going to marry him," Amy whispered in my ear.

"The two of you decided that quickly," I said.

"Oh, he doesn't know yet," Amy said. "I'll let him ask me when the time is right."

We laughed again.

"You're a devious woman, Amy," I said, half in jest and whole in earnest.

"Thank you, Robyn," Amy took the compliment at face value. "It's cold here. Let's get out of the river."

We began the cold paddle back to the pebble beach where we had left our boots and stockings. My weak ankle forced me to sit on the ground to pull on my stockings, and in that position, I saw the bird arrive. I heard the slow flap of its wings first, and then moonlight gleamed on something white and vaguely primeval landing on the slab we had so recently vacated.

"What are you looking at?" Amy asked. "It's only a bird."

"It's a heron," I said as the large bird perched on the flat stone and began to search the Lover's Pool for fish. I did not add that it was Adam Carmichael's bird. Anyway, he thought of me only as his duty, and I hated him for his occupation.

Didn't I?

When I looked at the heron again, I thought its eyes were mocking me, but that was only my imagination, brought on my Amy's silly game.

Chapter Twelve

"Well?" Mother asked when we returned home, for Amy was spending the night at Winter Lodge. "Did you see your husband in the Lover's Pool?"

"Amy said she saw hers." I was still confused by the night's events.

"Who did you see?" Mother asked.

"Derek Pringle," Amy's eyes were wide with wonder, making her look like a girl of 15 rather than a woman of 23. "I saw his face as clearly as I see yours, Mrs Moffat."

"Then that is your future assured, Amy. All you need do now is follow your heart and see if it leads to Mr Pringle."

"It will," Amy said.

Mother nodded. "Sometimes, these old practices are more helpful than we realise."

"I've never heard of that one before," I said, grumpily. "It's a silly superstition."

"Perhaps." Mother ushered us back up the stairs, with the flame of her candle sending flickering shadows across the wall. "But I think it helps focus your mind on who you want to see."

We waited until Amy withdrew into one of our guest bedrooms and closed the door before I spoke further.

"Amy said she saw Mr Pringle." I got ready for bed as Mother sat on my chair, listening.

"Than that is who she hopes to marry." Mother said. "Did you see anybody?"

"No," I said, crawling between the sheets, luxuriating in heat left by the warming-pan the maid had placed there earlier. I did not mention the heron. It had only been a bird.

"I saw Moffat." Mother blew out the candle.

"You saw Father?" I spoke into the sudden darkness. "You looked into the Lover's Pool?"

"Yes." Mother had not moved from the chair. "He followed me to the Pool and waited at the river bank. When I said the words, he jumped into the water and nearly drowned himself. The silly fool didn't know how deep it was."

I laughed, trying to imagine my respectable father acting in such a manner. "How unfortunate."

"Was it? It demonstrated our love," Mother said. "The Pool never seems to work as we expect. Are you sure you saw nothing?"

"I only saw a bird," I said reluctantly.

"Ah," Mother's voice came from the doorway. "Perhaps it was a pigeon carrying a message."

"It was a heron," I said, "hunting for a fish."

"A heron," Mother said. "Are you sure he wasn't hunting for a wife?" She closed the door, leaving me with my mind a whirl of confused thoughts. The surrounding darkness seemed to mirror the sombreness of my future. Yet as I lay there, I saw a man's face. It seemed to arrive unsought in my mind, as Amy claimed Derek Pringle's had appeared to her.

I sat up in bed with a jerk.

Matthew Juner. I had seen Matthew Juner in my mind; my future was tied to that steady-eyed, self-taught collier.

The realisation was comforting. I felt as if I had seen Matthew in person as if he was in Winter Lodge, and I was descending the stairs to greet him. I was smiling, wearing my favourite dress of deep red, edged in silver, and he stood at the door, holding something in his hand. I could not see what it was. I heard wedding bells in the background, the deep, near sonorous clatter of Gowkpen Church, and saw Matthew waiting at the altar, with the miners filling the pews and a woman walking up the aisle towards him.

"Is that me?" I asked the question. "Is that me?"

The bride turned to reply, but before she unveiled her face, I heard a terrible noise. The church dissolved into fragments, the people vanished and only Matthew remained, staring at me surrounded by dark water, with one hand held out in a desperate appeal for help. And then the shouting started. I was awake in my bed, and Winter Lodge was in turmoil.

"They've got him!" Agnes shouted shrill-voiced.

"Got who?" That was Cook's excited voice.

"The thief! The escapee! The messenger-at-arms captured him in our grounds!"

Being wakened suddenly is always a shock. But being wakened to such a noisy racket when one has hardly got to sleep is the worst of sensations. I lay there between the covers, trying to make sense of the situation. I heard my mother's voice calling for quiet.

"You'll waken the household!" Mother said. "You'll waken Miss Robyn and Miss Amy!"

"It's too late, Mother," I called. "I'm already awake." Dragging myself out of bed, I took hold of my walking stick and limped to the door. Amy peered out of her bedroom, her hair an explosion and her eyes startled.

Lanterns and candles bobbed across the corridor, showing servants rushing about in various stages of dress and undress. Only Sims was fully dressed, holding a single candle in a brass holder as he tried to organise the staff. Mother was in her night-gown, with an untidy turban on her head and her feet bare, while James, our younger male servant sported only long white underwear, until Mother sent him about his business with a flea in his ear.

"James! Make yourself decent before Miss Robyn sees you!"

"It's all right, Mother," I said. "I'm not shocked." I saw poor James scurry away, trying to cover himself with an outspread hand held behind. "What's to do?" I asked.

"It's nothing to concern you, Robyn." Mother ran up the stairs, candle in hand and her turban unravelling with every step. "You get back to bed."

Amy stepped into the corridor with her night-clothes in disarray and her eyes bleary from lack of sleep. "What's happening, Robyn? Is it morning already? Is it a fire?"

"It's that man, Miss." The 14-year-old Agnes had wonder in her eyes. She spoke to me even as she watched James in his state of undress. "The messenger caught him in our grounds."

"Which man, Agnes?" I pulled her attention entirely to me. At her age, she was too young to watch boys in their underwear, especially James, who was quite handsome and apparently well put together. "Explain more clearly, please."

Brushing back her blonde hair, Agnes took a deep breath, forced her gaze away from the retreating James and faced me. "That man, Miss Robyn, the one the police were after."

"Do you mean the collier?" I grasped Agnes by the shoulders. "Do you mean Matthew Juner, the collier?"

"Yes, miss, that's the one." Agnes nodded so eagerly her hair flopped across her face. "Matthew Juner, the collier."

I felt my heartbeat increase further. "What about him, Agnes?"

"The messenger caught him, Miss." Agnes nodded again to emphasise her words.

Restraining myself from slapping the foolish girl, I took a deep breath. "Which messenger?" I already guessed the answer.

"The Queen's messenger, Miss," Agnes slowed down. "The messenger-at-arms that's been chasing him all over Scotland. Mr Andrew Dewar saw Matthew Juner at church on Sunday and told the messenger, who caught him in our grounds, miss, and with things stolen from our house! They'll hang him for sure." Agnes twisted her head to one side, thrusting out her tongue in imitation of a man being hanged.

I was not sure what to think. "Go about your business." I pushed Agnes away.

"What fun!" Amy ran to me in high excitement. "Imagine a wanted criminal in your grounds. You do have such an exciting life, Robyn!"

"Everybody go back to bed," Mother took charge. "We'll see what's what in the morning. Go on! Get to your beds!"

Only Sims and I remained still as the other servants scurried away, talking among themselves.

"Mother," I said.

"Good night, Robyn," Mother said firmly.

"But, Mother…"

"Good night, Robyn. Go to bed."

"Good night." I retreated behind my bedroom door to think things through. I did not know what time it was, only that it was dark and my mind was too active to allow sleep. The messenger had captured Matthew. Was that the reason than Mr Carmichael had spent so much time with Father? Had he been waiting to trap Matthew? Had his pretended friendship with me only been for that single duty?

There were so many thoughts and images racing through my head that I could not put anything into order. I saw Matthew and Mr Carmichael, the Lover's Pool and Derek Pringle, mud and rain and the ranks of redcoats in Dalkeith. Lying on my face on the bed, I gripped the covers in my hand and fought my frustration. I knew Matthew had tried to create a combination of colliers, but a thief? Why? And what on earth had he stolen? No doubt I would find out in the morning.

I must have slept that night, for something wakened me, but in the morning I was as heavy of eye as I was of heart and staggered down to the breakfast room with my ankle as sore as it had been for days and all the servants excited with the news.

"The messenger caught him sneaking through the garden." Agnes was an expert in passing on information. Mother stood her at the foot of the table and questioned her.

"Are you sure it was Matthew Juner?" Mother asked.

"Yes, Mrs Moffat," Agnes confirmed, nodding vigorously.

"And he was stealing from us?"

"Yes, Mrs Moffat," Agnes said solemnly. "The messenger caught him with a whole bundle of things from the house. Dozens of them."

Mother indicated the door. "Thank you, Agnes. You may return to your duties."

"Yes, Mrs Moffat." Agnes bobbed in a curtsey.

"And that is how rumours start," Mother told us primly as Amy gobbled breakfast as if she had not seen food for weeks. Honestly, I have no idea how that woman keeps her figure. One of these days she will simply expand until no man, not even Derek horsey Pringle, will wish to be near her, I hope.

Mother continued. "Here is what happened, to the best of my knowledge. The authorities, in the presence of Andrew Dewar, arrested Matthew Juner in the grounds of our house last night. That much is correct. He was carrying one item of ours, I believe, certainly not a whole bundle. As far as I am aware, there was no messenger-at-arms involved."

"What did he have?" I asked.

"I do not know." Mother said with a shrug. "If you remember, Cook complained of various items of food going missing, and you lost your winter coat, I recall. Perhaps our Mr Juner has been methodically stealing from this house since he escaped from the police in Dalkeith."

I nodded, trying to hide my guilt. "What will happen to him now?"

"Mr Dewar took him to Dalkeith, from where he will be carried to jail in Edinburgh until his trial."

"His trial?"

"He is accused of using a combination to intimidate others, which is a serious offence, Robyn," Mother said, "and so is breaking into a house to steal."

I thought of Matthew emerging naked and vulnerable from the Winter Burn. "What could happen?"

"I'm not sure" Mother moderated her tone. "Maybe transportation to Van Diemen's Land, or penal servitude, or worse."

"Worse?" I heard the tremor in my voice.

"I believe the judge could sentence him to death," Mother said quietly.

"Oh." I could not think of anything to say.

Leaning across the table, Mother patted my arm. "He made his bed, Robyn, and now he must lie in it. There is nothing you could do to help. We can't allow thieves to go unpunished."

"He might not be a thief." I knew my words sounded weak.

"The court will decide on his guilt or innocence," Mother said. "Now, you have other matters to think about, I hope."

"Have I?"

"You have a decision to make and a husband to find."

Thinking of Matthew, I nodded. "Yes, Mother."

At the foot of the table, Amy looked up. "I don't have that worry," she said. "The Lover's Pool showed me my husband."

"Yes, dear," Mother said with infinite patience. "We know."

After that, there was only the sound of munching toast and the delicate clink of cups on saucers. Inside my mind, despair battled with a determination to get Matthew free. How could I do that?

I knew of only one man with legal experience, and he was so shy that he fled from my company the last occasion we had met. How on earth could I ask his advice when he was evidently scared of women?

I sat through that breakfast in misery as I tried to dredge up all that I knew of Hugh Beaton. What had Father once said about him? He played golf. Where did he play golf, I wondered? I did not know, and Father was not here to ask, but Amy was, and one thing was certain, Amy Peacock would know all there was to know about every eligible man in Midlothian.

"Amy," I asked after breakfast, "would you care for a walk with me?"

"I'd like nothing better," Amy said. "Unless you are planning one of your horrible expeditions to the top of Camp Hill."

"Not at all," I said. "A quiet stroll around the grounds only, to refresh our minds."

"And talk about Mr Pringle, no doubt," Mother said.

"He may come into the conversation," I said.

Naturally, we did talk about Derek Pringle. Indeed, it was hard to divert Amy's attention away from that less-than-fascinating subject once we were outside the house.

I led us around the grounds, keeping to the well-maintained paths and the neatly-cropped grass, where no stray colliers were hiding. After the first half-hour of Amy's gushing about how perfect Mr Pringle was, and how happy they would be together, I ventured to steer her on to the subject of Hugh Beaton.

"Ah." Amy caught on at once. "You have recovered from Mr Dewar then and are after other game. I never did like that man, despite his wealth – far too self-important for his position."

"I have quite forgotten about Andrew Dewar," I said.

"And now Mr Beaton occupies your thoughts," Amy put her small hand on my arm. "I have heard little bad about Mr Beaton," she said, "but little good either."

"What do you mean?" I asked.

"I mean I have heard little about him at all," Amy said. "He rarely attends social gatherings, never speaks to ladies, and when he is not studying for his legal profession, he is at his foolish golf."

"Ah," I said. "Mr Beaton's golf. Where does he play at golf?"

Amy stopped walking to consider. Evidently, it was hard for her to stroll and think at the same time. "I know he played at Bruntsfield Links in Edinburgh," she said, "for many of the legal profession meet there."

"Oh," I tried to hide my disappointment, for Father would not lend me the coach to travel into Edinburgh, and I did not know the capital well enough to walk from wherever the stagecoach stopped. "Bruntsfield Links in Edinburgh."

Amy shrugged and, with her thinking completed, continued her walking. "Yes. Edinburgh and on Musselburgh Links, of course."

"Of course," I said. "Musselburgh Links."

"Mr Beaton's cousin lives in Inveresk," Amy spoke as if everybody should know about Hugh Beaton's cousin. "I believe they play golf together every Tuesday morning, rain or shine."

"Ah," I said, suddenly eager to get to Musselburgh to view the Links. "That is near Fisherrow, is it not?"

"Where?" Amy turned a curious eye on me. "I have never heard of the place."

"Fisherrow," I said, "where the fisherfolk live."

"Oh," Amy said. "The fisherfolk. I have no idea where such people might live or if they live at all." She gave a small laugh at her attempt at humour.

"I'm sure it is nearby," I said. "Mother intends to do charitable work with them."

"Oh, I am sure they need it," Amy said, and returned to her favourite subject of Amy Peacock's romantic hopes and dreams.

* * *

"You wish to accompany me to Fisherrow?" Mother looked at me with suspicion. "Why the sudden reversal, lady?"

"I thought of our poor fisherfolk out on the Forth, battling the storms and seas every day," I gave the speech I had been rehearsing all day in front of the mirror. "And how lucky we are not facing the hardships they must endure."

"What's his name?" Mother ignored my words as if I had not spoken.

"Whose name?" I pretended innocence with no hope of success.

"The name of the young man whom you hope to see in Musselburgh?"

"Mr Hugh Beaton." I capitulated at once. "He has a cousin in Inveresk and plays golf at Musselburgh Links."

"I see.," Mother shook her head. "It's a sad thing to use charity as a pretext for a romantic liaison, Robyn."

"Yes, Mother," I agreed, "but you have encouraged me to use diligence in my search for a husband."

"Diligence, yes, deception, no." Mother did not smile. She shook her head in pretended sorrow at my duplicity. "You may come and welcome. I'll drop you off at the Links."

Musselburgh Golf Links claims to be one of the oldest in the world, although Leith and Bruntsfield may have something to say on that matter. It is an airy spot, hard by the shore of the Firth of Forth and, when Mother stopped the carriage to allow me to alight, what she called a fresh breeze nearly lifted the hat from my head. I gripped my walking stick firmly for, although my ankle was almost healed, I had grown used to carrying a stick.

"I'll be three hours," Mother said. "Are you certain you don't wish Agnes as a companion?"

"Yes, Mother," I said meekly, for the last thing I wanted was a chattering servant girl accompanying me when I spoke to Mr Beaton.

I was fortunate in the weather for, save for the wind, the day was dry and bright, which seemed to encourage the golfers to emerge from wherever they lived whenever not on the course. I watched, wondering about the appeal of whacking a small ball across a stretch of grass into a hole in the ground. The men seemed to take it very seriously, and then I saw Mr Beaton's angular form, playing with a tall, athletic-looking man who had his back to me.

Mr Beaton did not look as awkward on the golf course as he had elsewhere. I watched as he lined up his ball and smashed it a colossal distance, with his partner shading his eyes from the low sun to follow its progress. I wondered at the correct way to address a golfer during a match. Should I wave like an idiot, run across the green, or wait until the men finished their game, then seek Mr Beaton out?

In the event, I need not have worried, for Mr Beaton's golfing companion was not as accomplished at striking the ball as his appearance suggested. I watched as Mr Beaton's companion lined up his shot, lifted his club and fired the ball at right angles to the fairway, so it came within a few yards of where I stood.

I stood still while both players strolled towards me, and then I wished I had not. While Mr Beaton visibly shuddered at the sight of a woman next to the ball, his companion gave me a wide smile.

"Miss Moffat," he said. "What a lovely surprise to see you here! I hope your ankle is healing nicely."

I gave a small curtsey in reply to his bow, ignoring the sinking sensation inside my stomach. "It is, Mr Carmichael, thank you." I said. "Good morning, Mr Beaton."

"That is good. What brings you here?" Mr Carmichael asked while Mr Beaton studied the grass at his feet.

"I came to watch the golf," I said and quickly amended my words. "I also hoped to speak to Mr Beaton."

"Oh." I swear that Mr Carmichael looked disappointed for a moment before the habitual laughter returned to his eyes. "Well, here he is, Miss Moffat."

"Good morning, Mr Beaton." I curtseyed again, hoping to draw some conversation from the man.

"Good morning." Mr Beaton did not raise his gaze from the grass.

"Mr Beaton," I said, and stopped, unsure how to proceed with the messenger listening to every word I said.

"Is this a personal conversation?" Mr Carmichael showed more decorum than I had expected. Raising his hat, he stepped away. "I'll be beside my ball, Hugh, when you are ready."

Mr Beaton looked up, nodded and resumed his scrutiny of the ground.

Hugh? These two men were on first name terms, which was unusual in my experience, but if both were in the legal business, perhaps they frequently worked together.

"Mr Beaton," I began again, "I should wish your advice over a legal matter."

"A legal matter?" Mr Beaton looked up briefly. "What is that, pray?"

Taking a deep breath, I began my story. "There is a man in custody whom I would like to help."

"Does he have a name, this man?" Mr Beaton interrupted.

"Matthew Juner," I said. "He is a collier at Winterhill Pit."

"I know the name," Mr Beaton said at once.

"Do you know the facts of the case?" I asked.

Mr Beaton gave a brief nod. "Some." He looked at Mr Carmichael, who stood patiently beside his golf ball, waving another contesting pair on to the next hole. "Do you know anything that might help the unfortunate fellow?"

Torn between telling Mr Beaton the whole story and letting him continue with the match, I hesitated. "I might," I said.

"Then do so, Miss Moffat," Mr Beaton was no longer shy. "Any facts may save him from a long spell in prison, transportation, or even the rope."

"Would you pass my information on to whoever is his defence solicitor?" I asked.

"I am defending Mr Juner," Mr Beaton said. "Come now, Miss Moffat, tell me what you know."

"I am spoiling your game," I pointed out.

"The match is less important than poor Mr Juner's life," Mr Beaton said. "Wait here, Miss Moffat."

This Mr Beaton was not the shy man I thought I knew. He was both decisive and abrupt. Without another word he stalked to Mr Carmichael, returning in a few moments.

"Where are you staying?" Mr Beaton asked.

"I'm not staying in Musselburgh," I said. "I'm only in the area for a few hours."

"That will have to do," Mr Beaton said. "Adam, that is Mr Carmichael, and I have spent half the morning discussing Matthew Juner's case."

I raised my eyebrows, wondering what the defence solicitor had to discuss with the messenger-at-arms who had hunted for Matthew.

"How much time do you have?" Mr Beaton nearly snapped the words.

"My mother will be here at noon to collect me," I said.

Mr Beaton glanced at his watch. "That gives us the best part of three hours," he said. "I see you walk with a stick, but I have a carriage nearby. We can talk in Esk House, my cousin's place, if you are agreeable?"

Quite swept away by Mr Beaton's manner, I could only nod. Within a few moments, I was sitting inside his very comfortable carriage on the short drive to Esk House. Mr Beaton sat opposite, barely looking at me as he cradled his bag of golf clubs in his arms.

"Will your cousin not mind?" I asked.

"Not a bit of it." Mr Beaton dismissed the idea without a qualm as he ushered me through the front door of what was a substantial Georgian manor house with an impressive array of windows. Waving aside a uniformed butler, Mr Beaton showed me into a snug room where a variety of decanters was arranged on a side table beside half a dozen deep leather armchairs. In the corner beside the window, a long-case clock sounded away the minutes, its soft tick strangely comforting.

"Pray take a seat," Mr Beaton invited.

I did so, folding my skirt beneath me.

"Now," Mr Beaton sat directly opposite me, with his gaze as intense as anything I had ever encountered. "Tell me everything you know about Mr Juner." My shy Hugh Beaton had transformed into something more like a predatory stoat than a rabbit.

"I do not wish my information to be generally known," I said.

"I will treat anything you say with the utmost confidentiality," Mr Beaton said. "I promise to use only what is essential in helping Matthew Juner's situation."

So I told him. Starting from the riot in Dalkeith, I told Mr Beaton nearly everything about my dealings with Matthew Juner. Naturally, I did not mention the incident when I came across him coming out of the Trout Pool, nor did I mention my affection for the man.

Mr Beaton nodded throughout my discourse. "Thank you, Miss Moffat," he said. "I shall write down the salient points and perhaps use them when Juner's case comes up in the court." He raised his voice. "You may come in now, Adam."

Mr Carmichael looked slightly agitated when he hovered at the open door, or perhaps it was guilt that had eroded the laughter from his eyes.

"Have you completed your business, Miss Moffat?" Mr Carmichael asked.

"I have." I found it hard to meet the gaze of the man who had pursued Matthew, yet had proved so helpful on the day of the hunt.

"In that case, I may enter the room." Mr Carmichael's smile was unnaturally forced. "I don't like to enter when Beaton is working."

I nodded. "I suppose, in your line of work, it is better not to speak to the accused's defending solicitor."

"In my line of work?" Mr Carmichael shook his head. "I am afraid I cannot see the significance, Miss Moffat."

"Well, I certainly can," I said, with my temper growing hot. Mr Carmichael seemed to stir deep-seated emotions in me.

I swear that Mr Carmichael stepped back, either out of surprise at my outburst or shame at his actions. "Can you now?" he said. "Could you tell me how, Miss Moffat?"

"I am afraid that your answer will have to wait, Miss Moffat," Mr Beaton said, "for time has passed and your mother will be arriving to collect you soon."

I glanced at the clock. Mr Beaton was correct; it was a quarter short of noon, and I had been in that room for nearly two hours.

Mr Carmichael continued to look perplexed, as though trying to work something out.

"I'll be back in half an hour, Adam," Mr Beaton said.

Mr Carmichael gave the curtest of nods. "I'll be here, Hugh." He nodded to me. "Miss Moffat."

"Mr Carmichael," I said, walking past him holding my skirt held so the material would not touch him.

"Miss Moffat," Mr Carmichael said as Mr Beaton opened the door. "I appear to have offended you in some manner. I assure you it was not intentional."

"Good day, Mr Carmichael," I said, and for the life of me, I could not help adding. "You may return to your duty now." I left him with a look of puzzlement on his face as Mr Beaton ushered me into his carriage.

"Thank you for your help, Miss Moffat," Mr Beaton said as he helped me dismount at the place where I had watched the golf.

"I wish you every success in defending Mr Juner," I said, as I leaned on my walking stick with the wind playing merry games with my hair.

"Thank you," Mr Beaton said. "It seems that Matthew Juner's case is attracting some interest."

"Tell me," I asked, looking in vain for my mother's coach in the wind-blown links, "what made you choose to defend him?"

"I did not choose to," Mr Beaton said. "A gentleman of my acquaintance suggested I do so."

"Oh? Who?" I asked.

Mr Beaton looked away as his shyness returned. "I am obliged not to say. It is confidential."

"I should have known that." I saw my mother's coach rolling towards us, with George having the devil's own time keeping it from the ruts in the abominable track. "Well, thank you, Mr Beaton. I have been concerned about Matthew Juner. I am glad to know he has an able man to defend him."

Mr Beaton bowed and bowed again as Mother opened the door of her coach.

"Mrs Moffat," Mr Beaton said.

"Mr Beaton." Mother favoured him with a smile before addressing me. "Come, Robyn, the rain is following us."

"I trust you have a safe journey," Mr Beaton spoke to the wheel of our carriage, or perhaps to the horse for he looked anywhere except in my direction.

"Thank you, Mr Beaton." Mother replied for both of us. "Take us home, George, before the rain makes the roads unmanageable." She settled back in her seat as George cracked the reins and the coach lurched onward. "So you spoke to Mr Beaton, then?"

"Yes, Mother." When I looked out of the window, I saw Mr Beaton standing beside his carriage, staring at the horse as if he had never seen such an animal before, and I wondered what chance Matthew had in court.

"Now you may tell me why you had a sudden interest in Mr Beaton's golf." Mother asked.

"He is a legal man," I decided to tell as much of the truth as I could, "and I am worried about Mrs Juner's wayward son."

"Matthew Juner." Mother supplied the name I knew well.

"Yes." I glanced out of the window again and jerked back immediately, for Mr Carmichael was walking level with our coach.

"Robyn?" Mother leaned forward to see what had startled me. "Oh, it's only Mr Carmichael. Whatever is he doing here?"

"He was playing golf with Mr Beaton," I said.

Mr Carmichael lifted his hat in acknowledgement, gazing directly at me, and then we were past, with the carriage jolting most abominably and the first of the rain pattering on our roof.

"There now," Mother settled back in her seat. "There's the rain."

"Yes," I wondered if the men would continue to play golf in the wet, decided they probably would, and looked outside in misery.

"You are very quiet, Robyn." Mother, like nature, abhorred a vacuum of sound. "What were you and Mr Beaton talking about?"

"I told you. We were talking about Matthew Juner."

"You seem exceedingly interested in that unfortunate man," Mother said, "yet you have never met him, to my knowledge."

"I feel sorry for him."

"He is a collier, Robyn. You are the daughter of one of the oldest families in Midlothian." Mother's eyes were troubled. "I know you have read romantic tales of women running off with gypsies and suchlike, but it is always better to keep your own side of the wall."

I nodded. Mother was advising me not to become romantically involved with a man from a different social class. "Yes, Mother." *You are too late with your advice. I already think of Matthew 100 times a day.*

"What did Mr Beaton tell you about Juner?"

"Mr Beaton will be acting as Matthew Juner's defence when the case comes to court," I said. "Some mysterious man asked him to do so."

Mother nodded sagely. "Aye, kindness lies not aye on one side of the house."

I tried to work that out. "Do you mean that Mr Beaton is a kindly man?"

"Kindness knows no boundaries, either of place or class," Mother said. "Now tell me all that happened."

I did so, as Mother listened, nodding encouragement at all the right places.

After I finished, I screwed up my courage. "I want to be present at the court case," I said.

"Do you indeed?" Mother's eyes were searching my face. "Is Matthew Juner so important to you? Or is there some other reason?" She was silent for what seemed quite a long time as the coach rattled and jolted on the road back to Winter Lodge. At last Mother gave a sigh. "It is not Matthew Juner who interests you!" she said. "It is Mr Beaton! You are setting your cap at Mr Beaton."

"Mr Beaton!" I repeated the name to give me time to formulate a reply.

"Mr Beaton," Mother favoured me with her most knowing smile. "The same gentleman you journeyed to Musselburgh to see when you have never had any inclination towards golf, and the same gentleman who will be defending the unhappy Matthew Juner." Mother's smile could not have been more triumphant. "Until this very day, I have not noticed you having any interest in legal matters. Now that you find Mr Beaton practises law, you have developed an interest in the court and court cases."

I tried to appear abashed as if Mother had uncovered my deepest secret. It helped that I did have a passing interest in Mr Beaton.

"Mr Beaton is not as shy as he appears," I said.

"That may, or may not, be a good thing," Mother said.

"He was the perfect gentleman," I added hastily.

"'Do you understand what sort of people may be present in a courtroom?" Mother asked. "There will be relatives and friends of the accused, people of the worst possible type, people of the criminal classes and those who merely wish to gloat over the misfortunes of others."

"I understand that," I said, although in truth I had given no thought to the type of people who I might encounter on the public benches.

"I should accompany you," Mother said, "but I don't think you would appreciate my company if you are there to see Mr Beaton."

"Thank you, Mother," I accepted her words as qualified acceptance of my attendance at court. I knew well that, at 22, I was legally my own woman, but when one is used to seeking permission from one's parents, it is hard to break the habit.

Mother leaned back once more, smiling at some secret thought. "Hugh Beaton, then," she said and closed her eyes.

Chapter Thirteen

I had never been in a courtroom before, let alone the High Court in the heart of Edinburgh's Old Town, and the atmosphere struck me like a slap on the face. Even the surroundings had taken me by surprise for, when one is used to the quiet of the countryside or the relative bustle of Dalkeith, venturing into Scotland's capital city is a bit of an adventure. The noise, the crowds and even the smells were either unfamiliar or magnified a score-fold from what I knew in Midlothian. I felt very much like a country girl out of her environment and, more than once, I thought of turning back to my own world. However, I did not. I wanted to see Matthew again, so I took a deep breath, fought my nerves and continued.

When I came to the Old Town, I had to stop and stare. Such a confusion of buildings and people I had never seen before. Old and new, tumbledown and proudly polished, all stood cheek-by-jowl in Edinburgh's ancient centre, and it was all I could do to find my away around, let alone enter the Courthouse.

Luckily, I had what my mother called "a guid Scots tongue in my head", and I asked directions from a gentleman. He proved very amiable, although he seemed amused at my country accent, which was clearly much more pronounced than I realised.

"You go through that door," my friendly Edinburgh gentleman advised, "and you'll see two men in queer uniforms. They will guide you to the public galleries."

"Thank you, sir," I rewarded him with a curtsey, which also amused him, for curtseys were quite out of fashion in Edinburgh, it seemed. It appears that rural Midlothian was behind the times in terms of clothing, speech and manners.

Feeling confused and out of place, I followed the gentleman's directions and still got lost in the labyrinth of courts and passages, rooms and corridors. I tried a short-cut, rounded a corner and saw two men I instantly recognised.

When I saw Mr Carmichael talking to Mr Beaton, my emotions were decidedly mixed. One part of me wished to run towards these familiar faces amid so much unfamiliarity, while another part of me boiled with anger. No doubt Mr Carmichael was here to send Matthew to Van Diemen's Land or the gallows, so why was he engaging Matthew's defender in conversation? Were they not on opposite sides?

I looked away, not wishing Mr Carmichael to see me, for I had no wish to talk to a man who thought of me only as a duty. I did not like to admit, even to myself, how much that memory still hurt.

"This way to the public gallery, madam!" A uniformed flunkey opened a door for me. "No drinking or abusing the court officials."

"Thank you." Pushing aside any thoughts of Mr Carmichael, I entered the court. The courtroom was smaller than I had expected, with an array of people already present, from sombre-faced men who must have been court officials to a host of women and men in the public gallery. I took my place among the latter and felt my heart lurch as the judge entered, complete with wig and robes.

"All stand!" one of the stern-faced officials ordered, and we all obediently stood.

"That's Lord Cockburn," my neighbour, a middle-aged woman with a long face said. "He often sends culprits to the gallows." She seemed to relish the idea.

"Oh." I looked at Lord Cockburn. He seemed an open, kindly man beneath the wig. "Do you know much about trials?"

"I come here for every interesting trial," the woman said. "I am Mrs Grant. Mrs Lyndsay Grant." She said the name as if it should mean something to me. It did not.

"Miss Robyn Moffat," I introduced myself. "I have never been here before."

Mrs Grant bobbed her head. "You have not chosen the best of days," she said. "There are very few interesting cases. There is one case of house-breaking, one of theft and some political crime, one of child murder – that's the one I am most interested in – and one of wife-beating."

I sat among the crowd of mainly female spectators as two tall wardens, or whatever they were, escorted the wife-beater to a small box-like structure in front of the judge and his supporters. The man stood there, pallid of face, dressed in clean, if rough, clothes as he stared at the judge. I listened to the evidence with little interest, despite the gasps from the audience, for Matthew's predicament wholly occupied my mind.

"The jury found you guilty," Lord Cockburn's words came as no surprise. "You are nothing but a brute barbarian, treating your poor wife in such a manner. I think she will be relieved to be free of you for the five years in prison to which I sentence you. Next case!"

"What a horrible man," Mrs Grant whispered to me. "Imagine being married to such a brute."

"I don't know what I would do," I said.

"I would plunge a knife into him as he slept," Mrs Grant said, cheerfully, "and chance the hangman's rope." She entered into details that I had no wish to hear as I thought how terrible it would be to be married to a violent man, or a woman such as Mrs Grant.

Matthew's case was next.

I swallowed hard, trying to control my nerves as Matthew walked slowly to his place. The authorities must have considered him dangerous, for heavy iron manacles hung, clattering, from his wrists. He stood with his head up, either in dignity or defiance, I was not sure. I only knew that I felt a surge of pride when I watched him face the court.

"State your name, occupation and address," the Clerk of the Court ordered.

"I am Matthew Juner, a collier of Winterhill in Gowkpen Parish, Edinburghshire," Matthew spoke in a low if distinct tone. I had expected him to be scared in such a place, but as he spoke, he stood even more erect, with his great shoulders squared, facing Lord Cockburn as an equal.

Mrs Grant grunted in disapproval. "The impudence of the man." Others on the public benches were equally censorious, shaking their heads at Matthew's stance. However, as I looked around, I saw at least one other woman looking intently at Matthew. I nodded to her, letting her know she was not alone.

"Take the Bible in your right hand, Matthew Juner, and take the oath."

Holding out his manacled hands, Matthew took hold of the leather-covered Bible and intoned the words. "I swear by Almighty God that I will tell the truth, the whole truth and nothing but the truth."

"You are charged with creating a combination with the intent to incite disorder and threaten and intimidate others. How do you plead?"

"Not guilty." Matthew's voice remained steady.

"You are charged with breaking and entering and with theft, in that, on the 15th November current, you did break into the residence known as Winter Lodge in Midlothian and did steal a woman's coat. How do you plead?"

"Not guilty," Matthew said, with his voice now less strong.

I felt my heartbeat increase. The charge referred to my greatcoat. The court was charging Matthew with stealing the coat that I had freely given him. What should I do? Should I remain quiet and see Matthew accused of a crime he did not commit? Or should I stand up in court and admit to helping a man wanted by the police, thereby damaging my reputation and that of my father, with possible repercussions on his business? With my mind in an agony of indecision, I remained where I was, twisting my handkerchief between my fingers as I watched the court's proceedings.

"Now we'll see," Mrs Grant leaned forward. "I don't like these combinations. Folk should know their place and submit to lawful authority."

"Mr Johnson, would you please continue?" Lord Cockburn sounded weary.

The prosecutor stood to give his address. He was a large man in his late forties or early fifties, with a red-tinged nose that spoke of excess drinking. "This man, Matthew Juner, is a known rogue," the prosecutor spoke quickly and with passion as if Matthew was his personal enemy. "Not only is he responsible for using a combination of the colliers to force others to withdraw their labour at a time of trade depression when mine owners struggle to keep their businesses alive but he is also a thief."

The prosecutor halted there to impress the terribleness of Matthew to his audience. I studied the jury, 15 earnest, well-fed faces, none of which, I guessed, had ever seen a pit-shaft or the terrible conditions in which colliers and their families had to live and work. I began to feel despondent, a feeling which increased when I looked at Mr Beaton, who was studying his boots rather than listening to the case.

Matthew stared straight ahead. From the position where I sat, I could not see his face, so I could not read his expression.

I sat there as the prosecutor continued his verbal assault on a man for whom I had great affection. The jury listened, some nodding or otherwise showing their approval of the prosecutor's words.

"That is the case for the prosecution, your Honour," the prosecutor said after he had tried to destroy Matthew's name, honour and reputation in every way possible. Over the past half hour, I had gained a healthy hatred for that man and his smoothly unpleasant words and resolved to do him ill at the first opportunity.

"Do you have any witnesses to call, Mr Johnson?"

I would remember that name and that face. My anger was mounting by the minute as I watched Mr Beaton do nothing to help his client, my friend. Had Mr Carmichael said something to prevent Mr Beaton from defending Matthew?

"I have only one witness," Mr Johnson said. "As the defendant is evidently guilty to the charge of helping form a combination, I do not need any witnesses on that count. To save the court's time," my sleekit adversary continued, bowing to the court and smirking, "I will be as brief as possible. After all, there is no doubt about the panel's guilt."

"Whom do you call, Mr Johnson?" Lord Cockburn sounded even wearier.

"I call Mr Andrew Dewar, your honour."

I must admit that I started at the name and shrank into my seat, trying to appear as invisible as possible, although Andrew never glanced in my direction.

Andrew had taken pains with his appearance, wearing a very smart dark suit with a sober waistcoat. He bowed to Lord Cockburn, took the oath as solemnly as a man determined to do his duty, barely glanced at Matthew and faced Mr Johnson.

"State your name and occupation," Mr Johnson invited.

"I am Andrew Dewar of Dewar House." Andrew made it evident that he was a gentleman with no need for a profession of any sort.

"I believe you are also a Special Constable, Mr Dewar." Mr Johnson said.

"I am, sir. In this present climate of unrest, I believe it is every man's duty to try to maintain the rule of law." Andrew addressed Lord Cockburn rather than the jury.

I stared at Andrew, wondering what I had ever seen in this pompous, self-righteous man. Either he or I had changed a great deal. I was pleased to see that Lord Cockburn did not seem impressed by Andrew's words as he scribbled a note on a pad in front of him.

"In your capacity of Special Constable," Mr Johnson said, "what do your duties entail?"

"I help the County Police maintain law and order within the county of Edinburghshire," Andrew said.

"While doing this admirable duty," Mr Johnson's voice was as smooth as the finest China silk, "did you ever encounter the panel?"

Andrew looked as confused as I felt. "The panel?"

"By the panel, I mean the accused man, Matthew Juner," Mr Johnson explained.

"Yes, sir. While executing my duty, I saw the panel on three separate occasions."

I waited for Mr Beaton to protect Matthew. I might as well have tried to catch moonbeams in a fishing net, for Mr Beaton continued to study the floor. What had happened to the ardent man who had questioned me? Once again, I wondered what Mr Carmichael had said to him.

Mr Johnson wrapped a honeyed smile around Andrew. "Could you please tell the court what these occasions were, Mr Dewar when you saw the panel?"

I think it was then that Andrew first noticed me in the public gallery, for I saw him start. He stared fixedly at me for what seemed a long time before he responded to Mr Johnson.

"The first occasion, I was on duty in Dalkeith, and I saw Juner, the panel, addressing a rally of colliers in the High Street."

"You saw the panel addressing a rally of colliers," Mr Johnson repeated slowly as if that was a crime worse than regicide.

"Yes, sir." Andrew seemed quite smug with his answer.

I was surprised when Mr Beaton eventually realised he should do something. He slowly got to his feet, sighed and spoke in a low voice. "Mr Dewar, did you hear what the panel was saying to these colliers?"

"I am sure he was exhorting them to violence," Andrew said, to the fervent nods of Mr Johnson.

"Ah," Mr Beaton said and was silent for a moment as some members of the jury shuffled on their seats. "Could you please tell the court what the panel said that was so inflammatory."

Andrew looked confused. "I can't," he admitted.

"You can't?" Mr Beaton repeated. "Pray tell the court why you cannot tell us what the panel said that you were sure was inflammatory."

"I was too far away to hear the actual words," Andrew said and added with a rush. "I know they were inflammatory though, for he had his arms in the air and he was shouting."

"I see," Mr Beaton spoke crisply in comparison to Mr Johnson's honeyed tones. "You could not hear, yet you knew the words incited the colliers to violence." He paused. "What happened after the panel spoke, Mr Dewar? Was there an immediate riot? A rush along the High Street, murder and mayhem through Dalkeith?"

"No." Andrew admitted.

"'So Mr Juner's words, which you did not hear, did not succeed in inciting violence. What did the miners do?"

"They went home," Andrew said, sullenly. "And later they withdrew their labour."

"In a violent manner?" Mr Beaton asked, and when Andrew remained silent, added, "I remind you that you are under oath, Mr Dewar. After the panel spoke to them, did the colliers act in a violent manner?"

"No." Andrew sounded sullen.

"No," Mr Beaton repeated, sat down and continued his examination of the floor.

Neatly done, I thought. *There was more to Hugh Beaton than a shy appearance and ability to browbeat lone women.* For the first time, I saw a glimmer of hope for Matthew.

Mr Johnson resumed his questioning as Andrew, now white-faced, tried to regain the position he had lost.

"You said you saw Mr Juner on three occasions," Mr Johnson said. "Could you tell the court about the second, please?"

Glancing rather sulkily at Mr Beaton, Andrew said: "I was waiting outside the Freemasons' Hall in Dalkeith when the miners held a meeting inside. We had an arrest warrant for some of the colliers."

"How was this arrest warrant conveyed, Mr Dewar?" Mr Johnson was back to his silk-tonged best.

"A messenger-at-arms had it, sir," Andrew said. "He had been in the area for some time, helping us identify the wanted men."

Mr Johnson nodded. "Thank you, Mr Dewar. I will not be calling the messenger-at-arms as a witness. My case is sufficiently clear without disturbing such a busy man."

I saw some members of the jury nod their agreement, as did some of the heads on the public benches. I started when I saw Mr Carmichael sitting near the front, as erect as a guardsman, enjoying the drama he had helped create.

Mr Johnson held up his hand. "Mr Dewar, please tell the court what the arrest warrants were for?"

Andrew visibly grew in confidence as he answered. "Certainly, sir. The arrest warrants were for three colliers who were leading members of the combination. These wanted colliers were also accused of intimidating mine-owners and those colliers who refused to join the combination."

"I see," Mr Johnson said. "They sound like unpleasant fellows. Can you see any of these desperate men in the court?"

Andrew nodded. "Yes, sir. I see the panel."

"You see the panel," Mr Johnson repeated slowly, as I twisted my handkerchief into an unrecognisable rope under the bench. I could hardly look at Mr Johnson – my dislike was so intense.

"I do, sir. I see Matthew Juner."

My dislike transferred from Mr Johnson to Andrew. At that moment, I could have condemned all three of them, Andrew Dewar, Mr Johnson and Adam Carmichael, to whatever torments the devil maintained for the most atrocious of evil sinners.

Lord Cockburn sighed. "I think we are all aware of the panel's identity, Mr Johnson. Please hurry along."

"Yes, Your Lordship," Mr Johnson said. "And did you succeed in arresting the panel?"

"Not at that time, sir." Andrew fixed Matthew with a glower. "When we moved to arrest them, the panel escaped."

"I see. The panel chose to avoid the consequences of his actions. Pray inform the court of the third occasion you saw the panel?"

"I saw the panel in Gowkpen Church during the Harvest Festival," Andrew said. "I did not wish to arrest him in the church, so hunted for him in the vicinity. I had heard there had been several thefts from Winter Lodge so waited in the grounds there, where I caught him with stolen property."

"Thank you, Mr Dewar," Mr Johnson said. "I have no further questions."

"I have some questions, if it pleases your Lordship." Mr Beaton stood again, shuffled his papers, dropped them, skiffed them up and apologised to the court while Andrew stood with an expression on his face like a man waiting for execution. "Mr Dewar, could you tell the court who it was that the panel is supposed to have threatened?"

"Juner threatened the mine owners." Andrew looked to Mr Johnson for help. *Aye*, I thought, quoting one of Mother's sayings to myself. *You are seeking grace at a graceless face. That man would not help his mother unless he profited by it.*

"'Do you have proof of these threats, Mr Dewar?" Mr Beaton was remorseless.

Andrew glanced at Mr Johnson, who managed to avoid his eye. "It was well known."

"Do you have proof?" Mr Beaton persisted as my respect for him grew into liking.

"The mine owners spoke of it." Andrew said.

"Thank you, Mr Dewar. I dismiss you for now, but I'll recall you later." Mr Beaton stretched to his full six-feet odd of angular manhood. "May I call my witness, Your Honour?"

"You may," Lord Cockburn glanced at his fob watch in an unmistakeable warning not to waste time.

"Please call Mr Thomas Moffat," Mr Beaton said.

I started at that and tried to shrink into invisibility as Father lumbered to the witness box. He wore decent clothes, but not his best, and took the oath without any added emphasis.

"You are Mr Thomas Moffat of Winter Lodge?" Mr Beaton asked.

"I am," Father agreed.

"And are you the proprietor of Winterhill Pit."

"I am," Father said.

"I ask you to look around the court and tell me if you see anybody you know."

Father did so, with his eyes narrowing when he saw me in the audience. Thankfully his gaze passed on until it rested on Matthew, standing manacled and expressionless in the dock.

"I see the panel," Father said, "I see Matthew Juner."

There was a gasp from the public gallery, and I saw some of the jury nodding in smug understanding.

"Thank you, Mr Moffat," Mr Beaton said. "Please tell the court in what capacity you know the panel."

Silence descended as everybody in the court waited for Father's reply.

"Matthew Juner is one of my tenants," Father said. "He is a collier at the Winterhill Pit."

"Do you know him in any other capacity?"

"No," Father said, shortly.

"Has he ever threatened you?"

"No," Father said.

"Has he threatened you in any way?" Mr Beaton persisted.

Father frowned at the repeated question. "Not in any way," he said.

"Thank you, Mr Moffat." Mr Beaton addressed the court. "I think that disposes of that charge. We are already aware that the panel spoke to his fellow colliers in Dalkeith, and afterwards, they dispersed peacefully, which disposes of the charge of inciting violence. Mr Moffat has helped clear any charge of threatening the mine-owner, and now only the nonsensical charge of theft remains."

Father said nothing as his eyes sought me on the public benches. I gave a weak smile in response to his glower.

"On the night of the alleged theft, Mr Moffat, did you examine the house for any sign of a break-in?"

"I did." Father returned his attention to Mr Beaton.

"Did you find anything?"

"Not a thing."

"No open doors or windows, broken shutters or the like?"

"Not a thing." Father did not like repeating his words.

"Thank you, Mr Moffat. Please ask Mr Dewar to return to the stand."

As Father gave me a last glance and left the courtroom, I began to think that Matthew might walk away from all the charges.

Andrew looked even more sheepish when he stood under Mr Beaton's deceptively mild gaze.

"Now, Mr Dewar." Mr Beaton spoke so softly that I had to strain to hear him. "You said that you saw the panel in church and searched for him in the neighbourhood."

"That's right." Andrew sounded very defensive.

"Did you have Mr Moffat's permission to wander in his grounds?"

"I know Mr Moffat," Andrew said.

"Ah." Mr Beaton nodded his understanding. "He will have given his permission at once, then. Did he?"

"I did not need to ask," Andrew said.

Mr Beaton shook his head. "You did not have permission then. I will pass over your trespassing for now – after all, you are not on trial today."

"Mr Dewar is not on trial," Lord Cockburn confirmed.

"Thank you, my Lord," Mr Beaton said. "Now, Mr Dewar, did you witness the panel steal the article in question?"

Andrew looked decidedly uncomfortable. "I saw him with it."

"That was not my question. If you saw the panel steal the coat, you must have been inside the house, again without the permission of Mr Moffat. Did you witness the panel stealing the item?"

"No." Andrew said. "But he stole it right enough. How else would he have it?"

"You did not see him take it," Mr Beaton spoke slowly to emphasise the point he was making. "When you found him, in which direction was he walking?"

Andrew opened his mouth, closed it again and looked downward. "I can't recall."

"Come, Mr Dewar. You are under oath. In which direction was the panel walking?"

"Towards Winter Lodge," Andrew said.

"The panel was walking towards Winter Lodge," Mr Beaton said slowly, emphasising the word "towards". "Is it possible that the panel had found the item, a woman's winter coat, and was returning it to the house?"

"Why would he do that?"

"Why would he walk towards the house carrying an item he had allegedly stolen from the house, a feat that he apparently achieved without opening a single door or window?" Mr Beaton faced the court. "We have heard Mr Moffat's testimony that no window or door was open. I ask again, is it possible the panel had found the item and intended to return it to the house?"

"I do not know," Andrew said.

"Nor do I." Mr Beaton was rapidly gaining my affection, whatever the men of the jury thought. "And I am sure the jury also finds your testimony hard to believe. Thank you, Mr Dewar."

Matthew was next on the stand. He stood there, impassive and unemotional as he answered every question without hesitation.

Yes, he helped organise the local colliers' combination. No, he had never incited anybody to violence. No, he had not threatened Mr Moffat. No, he had not stolen the woman's coat. He was returning it when the Special constable arrested him.

After thanking Matthew for his words, Mr Beaton sat down. "That ends the case for the defence."

Mr Johnson immediately stood up. "From where did the panel obtain the coat if he did not steal it?"

"I'd rather not say," Matthew said.

"You are under oath," Mr Johnson reminded. "If you do not say, then the court will draw its own conclusions."

"I'd rather not say," Matthew stood erect.

I knew he was protecting me and I wondered what to do. Lord Cockburn helped my decision as he leaned forward in his seat.

"Matthew Juner," he said, and I think he was trying to be kind. "If you refuse to say, the jury can only conclude that you did steal the coat. If you are found guilty of theft, then the least sentence I can hand down is transportation."

I saw Matthew flinch at the words. "Thank you for the advice, Your Lordship, but I abide by my decision."

I could feel the atmosphere in the court alter as the jury turned against Matthew. I could not help myself. I could not allow Matthew to be transported over a coat that I had lent him.

"Your Lordship," I said, standing up. "May I speak?"

Chapter Fourteen

It was amazingly lonely, standing in that courtroom with everybody staring at me. I felt the queerest prickle at the nape of my neck as Lord Cockburn lifted his head.

"Who are you, madam?"

"I am Miss Robyn Moffat of Winter Lodge, Your Lordship, and the owner of the coat that Matthew Juner is accused of stealing."

"Pray come to the stand, Miss Moffat," Lord Cockburn invited.

Before I could say more, two court officials escorted me to the witness box, where I stood in splendid isolation as Lord Cockburn encouraged both advocates to interrogate me. Mr Beaton was first, and within a few moments he had found out for the court that I was indeed Robyn Moffat, that I lived in Winter Lodge and that I owned the coat – all of which I had already told them.

"Now, Miss Moffat." Mr Beaton faced me. "Can you tell the court how the panel came into possession of your greatcoat?"

"Yes, sir," I was unsure what to call Mr Beaton. "I gave it to him." I was glad Mr Beaton did not demand details.

"Why did you give the panel your coat, Miss Moffat?"

"He was cold and wet, sir. He needed something to protect him from the weather."

Mr Beaton studied the floor before asking the next question. "Did you give the panel the coat freely, Miss Moffat?"

"Yes," I said. "He needed help and I had the means to provide it."

I could see the gratitude in Matthew's face.

"Thank you, Miss Moffat," Mr Beaton said. "I have no further questions."

I suddenly became aware that Mr Carmichael had sat in the public gallery and was studying me with the most curious expression on his face. I was glad I had not noticed him earlier, or I would have been too nervous to continue with my declarations. Duty indeed! Honestly, I could not have despised that man more if his name had been Napoleon Bonaparte or he had been a grave robber.

When the obnoxious Mr Johnson had no questions for me, I thankfully made my way back to my previous position, where I found I was suddenly important.

"You should have allowed him to hang," Mrs Grant said. "I like a good hanging."

With all the evidence presented, Lord Cockburn summed up the case in a few short sentences and sent the jury away to consider their verdict.

"This could take hours," Mrs Grant whispered to me. "Most often, I cross the road to a public about now."

As I had no intention of spending time in a public house, I turned down Mrs Grant's generous offer of allowing me to buy her refreshment and instead waited in the rapidly emptying public gallery. I had no sooner reconciled myself to a long and tedious wait than the foreman of the jury returned.

"Have you reached your verdict?" Lord Cockburn asked formally.

"We have, Your Lordship."

I listened, not at all comprehending all the legal terminology until the foreman intoned the final words.

"On the charge of breaking, entering and theft, we find the panel not guilty."

I felt my heart flutter with relief that my testimony had helped.

"On the charge of attempting to intimidate a mine owner, we find the panel not guilty."

I could feel my heart fluttering. Matthew would walk free today.

"On the charge of inciting disorder, we find the panel guilty."

Guilty. I felt my heart race. *Oh, Lord, no!*

Lord Cockburn sighed. "Prisoner at the bar,' he said, 'you have been found guilty of being involved in inciting disorder. I have no choice but to order you to be transported to one of her Majesty's Penal Settlements for the period of 14 years."

Fourteen years!

I felt a ripple run around the court. Fourteen years' transportation was a harsh sentence. I sat in numb silence as two bully officials escorted Matthew away with the clanking of his manacles a reminder of what was to come.

Fourteen years!

***

Father listened, tapping his fingers on the desk as I explained about Matthew. "I see," he said at length. "All the time that I had men searching the grounds, you had this fellow secreted away."

"Yes, Father," I admitted my guilt.

"Where?"

"In the old folly overlooking the Winter Burn."

"I sent Andrew Dewar and his men to scour that area," Father said.

"Yes, Father." I did not say that I led Andrew astray. I was in enough trouble as it stood. Nor did I say that I harboured feelings for Matthew. In truth, I was so confused that I could hardly say anything at all.

Father looked away. "You should not have deceived me," he said.

"I did not know how you would act," I said.

Father took a deep breath. "Do you think I would have persecuted this fellow?"

"You would have done your civic duty," I said, and could not help adding, "as Mr Carmichael did his."

"Carmichael?" Father frowned. "What the devil has he to do with this?"

"I think you know that, Father," I said.

"I am at a loss to understand," Father said. "But be that as it may, Robyn, I wish you to promise that you will not hide such things from me again."

That was an easy promise to make, for I doubted that any further colliers would hide in our policies.

"Good." Father seemed satisfied with my word. "I have two more things to say before we close this unhappy affair."

"Yes, Father," I waited for the criticism.

"Firstly, I am very proud of you, both for helping a man in need and for standing up in court. That took considerable courage."

I started. "Thank you, Father." I had not expected praise.

"And secondly, you seem upset by the trial and the result of the trial."

"Yes, Father. I feel sympathy for the unfortunate man." I did not say that I had spent the previous night soaking the pillow with my tears.

"I can see that, Robyn and, although I understand your feelings, justice must take its course. Juner had a fair trial and an able defence. Your friend Beaton argued well for him."

"He did," I agreed. My slight admiration for Hugh Beaton had grown into a spark of affection.

"I have never previously found Beaton to be the most loquacious of men," Father said. "I should inform you that he will be present at the Pringles' winter ball."

"Oh?" The rapid change of subject took me by surprise.

"I have already accepted Pringle's invitation on your behalf," Father said. "You need something to distract you from your lowness of spirit."

For once, I was at a loss for words. "Thank you, Father," was all I could manage although, in truth, I was seldom less inclined to attend a social event than I was at that moment.

*　*　*

In our somewhat limited social circle, the winter ball was a highlight. Everybody who was anybody, or who wanted to be considered as somebody, attended, and much of the time was spent in posturing or trying to outdo one's neighbours and friends. I did not usually care for such events, but after my painfully dramatic autumn, I was glad to lose myself in the frothy nothings of socialising.

The Pringles' Beaumont House was a splendid mansion that put Winter Lodge to shame in the matter of size, although their taste left much to be desired. Poor Mrs Pringle had passed away some years ago, leaving her husband to care for three unruly sons. The elder Mr Pringle had coped by packing them all off to boarding school, from where one had promptly joined the army, another had joined John Company in India and Derek had returned to infest the house and county with his sporting prowess.

In consequence, the Pringle house was a mish-mash of furniture from Mrs Pringle's time, sporting trophies, golf clubs and other masculine knick-knacks that ought to have been confined to the study or the gun room. Despite the surroundings, and the snow that was beginning to fall, people assembled at Pringle House, for the ball was a welcome break in the monotony of early winter.

Amy was there of course and, as the current favourite of Mr Derek Pringle, was quite the belle of the ball, showing off a splendid new ring whose stone sparkled nearly as much as her personality. The central diamond was the largest I had ever seen, making me wonder how much of the Pringles' remaining wealth had gone into its purchase.

"You and Mr Pringle seem well suited," I said as I admired the ring for the third or fourth time.

"Thank you, Robyn," Amy had affected an ivory fan, with which she tapped me on the shoulder. "Is it not about time you found yourself a suitable match?"

"Time enough," I said, "when the right man appears."

"Time is passing." Amy looked distracted as she raised her fan in languid acknowledgement of a man I did not know. "I hunted my man down quite determinedly," she said. "Perhaps you ought to do the same."

"You were certainly active at the hunt." I wished I had not come.

"There is Mr Dunedin." Amy helpfully pointed her fan at the young man to whom she had waved. "He is free of any attachment."

I glanced at the spotty young man Amy had indicated. "And that is not surprising," I said. "He must be all of 19 years old."

"And heir to his father's fortune," Amy said. "He would be happy for any sort of catch."

"Perhaps so," I said, "yet I am not happy to be just any sort of catch."

Amy ignored my words. "Or there is Mr Beaton, whom you already know. A man of few words but perhaps some advantages."

Mr Beaton stood in the corner of the room, half-hidden behind the swirl of satin, silk and sugary smiles. He looked as awkward as I felt.

"A landward lad is aye bashful," I said and walked away before Amy asked for an explanation. It was true, though, young men from the country were usually shyer than their city counterparts. Derek Pringle, of course, was an anomaly.

As usual, Mr Beaton was studying the floor with great intensity. "Good evening, Mr Beaton." I dropped in a curtsey that was lower than usual.

"Good evening, Miss Moffat." Mr Beaton sounded surprised that somebody had actually spoken to him. He looked at me, flushed and looked away quickly.

We stood in an oasis of quiet among a confusion of noise, polite laughter and people jostling for position. "Thank you for trying to defend Matthew Juner," I said.

"I am afraid it did little good," Mr Beaton said to the floor. "The jury was not convinced."

"You got him off the theft charge," I reminded.

"Your testimony did that," Mr Beaton looked up, smiled briefly and looked away.

"Your arguments did more." I found this conversation immensely hard work, yet I wished to thank Mr Beaton and possibly get to know him better. "Do you know where Matthew Juner is now?"

"Calton Jail in Edinburgh, I believe," Mr Beaton said. "He'll be shipped to the hulks soon and then off to Van Diemen's Land or some other penal colony. There are hard times ahead for him, I fear."

I thought of poor Matthew suffering under the lash of a brutal prison guard. "Can I help him in any way?"

Mr Beaton's gaze searched my face as he considered the question. "You could write to the Home Secretary or even the Queen requesting clemency," he said. "Or you could ask me to compose a letter for you."

"Is that possible?" I asked.

"It is possible," Mr Beaton said, "although I can see little likelihood of success."

"I would do anything to help him," I said.

"Anything?" Mr Beaton raised his eyebrows. "Is his case so important to you? I thought he was only one of your father's tenants."

"Yes, Matthew Juner's welfare is important to me," I said. I had been aware of a third person joining our group, but only then did I realise it was Mr Carmichael. I stiffened. "Excuse me, Mr Beaton," I said, with a small curtsey. "I find I must leave you now."

Whisking my skirt aside from Mr Carmichael, I stepped around him, responded to his bow with the briefest of nods and swept away with as much display of dignity as I could muster. Even after that very short encounter, I felt my legs shaking, so I sought a chair to sit on. I was fortunate that I could claim that my injured ankle was still weak, although, in truth, it was entirely as strong as its partner.

"Are you all right, Robyn?" Amy pretended concern as she dragged a chair to my side.

"My ankle is paining me a little." I rubbed at it to enhance my pretence.

"Perhaps you had best return home," Amy said. "Certainly, you should not put further strain on it by attempting to dance."

I nodded. I had not expected to see Mr Carmichael in the Pringles' place, and now my nerves were all a-jangle. "You are right, Amy. Please tell my mother than I have returned home."

Now, it is an easy matter to enter a ball, but harder to leave before the dancing has begun. There is the host to inform, and outer coats to reclaim from the cloakroom, and transport to arrange, even when one's driver was warmly ensconced in the Pringle's kitchen, cradling a pot of ale while making friends with a plump maid.

However, with help and impatience, I arranged things. Derek Pringle was not in the least put out by my decision, the servant in the cloakroom was highly organised, and the plump maid was full of sympathy for me with my now-heavy limp.

"Go on, George, you great lump." She pushed our driver off his chair. "The poor mite is feeling unwell, and her with her ankle broken near in two!"

Favouring me with a glower, George placed his ale on the deal table and shuffled away, mumbling about young women who could not make their minds up whether they were coming or going. Still grumbling, George drove the coach around to the front of the house, and I bundled myself outside, putting on a terrible limp and gasping theatrically, to find the snow still falling.

"Back home, Miss Moffat?" George asked, raising a hand to the plump maid, who had come to the front of the house to see him off.

"Yes, please, George." I feigned a wince. "It's my ankle."

"Aye, chancy things, ankles," George said. "We'll have you home in two shakes of a lamb's tail, provided the front wheels hold out."

I nodded, knowing that George used weak front wheels as his excuse for driving slowly, as I used my no-longer-injured ankle to escape from unpleasant situations. I understood his reasoning.

The snow was growing heavier as we drove through the always-wedged-open gates and on to the road outside. Within 10 minutes, we were sliding and slithering between winter-bare trees with snow already forming patterns on the windows and a rising wind rocking the body of the coach from side to side. Within 20 minutes we were driving so slowly I swear I could have walked faster, blindfolded and with one leg.

"Hold on, Miss Moffat!" George roared from the driver's seat. "The road is a bit slippery."

He did not have to tell me as I could feel the wheels slithering as the horse struggled to keep its footing.

"Maybe we'd better return," I shouted.

"If we do we'd likely be stranded in the Pringle place all night," George said. "We're about halfway, so it's as well to go on as to go back."

"All right," I said, relying on George's experience.

We rolled on, with the snow increasing by the minute and the coach slowing to less than walking speed. Peering outside the windows, I shuddered. The lamps pooled faint yellow light on a landscape that could have belonged to the Arctic rather than Lowland Scotland. Honestly, I had never known snow to come down so thickly so early in the season as it did that evening.

I saw the figure plodding, head-down, through the fields. He was only a dark shape caught on the periphery of the lamplight, one minute there and the next gone. Rubbing a circle clear of condensation on the window, I peered outside. The man was still there, walking determinedly towards the road.

"There's somebody walking in the snow!" I shouted to George, for I knew he would be too preoccupied with driving the coach to have any attention for anything else.

"Where about?" George glanced around. "I can't see anybody!" He had to shout above the roar of the wind.

"I'm sure I saw somebody," I opened the door to get a better look and shuddered as a blast of wind nearly tore it out of my hands. "Over there!" I pointed to the right.

Slowing the horse to a crawl, George peered over his shoulder. "This is no night for a man to be walking," he shouted.

"I know," I yelled. "We must stop and give the poor fellow shelter!"

"Halloa!" George raised his voice further. "Halloa out there!"

"Halloa yourself!" The man replied, with the wind and snow distorting his voice.

"Come out of the weather!" George yelled.

The man emerged from the dark. Tall and broad, he walked round-shouldered against the wind. "What's to do? Where are you headed?"

"Winter Lodge!" George said. "You'd be better with us than out here."

"That is extremely Christian of you," the man said, and my heart lurched when I realised it was Mr Carmichael.

Of all the people I least wanted to share a carriage with, Adam Carmichael was top of the list. I wondered if there was some way I could retract my words, but it was too late. Mr Carmichael was already stepping on board the coach, removing the top hat that had once adorned my head and dropping wet snow on to the fresh straw we had on the floor for warmth.

"Miss Moffat!" He favoured me with a quick bow. "How pleasant to meet you again. I must express my gratitude for your kindness."

"It is only my Christian duty," I said coldly, hoping he recognised the words.

"May I sit down?" Balancing within the swaying coach, Mr Carmichael indicated the seat opposite me.

"If you don't," I said, "you will surely topple over the moment we move again."

"Thank you." Mr Carmichael sat down with his knees uncomfortably close to mine and his eyes examining me. "I am surprised you stopped for me, Miss Moffat."

I wondered how best to respond. "It was my Christian duty, I thought it best to repeat my words.

"What have I done to offend you, Miss Moffat?" Mr Carmichael was nothing if not direct.

I sidestepped the question. "Where are you heading, Mr Carmichael?"

"Here," Mr Carmichael said. "I was hoping to intercept you."

I could not have been more surprised if Mr Carmichael had said he was the man in the moon. "What on earth for?" I gasped as the coach jerked to the side, throwing me hard against the door.

"Careful now!" Mr Carmichael took hold of my arm. "Are you all right?"

"Yes, thank you." I grabbed hold of the leather strap inside the door to ensure I did not require Mr Carmichael's assistance again. This journey already seemed interminable. "May I ask why were you hoping to intercept me, Mr Carmichael?"

"To talk to you, Miss Moffat." With both of us holding on to a leather strap, we endured the sliding, battering journey. "I heard you say you wished to help Matthew Juner." Mr Carmichael's eyes were hard as flint once more.

I nodded, wondering if wishing to help a guilty man was illegal. "I do."

"Why?" Mr Carmichael snapped the question.

"I like the fellow." I held Mr Carmichael's gaze, refusing to be intimidated. "And I believe the authorities have treated him very badly." I hoped my words stung this representative of authority.

"Do you, indeed?" Mr Carmichael looked strangely at me, as well he might.

"I do, indeed," I matched his words, nearly daring him to condemn me. I have seldom been angrier with a man I scarcely knew.

Mr Carmichael cocked his head to one side, rather like a cat surveying itself in a mirror. "Tell me, Miss Moffat, how well do you like this Juner fellow?"

I lifted my chin. "I like him very well," I said.

"Enough to break the law and put yourself in danger?" Mr Carmichael seemed to be musing.

"If need be." I said, wondering if Mr Carmichael was setting a trap to catch me, before tossing me in jail beside Matthew.

Mr Carmichael nodded slowly. "A man would consider himself fortunate to have a lady say that."

"I would not consider Mr Juner very fortunate in his present unhappy position." I wondered if Mr Carmichael was paying me a compliment, or quite the reverse.

"I might be willing to help you," Mr Carmichael said.

At that point the carriage slithered to one side, George swore foully and immediately apologised. The coach righted itself and continued, now at a steep angle as George negotiated the slope of Roman Camp Hill.

"Why?" I asked Mr Carmichael. "You don't even like the man."

"No, I don't," Mr Carmichael said. "I find him conceited, arrogant and trouble making."

"Then why might you help me?"

"Can't you guess?" Mr Carmichael sounded almost plaintive.

Before I could reply, the coach stopped, then slowly slid backwards.

"What the devil?" Mr Carmichael stared at me.

"We can't make the hill," George shouted. "The road is too slippery-steep for old Charlie to manage."

With old Charlie being the horse, I knew there was only one thing we could do. "My apologies, Mr Carmichael, I am afraid we shall have to leave our shelter to help Charlie pull the chariot."

"There is no need to apologise," Mr Carmichael said. "You did not bring the snow."

The instant we left the carriage, the bite of the wind caused me to huddle deeper into my greatcoat.

"God help poor sailor men on a night like this," Mr Carmichael said, although what sailors had to do with anything I could not imagine.

The snow was thicker than ever, lying two feet deep so I could not tell where the road ended and the fields on either side began. I stamped my feet, looking for familiar landmarks in this world of black night and white snow.

"I'll lead Charlie," George said. "I'm afraid, Miss Moffat, you and Mr Carmichael will have to walk the distance to Winter Lodge."

"Of course," I said, "but I'll need my stick."

"I'll get it." Mr Carmichael passed it on to me. We stood side by side in silence as the snow whirled down and George led Charlie and the coach slowly, step by laborious, plodding step, up the hill.

"Are you sure you are willing to break the law for Juner's sake?" Mr Carmichael tapped his hat in place. He moved to shelter me from the wind, as was his duty as a gentleman.

"Yes." I watched the coach slide slowly up the hill, with George urging Charlie and occasionally pulling at the front wheel.

"Then I am willing to help you," Mr Carmichael said. We were silent again. Mr Carmichael removed his hat and placed it on my head. "I still think my hat suits you."

"Thank you," I said, as my dislike for this man dissipated a little. "We'd best get up to the house." I returned his hat.

Mr Carmichael nodded. "Your man George is struggling," he said. Without another word, he stepped forward, put his shoulder to the coach and pushed. His weight might have made a difference for the coach straightened up slightly.

"Oh well," I sighed, and lent my slight strength to the problem.

"Miss Moffat, Mr Carmichael!" George sounded upset. "It's not your place to push a coach!"

"Nonsense," Mr Carmichael said. "Everyone should help in an emergency. There are no atheists in a storm."

Once again, I felt a spark of liking for this man I was determined not to like at all.

"Well done," Mr Carmichael mouthed to me as we pushed together with our feet slipping on the snow and both of us tripping over the deep ruts the wheels left. I smiled back to him, quite enjoying the physical activity even although we made little difference to the outcome. I doubt the coach moved more than a foot or two upwards.

"We might have to abandon her here," George said. "Who's this now?"

I saw the figure emerge from the snow to our left. Tall and slender, he seemed to come from nowhere.

"Good evening Miss Moffat." He nodded to me, with snow dropping from his bare head and around his beard.

"Good evening, Will," I said as if it was normal for Wild Will to appear before me in the middle of a snowstorm.

"You need my help." Without another word, Will put his shoulder to the body of the coach and pushed. The coach moved slightly, and we all doubled our efforts, so the coach slowly ascended the hill. Twice we stopped as the wheels locked and we slipped sideways, but each time George, Charlie, Will and Mr Carmichael righted us by brute force and cunning skill, while I gave my slender aid. From time to time, Mr Carmichael murmured encouragement to me while Will watched, saying nothing.

"Well done, Miss Moffat," Mr Carmichael would say. "Don't overstrain yourself, now."

"I won't," I promised, "for you three gentlemen are bearing the brunt of the work."

It took us the best part of an hour to reach the gates to the policies where the road levelled out, and by that time we were all soaked with the snow, muddied from the thighs downward and panting with effort. Yet for all that, I was happy to achieve something, however mundane. Physical work can be extremely satisfying when there is an end result. We grinned to each other with the fellowship that a successful enterprise creates.

"There we are." Will gave a strange little bow in my direction. "I'll be leaving you now, Miss Moffat."

"Thank you, Will," I said. "Won't you come inside to get dry and something warming?"

Will shuddered. "I don't go indoors," he said and turned away.

"At least let me bring you out a hot drink and a bite." I spoke to emptiness, for Will had already disappeared, leaving hardly a footprint in the snow.

"Who was that fellow? He never said a word to me," Mr Carmichael said.

"That's Will," I told him. "He's a friend of mine."

"You befriend the strangest of people," Mr Carmichael shook his head. "All the waifs and strays of society."

"Yes," I said and quickly changed the subject. "I'm not meeting you again, Mr Carmichael," I said, with what I hoped was humour. "Every time I see you, I end up wet and cold."

He smiled at me, realising I was joking. "I could say the same about you."

"Last time," I said, "you looked after me. This time I can play the host and get you dried off in Winter Lodge."

The mockery was back in Mr Carmichael's eyes as he bowed. "I look forward to it, Miss Moffat."

George patted old Charlie, showing his affection for the horse. "Thank you, Miss Moffat, thank you, Mr Carmichael." That was the first time I had ever heard George genuinely grateful, for he was usually a grumpy old soul.

I smiled over to Mr Carmichael again, nearly prepared to rekindle my liking for the man, when he spoiled things once again. "It's our Christian duty to help those in need," he said.

These words burned inside me, undoing all the good fellowship we had created pushing the coach up the hill. *Duty! Why did that man have to say that word? Did he do nothing for its own sake? Did he do anything for the sheer joy of helping people, rather than because duty compelled him?* The look I gave Mr Carmichael was colder than the snow in which we stood.

"It was my pleasure, George." When I contradicted Mr Carmichael's words, he knew that my feelings of only a few moments before had changed. The remainder of the short journey to the house had a different atmosphere as I gave monosyllabic replies to Mr Carmichael's attempts at conversation.

"The snow's falling fast now," Mr Carmichael said when we stopped at the front door. "I'll come with you to the Pringles' place, George when you pick up Mrs Moffat. It's easier with two on these roads."

George touched his hat in what was, for him, a show of respect rather than deference. "Thank you, Mr Carmichael."

"I believed we had things to discuss, Mr Carmichael," I kept my voice cold.

"They will keep, Miss Moffat." Mr Carmichael's bow was as formal as his voice. "George's need is greater than ours at present."

"I see." I could only watch as George turned the coach around and Mr Carmichael joined him in leading old Charlie. At that moment, I felt as lonely and desolate as I had ever been in my life, although I did not know why. Limping into the house, I had to fight my tears.

Chapter Fifteen

It was a couple of weeks before I saw Mr Carmichael again. I watched our drive in the hope, if not the expectation, of seeing him riding up on Chetak, but experienced only disappointment. Nobody arrived except visitors for mother and the occasional businessman to see Father. Strangely, although I disliked Mr Carmichael, I also looked forward to his company. I did not understand those contrasting emotions. I knew only that they confused me. All my efforts at fathoming myself led to one stark conclusion. I wanted Mr Carmichael's presence because I want him to help Matthew. There was no other reason, and with that, I had to be satisfied.

Every day I scanned the newspapers for news of Matthew and found none. His case had earned a few lines in the court pages, and then there was utter silence. He had been tried and condemned, and the world moved on to more dramatic affairs. It was around two weeks after the Winter Ball that I again approached Hugh Beaton to ask his help composing a letter to try and free Matthew.

"You're seeing a lot of Hugh Beaton now," Mother said hopefully, as we sat in the drawing-room, reading by lamplight.

"Yes, Mother," I said.

"Should I prepare for any news?" Placing a finger on the page to mark her place, Mother looked up,

"No, Mother," I said. "He is only a friend. He is helping me write an appeal for Matthew Juner."

"That is good of him," Mother kept her finger on the page. "Should Moffat expect the account for his services?"

"The account?"

"Solicitors don't work for nothing," Mother said. "Who paid him to defend Matthew Juner at the trial?"

I shook my head. "I don't know," I said. "I had not thought about it."

Mother returned to her book. "It would be better to find out who is paying for Mr Beaton's time before you proceed further. Moffat will be discomposed if he finds a large legal account on his desk."

"Yes, Mother." I was less than happy with that news and, when I arrived at Mr Beaton's house, I approached the subject with as much diplomacy as I was capable.

"Mr Beaton," I began as we sat on opposite sides of his desk with the long-case clock ticking away behind me and a feeling of dread in my stomach. "There is the matter of payment."

"Payment?" Mr Beaton looked up in some surprise. "That's already taken care of."

"How can that be?" I asked. "I have not paid you a penny. Did old Mrs Juner pay?"

"Mrs Juner did not pay me anything," Mr Beaton said. "It was quite another party entirely."

"Oh? May I enquire who?"

"You may not." Mr Beaton became nearly aggressive in his manner. "My clients' business is and always will be confidential."

"Yes, Mr Beaton." I accepted the rebuke quietly. Although we returned to the task of composing the appeal, my mind was racing as I wondered who was financing this legal work. "Is it the combination?" I asked at last. "Are the other colliers helping Mr Juner?"

"Confidential!" Mr Beaton said sternly. "Pray, do not ask me again."

"You would be a good man to tell a secret to, and keep it safe."

"One does not reveal secrets to anybody," Mr Beaton said. "Now, listen to this sentence, Miss Moffat, and tell me if you agree with the spirit of the words."

I found that prising intelligence from Mr Beaton was impossible. He was impervious to my hopeful charms, resistant to my womanly wiles, invulnerable to both sulks and pleas. Once I realised the hopelessness of my position, I concentrated solely on the task in hand, although I was seething with curiosity within.

Eventually, we had the appeals completed, one to Sir James Graham, a fellow Scot and the Home Secretary, and the other to Her Majesty. Mr Beaton had done most of the work and wrote the final note in a beautiful flowing hand on the best quality paper I had ever seen. I will not quote the text here, for Mr Beaton filled it with legal language that, quite frankly, I did not understand, but it was an elegant address appealing for clemency for the unhappy Matthew Juner.

"I'll have these in the post today," Mr Beaton applied the seals with a gesture of finality that in itself should have secured Matthew's freedom.

"I don't know how to thank you, Mr Beaton," I said.

"Mr Juner is a fortunate man to have a woman such as you caring for him," Mr Beaton looked directly at me. Mr Carmichael had said something similar.

"Thank you."

"I would consider myself extremely fortunate if any woman cared half as much for me," Mr Beaton said.

"I am sure that a better woman will come for you," I said, knowing that I was not the woman for Mr Beaton. However much I admired his legal skill, I did not feel that my affection could ever develop into love. I offered him the only consolation prize I could. "You are a good man." I said.

When I saw the sudden gleam of gratitude in Mr Beaton's eyes, I leaned forward across the desk, placed one hand against his cheek and kissed him on the forehead. "You are a good man, Mr Beaton." I repeated softly.

For one moment, I saw the man behind both the shyness and the legal front. For that moment, I saw a man desperate for affection, hoping to be recognised as a warm human being. I was correct – although Mr Beaton was not the man for me, he could be a loyal husband to some woman.

"Miss Moffat." Mr Beaton said as I returned to my previous position. He touched the spot I had kissed. "Thank you." I am sure I saw something glint damply in his eyes, a second before he looked away.

I listened to the sonorous ticking of the clock, not sure what to do.

"I'll have those letters posted today," Mr Beaton repeated his earlier words, speaking to the legs of his desk.

"Thank you," I accepted the words as a polite dismissal, rose and left the room. I had done all I could do for poor Matthew and had travelled as far as I could with Mr Beaton. My hunt for a suitable husband must continue in another direction.

* * *

Father lowered his newspaper. "Here's something that might interest you, Robyn."

It was so unusual for Father to mention anything in his newspaper that both Mother and I looked up in astonishment. I am sure that Agnes nearly dropped another cup in her surprise.

"What's that, Father?" I asked, carefully placing my cup in its saucer.

"That fellow Juner has escaped from confinement."

Mother and I exchanged looks before I asked for more details. I tried to conceal the sudden racing of my heart.

"It seems Juner was on a coach travelling from the Calton Jail to Leith docks," Father paraphrased the article for our benefit. "The coach held three other convicts, Smith, Hogarth and O'Brien, and all four were going to be put on a steamer for the Thames, then transported to Australia."

I pictured the scene, the four men, pale-faced, thin from prison food, chained together on the outside of the coach as it rattled from the austere Georgian Calton Prison down Leith Street towards the docks. Matthew would look around him, savouring the fresh winter air, knowing he might never see his homeland again.

"What happened, Moffat?" Mother asked, eager for any hint of scandal.

"They travelled at night to avoid being seen," Father said. "Apparently, the coach was part way down Leith Walk – that is the main thoroughfare between Edinburgh and Leith - when an armed man appeared, an old-fashioned highwayman, for heaven's sake, and stopped the coach."

"Good Lord!" Mother said, with a slice of toast halfway between the plate and her mouth. "In this day and age!"

I could see the highwayman, dressed all in black with his hat pulled low over his head. He would appear from one of the side streets, perhaps from one of the many hostelries, on a dark horse, present a large-bored pistol to the driver and demand the coach should stop.

"Apparently the highwayman – I can call him nothing else – wore a yellow neckerchief across the lower half of his face. He stopped the prison wagon, cut Juner's chains and made off in a single-horse closed coach."

Not a horseman then. I altered my mental picture to a man in a yellow mask, driving a closed coach.

"Only with Matthew Juner?" I asked.

"Only with Matthew Juner," Father confirmed.

"That is interesting," I said. "Are there any further details?"

"No." Father had returned to the sanctuary of his newspaper, leaving Mother and me to exchange wondering glances.

"It will be that combination," Mother said. "I've never liked the idea of men combining against lawful authority."

"They're not combining against anybody," I said. "The colliers are combining to help themselves and their families."

Father lowered his paper for sufficient time to send a glower in my direction, gave a single expressive grunt and raised it again. He rustled the pages and said no more.

I ate the rest of that meal in silence, wondering about Matthew, and if I would ever see him again. Mother was anything but silent as she speculated on who had rescued Matthew, and why, and what she might do to them if ever they tried to hold her up on her lawful journey to Leith.

"No, Mrs Moffat." Father spoke from behind the newspaper. "No highwayman would dare try to hold you up."

"They'd better not try," Mother said.

"Your incessant chatter would talk them to despair so they would hand themselves in to the police before the day was done," Father said.

I did not even smile, I was so intent with thinking about Matthew that I could not react to this rare example of humour from Father. Mother gave a most unladylike snort and returned to her breakfast without another word.

Chapter Sixteen

"Mr Moffat." Mr Carmichael gave a bow, much to Father's surprise. Sims had replied to the knock at the door for him just as Father walked across the hall.

"Yes, Carmichael." Father dismissed Sims and stood with a small pile of documents in his hand. "Why the formality?"

"I have something to ask that you may not wish to hear," Mr Carmichael said.

Standing in the drawing-room with the door ajar, I watched the meeting, with Mother breathing heavily at my shoulder.

"What is that, pray?" I heard the caution in Father's voice.

When Mr Carmichael said, "It concerns your daughter," Mother squeezed my arm painfully.

"It's about you," Mother whispered as if deafness had suddenly stricken me.

"What about Robyn?" There was caution in Father's voice.

"I pray your permission to take Miss Moffat to an orchestral concert in Edinburgh." Mr Carmichael said.

Mother's hand nearly crushed my arm. "An orchestral concert!" She repeated, sufficiently loud to be heard in Dalkeith.

I saw Father's face relax. "I am sure you may ask Robyn," he said. "She is of age, you know and quite capable of making her own decision."

"I am aware of that, sir." Mr Carmichael said. "But as she lives in your household, I thought it polite to ask your permission."

"Come, Carmichael." Father said. "You have helped Robyn on more than one occasion in the past. I am sure she will entertain your invitation."

"Or be entertained by it," Mr Carmichael said. "I am afraid that your daughter does not have a high opinion of me."

"Come, come, Carmichael. You must ask and see her response."

"Robyn!" Mother steered me away from the door and sat me down near the fire. "Look busy – and say yes when Mr Carmichael asks you."

"Mother!" I hissed. "I don't like the man."

"He evidently likes you," Mother said. "Hush now!"

I returned to the book I was reading, but the words seemed to dance in circles across the page like so many ballerinas, making no sense whatsoever.

"Ah, Robyn," Father sounded more nervous than I had ever heard him. "Here is Mr Carmichael to ask you a question."

I stood up, curtseyed politely and waited as Mr Carmichael approached me, looking as though he was leading the forlorn hope at the siege of Badajoz.

"Miss Moffat," Mr Carmichael said. "Your father has given me permission to approach you."

I nodded, fighting the increased hammer of my heart. "Yes, Mr Carmichael?"

"I'll come straight out with it," Mr Carmichael said. "I would be greatly obliged if you would agree to accompany me to an orchestral concert in Edinburgh."

I had my reply ready. "Thank you, Mr Carmichael. It is very good of you to invite me." I could feel my Mother's eyes as she watched me. "I should be delighted to accept your invitation."

I was surprised that Mr Carmichael's eyes brightened as if he genuinely wished for my company.

"If you agree," Mr Carmichael seemed to address Father as much as he spoke to me, "I will arrange for accommodation in the city after the concert. It would save a long drive back in the dark."

"What type of accommodation, Mr Carmichael?" Instantly suspicious, Mother asked the question.

"I have a place in Edinburgh," Mr Carmichael said. "Miss Moffat can stay in one of the guest bedrooms. I assure you I have nothing untoward in mind."

I could have sliced the tension in the room with a blunt knife. Instead, I smiled. "That is a very kind offer, Mr Carmichael. I have complete trust in you as a gentleman." I raised my voice slightly. "If you had been less than a gentleman, you could have taken advantage of me in the church at Balantrodoch."

I saw Mother's frown clear. She nodded agreement as Mr Carmichael bowed in my direction, saying nothing.

"Then that is settled." Father sounded relieved. "When is this concert?"

"Tomorrow night," Mr Carmichael said. "I do apologise for the short notice."

Naturally that evening and the next day, Mother was full of questions, statements and mild panic about her daughter going into the city with a man.

"It's all right, Mother," I said, in between packing sufficient clothes into a bag to last me a week in Greenland, let alone a day in Edinburgh. "I trust Mr Carmichael."

"You told me you did not like the man," Mother reminded.

"I don't," I said, "I am taking your advice. Besides, I am wild to see where Mr Carmichael lives."

"You will take care," Mother said, "and tell me everything that happens."

"I will," I said, and added, mischievously, "every last kiss."

"There will be no kissing!" Mother said sternly.

"Not even one little peck?" I teased.

"Not until you are decently married," Mother said.

"I shall not be marrying Mr Carmichael," I said firmly.

"Enjoy the orchestra," Mother replied, with a smile.

Mother waited at my side when Mr Carmichael rolled up in a green-and-yellow gig. Scotland being what it is, the early snow had come and gone, the sun had broken through and the day was as warm as April.

Mr Carmichael jumped down to help load my bags. "We're not going to Africa, Miss Moffat."

"I like to be sure," I said. "After all, remember what happened when I went hunting with you."

"I remember," Mr Carmichael said. "I shall never forget."

We rolled away from Winter Lodge with the Pentland Ridge hard defined against a brilliant blue sky and a clamour of rooks calling from the nearest copse.

"You may have guessed that our journey is not solely for recreation." Mr Carmichael's expression altered the minute we left the gates.

"I wondered," I said. "It is hardly your duty to invite me to a concert."

"My duty?" Mr Carmichael looked puzzled for a moment. "Never mind. I have some news about your friend Mr Juner."

"I heard about him," I said. "The colliers rescued him on the way to the boat for London."

Mr Carmichael raised his eyebrows. "Is that what happened?"

"I believe so," I said.

"Do you still wish to help Mr Juner?" Mr Carmichael turned from the driving seat to face me.

"Yes," I said immediately.

"It is breaking the law meeting an escaped prisoner," Mr Carmichael warned.

"I wish to help," I said.

I thought I saw respect in Mr Carmichael's expression. "I've said this before, Miss Moffat, and I mean it. Matthew Juner is a fortunate man to have a woman such as you worrying about him."

I looked away without replying. I could not understand Mr Carmichael. Sometimes I thought he liked me, yet I knew he considered looking after me as only as part of his duty. Was that his Christian duty or his duty to the court and Crown? But why was he trying to help me with Matthew, a man the Crown employed him to arrest?

I shook my head.

"Do you not wish to know how you can help?" Mr Carmichael asked.

"Yes, I do," I said.

"I happen to know where Mr Juner is," Mr Carmichael said. "I also know where he can be safe."

"What do you wish me to do?" I asked.

"If you are willing, you can help convey Mr Juner from where he is now, to where he is safe."

Once again, I thought of Matthew's steady gaze and the good he was trying to do. "Yes," I said. "I am willing, but how do you know where he is?"

"A man in my position learns certain things," Mr Carmichael said.

A messenger-at-arms must be at the centre of affairs, I told myself. *He must know people in both the legal and the criminal world.* "I imagine so," I said.

"You're a brave girl," Mr Carmichael negotiated a bend with less skill than George, then accelerated on to a straight. To our left, the hills were bold against the sky, while ahead I could see the crouching lion shape of Arthur's Seat, the great hill around which generations of Scottish royalty had hunted while living in Edinburgh. Now I was bound to the same destination to help a hunted man escape his pursuers.

"It is my Christian duty," I tried to spur Mr Carmichael with his own words.

"Sometimes duty can be a pleasure as well as a necessity," he said, with a glance at me, "while at other times it leads one into treacherous waters."

"Yes," I was unsure what he meant.

"Let us hope that we can sail through any storms without mishap," Mr Carmichael continued his nautical analogy.

"That must depend on the skill of the captain," I replied.

"And the courage of the first mate," Mr Carmichael eased us through the toll gate at Eskbank, waving to the keeper as to an old friend.

"And the behaviour of the cargo," I was rather enjoying playing with words.

"That most of all, perhaps."

We travelled at a great rate so that the countryside sped past. I sat on my seat, held on to my hat and survived Mr Carmichael's driving as we left Midlothian behind and entered the environs of the capital.

"Where are we going?" I asked, peering about me, for I found Edinburgh endlessly fascinating as well as slightly frightening.

"A house in the New Town," Mr Carmichael said. "Mr Juner is already there."

I had hardly ever visited the New Town, that area of classical squares and streets that lies to the north of the ancient heart of Edinburgh. As the gig rattled over the cobbles, I could only admire the serene symmetry of the architecture and the atmosphere of respectability and security, so different from the bawdy confusion of the Old Town.

"Here we are." Mr Carmichael eased into a lane between two rows of identical houses and stopped at the broad doors of a stable. "Wait here."

The stables were smaller than ours at Winter Lodge but immaculately kept. Mr Carmichael drove the gig inside, pulling up beside a dark-painted closed carriage.

"It's a bit of a squeeze," he said.

I treated Mr Carmichael to a smile as I alighted with the help of his hand and my trusty walking stick.

"This way," Mr Carmichael led me from the stables across a narrow walled garden and through the back door of a townhouse. I looked around, not quite so happy now I was indoors. The house seemed dull as Mr Carmichael led me up a flight of stone stairs and into another world.

From darkness, we entered a fairyland of light and colour, with a huge mirror reflecting lantern light and carpets that must have come from exotic places. The furniture was like nothing I had ever seen, while pictures of strange foreign views adorned the walls.

"I can be a bit eccentric in my taste." Mr Carmichael stood, watching me. "Do you like it?" He sounded anxious, as if he cared about my opinion.

Did I like it? "Yes," I decided. "It's unlike anything I have seen before. It's like opening a gate into an entirely new realm."

"I'm glad you like it," Mr Carmichael said. "Most of the items my father picked up on his travels, or I found on mine."

"You must travel a great deal," I said.

"It's necessary with my business," Mr Carmichael sounded slightly puzzled.

"I knew you operated all over Scotland," I said. "I did not know you also worked overseas."

Mr Carmichael's face was a picture. "Our business takes us to the four corners of the world," he said.

"I had no idea." I said.

"I will have to tell you some of my stories sometime," Mr Carmichael said. "If you are interested."

"I am," I stared at a picture of some exotic city. "Where is this?"

"Marseilles," Mr Carmichael said, "in the south of France."

"And this?" A large city with a busy harbour.

"Madras in India." Mr Carmichael smiled with an old memory. "It's sweltering hot there, and smells of spices."

I had a sudden urge to visit these outlandish places. "Have you been there?"

"Yes," Mr Carmichael said. "Would you like to go?"

"Very much,"' I said. "Your business is evidently more interesting than I imagined."

"What did you think I did?" Mr Carmichael sounded slightly amused, "studied account books and bills of ladling all day long?"

"No," I faced Mr Carmichael, lifting my chin. "I think you hunt down men like Matthew Juner and take them to jail. Was that not what you were doing in Midlothian?"

"'Good God!" It was the first time I had seen Mr Carmichael looked visibly shocked.

"What do you believe I am?"

"You are a messenger-at-arms," I said.

Mr Carmichael took a step backwards. "Good God," he repeated, weakly. "Whatever gave you that idea?"

"Are you not?" I wondered if I was mistaken. "I heard Father call you a messenger, you asked about the colliers and you carry a pistol."

"Well now," Mr Carmichael shook his head. "That is a row of frail pegs on which to hang a man. I can assure you, Miss Moffat, that I am not, and never have been, a messenger-at-arms."

"Oh." I was unsure what to say.

"I was a messenger, sent by my father, Mr James Carmichael, to arrange a business deal with your father."

"Oh." I said again, wondering how I could have made such a mighty fool of myself. "You asked about the colliers."

"I did. My business depends on a regular supply of coal, which was what I was trying to arrange with your father, until another matter distracted me, somewhat."

"Oh," I said for the third time. "Pray, Mr Carmichael, pray tell me what is your business?"

"I am a partner in my father's steam shipping line, James Carmichael and Son. We trade to Europe, India and North America."

"Oh," I said yet again, as everything clicked into place. "But you carry a gun?"

"I do," Mr Carmichael said. "It was a habit I got into travelling in foreign parts. A pistol is a necessity in some of the places we trade."

"Oh," I said. "Mr Carmichael, I have done you a massive injustice. I owe you an apology for what I have thought."

"Thoughts can do no harm unless they turn into words or deeds," Mr Carmichael said. "We can discuss things later; I am only pleased, very pleased, to have cleared up that little misunderstanding. Now, I have a man waiting upstairs."

"Mr Juner!" In the excitement of discovering the truth about Mr Carmichael, I had quite forgotten the plight of poor Matthew. "Where is he?"

"This way, Miss Moffat." Mr Carmichael ascended a flight of stairs that led to the upper storey, with his feet as light as a bird.

Matthew looked up when Mr Carmichael opened his door. He sat on a solid armchair in a very comfortable bedroom, reading a book. Since I had last seen him, he had grown a small beard, and his hair was a little longer, curling over his ears most engagingly. "Miss Moffat! What are you doing here?"

"Miss Moffat is here to help you escape," Mr Carmichael replied for me.

"You cannot," Matthew said. "You have both already done more than sufficient for me."

Looking at Matthew's open face with his steady grey eyes, I felt again that surge of affection I had experienced when he was at the folly. "I should like to do more," I said, sensing Mr Carmichael watching me.

"What do you have in mind, Adam?" Matthew surprised me by his casual use of Mr Carmichael's Christian name.

"There is a ship in Leith Docks," Mr Carmichael said at once, "bound for North America. You will be safe there, until the situation here improves, and mark me, it will improve in time."

"I cannot leave the country." Matthew said. "My people need me."

"It won't be for long," Mr Carmichael said. "You can gather support and finances before you return."

"You cannot stay here," I encouraged. "Not with the police and the messenger-at-arms hunting for you." I glanced at Mr Carmichael. "I hear that the messenger is an abominably cruel man."

Matthew was silent for a few moments. "How would I get back?"

"Contact me when you are ready," Mr Carmichael said. "Our shipping company has offices in New York and Boston."

"Thank you." Matthew said.

"It's not me you should be thanking, it's Miss Moffat." Mr Carmichael nodded in my direction.

"I hardly think so," I retorted. "I believe the combination had something to do with rescuing you."

"Never mind that now," Mr Carmichael said. "Time is passing. We have to get you on to *Heron's Pride*, Matthew. I have held her back from sailing until you are aboard. I cannot hold her any longer for we have obligations to fulfil so, whatever happens, she sails on the tide this evening."

"Is it so difficult to get Matthew on board a ship?" I asked. "Can he not just walk on board?"

Mr Carmichael sighed. "Normally he could, but the police are proving very diligent in their duties. They expect Matthew to leave by sea, so have men posted at all the docks, with sketches of Matthew's likeness. The Leith Police have even brought in some men from Midlothian to help identify Matthew."

I had not expected such a busy response by the police. "How can I help?"

"You should not," Matthew said. "You have already done too much, Miss Moffat."

"I wish to help."

"We have to smuggle Matthew past the police and on to the ship," Mr Carmichael said.

Despite the seriousness of the situation, I felt a surge of excitement. "That sounds very romantic."

"Very dangerous," Mr Carmichael said. "If the police catch us, it would be the jail for sure."

"What do you want me to do?" I asked.

"As you see, Matthew has altered his appearance," Mr Carmichael indicated Matthew's burgeoning beard. "Which might help. I intend to disguise Matthew as a seaman and distract the police." He hesitated for a moment. "I would like you to provide the distraction."

"Of course," I had no idea what he meant. "What should I do?"

"I wish you to act as Matthew's girl." There was no humour in Mr Carmichael's eyes as he faced me. "You will be a seaman's doxy, Miss Moffat. I warn you that the police are not gentle with such women."

I took a deep breath. "I can do that." I said.

Chapter Seventeen

"You are a brave woman," Mr Carmichael said.

"Why?" Matthew asked. "Why are you doing this for me?"

"Can't you guess?" I asked. I was suddenly aware of strange anguish in Mr Carmichael's face.

"We've no time for this," Mr Carmichael's voice was rougher than usual. "If you are sure, Miss Moffat, then we shall go ahead."

"I am sure," I heard the tremor in my voice.

"All right then. If you care to come with me, you can change in the next room. Nobody will see you."

"Change?" I indicated the bag I had brought from Winter Lodge.

"Not into your own clothes, Miss Moffat. You will have to change into the sort of clothes a seaman's doxy would wear," Mr Carmichael said.

"Of course." I looked down at myself. I had taken pains dressing this morning, wearing my most favourite creation in red and gold, with the velvet band around the hips. Now, all that effort was going to waste. I sighed. Honestly, the things we women do for love. Men have no idea.

"This way." Mr Carmichael escorted me into a small room replete with chests and walnut furniture. A full-length mirror stood in one corner, reflecting the light that entered through the tall window. "I took the liberty of buying a selection of women's clothing. I was not sure of your size."

"I'm sure I will find something," I said.

"Nobody will disturb you," Mr Carmichael said. "I don't keep servants here. Indeed, I rarely visit this house at all." He closed the door quietly behind him.

I stood still for a moment, getting used to my surroundings, and then I opened the chest to see what sort of clothes Mr Carmichael thought a sailor's doxy should wear. I smiled at the array of gaudy ribbons and bright colours, while some of the dresses were so low-cut as to be positively indecent, yet strangely alluring at the same time.

Leaving the chest, I surrendered to my curiosity and opened all the drawers to see what else the room held. Most were full of items of men's clothing, while the top drawer was empty except for a couple of documents and a single swathe of yellow silk. I lifted the silk first, wondering to what use it could be put and returned it with a shrug. There were too many clothes to take my attention for one stretch of silk to hold my interest for long. The documents were more interesting, for Hugh Beaton's name was on top, and they were both invoices for services rendered. The first was for an astronomical sum as payment for defending Matthew Juner in court. The second was for a much smaller, if still formidable, figure for penning the appeal letters.

I raised my eyebrows in astonishment. So Mr Carmichael was the mysterious benefactor who had tried to help Matthew. He was a man of many surprises, and I vowed to question him closely whenever the opportunity presented itself.

First, though, I had to find suitable attire for my role as a sailor's ladybird. I must admit that I thoroughly enjoyed trying on an assortment of clothes, parading in front of the mirror and smiling to see how I looked in various guises. There were skirts so short they were absolutely suggestive and tops so low that they revealed much of my upper person to all and sundry. Smiling, I wondered if I could have been such a woman if I had been born in a different station, and was so taken up with admiring myself that I forgot the time so that Mr Carmichael had to tap on the door and gently enquire if I was all right.

"I'll be there directly," I said, giving myself a final look to ensure I was at least slightly respectable. I had chosen a flaring green and gold skirt and a top that covered me, if only just. I added a profusion of ribbons around my upper parts, pulled the dress down to conceal as much of my calf and ankle as possible, grimaced at my reflection and left the room.

My nerves were jumping so much I felt physically sick as I walked into the guest room and waited for Matthew and Mr Carmichael's comments on my appearance.

Mr Carmichael's eyes widened as he saw me. "My word." His gaze slid up and down me, from my nearly exposed ankles to my face and back. "My word, indeed."

"Yes," Matthew was less expressive. "Perhaps you are wearing a little too much."

"Well, I'm certainly not wearing any less," I snapped.

"No, you're not," Mr Carmichael agreed with me, thankfully, although I noticed that his man's eyes were still busy.

"When are we leaving?" Matthew asked.

"Late afternoon," Mr Carmichael said. "The tide is right for *Heron's Pride* just after dusk, so we want to arrive at the docks before then, but when the light is fading. Timing is crucial."

I nodded as the fun seemed to disappear. I realised what a perilous mission we were undertaking with a man's liberty and my reputation, if nothing else, at stake.

"We'll have something to eat," Mr Carmichael decided for us all. "It could be a long night." He gave me a slightly twisted smile. "It won't be anything fancy, Miss Moffat."

"Ship's biscuits and cold water will suit me well," I said, remembering our small adventure on the day of the hunt.

Mr Carmichael's smile straightened out. "I can maybe manage something a little better than that."

"Whatever it is will be grand." I was not in the least hungry as my nerves were sending butterflies to flutter around my stomach.

We had thick slices of bread and cheese, with mugs of sweet tea so strong one could nearly dance on the brew. It sounds plain, perhaps but, when the three of us ate together, I felt part of something important, as if I were assisting the Scarlet Pimpernel rescue a captive aristocrat, or Flora MacDonald smuggling Prince Charlie across the sea.

"I've no sugar," Mr Carmichael said, "so I sweetened the tea with rum."

I nodded, not caring what he had used as I thought of the perilous expedition on which we were embarking. Aware that Mr Carmichael was watching me closely, I swallowed the queer-tasting tea while Mr Carmichael gave us unhurried instruction on the parts we had to play.

I listened, trying not to let my tenseness show. "That does not sound too difficult," I tried to sound confident.

"Keep your nerve, and you will be all right," Mr Carmichael said.

I nodded, sipping more of the tea-and-rum.

"Come on, Matthew, we'd best get ready." Mr Carmichael answered my nod with a brief inclination of his head. "We won't be long, Miss Moffat."

When the men left, I took a deep breath to help steady myself. I wondered what Amy would think of me now. I suddenly realised that I realised I was sharing an audacious exploit with two of the three men who mattered most in my life. Until this day, I had refused to admit that I had never lost my affection for Mr Carmichael, only buried it behind disappointment.

That realisation shook me. I would have liked more time to work out my feelings, but the men were ready, the afternoon was fast sliding away, and adventure awaited us all.

"Something is missing." Mr Carmichael examined me with a critical eye. "You look the part but smell like the lady you are."

I frowned. "What do you mean, sir?"

"You should smell of cheap scent." Mr Carmichael sounded apologetic.

"Should I, indeed?" I shook my head. "No, sir, I will not cover myself in cheap scent. I will stay as I am."

Mr Carmichael gave a small bow, with the humour back in his eyes. "As you wish, Miss Moffat."

"Indeed, Mr Carmichael." I do not know why I responded with a low curtsey, but I did.

Dressed more gaudily than I had ever been in my life, I felt extremely self-conscious when we left the house by the back door and returned to the stables. Matthew was in the dress of an outward-bound sailor, with trousers tight around his hips and a short jacket straining across his broad shoulders. He carried a heavy bag that must have contained his possessions. Mr Carmichael, I was interested to see, wore dark trousers and a long coat, with a low crowned hat pulled down over his head, partly concealing his face. He looked the part of an adventurer, as he had looked the part of a gentleman. I wondered, briefly, which was the real man behind the acting. Who was the Adam beyond the apparel?

When we entered the stables, I had expected to board the gig, but instead, Mr Carmichael placed the horse with the covered carriage while Matthew opened the stable door. Grey light flooded in, and I hurried into the carriage before anybody saw me in my ribbons and frills.

"Thank you again, Miss Moffat," Matthew said as he took his place opposite me in the coach. "I hope you do not get into any trouble because of this evening."

"I am sure the evening will go well," I said. It was strange to be alone with Matthew again. I found myself tongue-tied, which was highly unusual for me.

Matthew looked out of the window as the carriage left the mews lane and grumbled along the cobbles. "I hope I can help the combination," he said.

"I hope so, too," I said, although I was more hoping that he would take some interest in me. "We may not see each other for quite some time," I said, trying to jog some reaction from him.

"No," Matthew was too preoccupied to say more.

"I will miss you." I knew I was pushing too hard, but wanted something to treasure when Matthew was away.

"The combination will miss me more," Matthew said. "I hope they will continue the struggle."

"I am sure they will," I said.

"I hope so," Matthew said. Producing a bottle of whisky, he rubbed some into his beard, took a swig and handed the bottle to me.

"You'd better smell the part," Matthew advised. "The police will expect you to smell of perfume or spirits and you've refused perfume."

I did as he advised. Although I objected to being showered with scent, I could see the sense of smelling of spirits.

"Nearly there," Mr Carmichael called from the driving seat. He crunched the coach to a stop. He was not as skilful as George, I thought. "Right, you two. Out you get."

We alighted in a narrow street of tall tenements with ship's chandlers and dark public houses at street level. A knot of vaguely maritime men clustered around a doorway, talking loudly through a cloud of tobacco smoke as two dogs snarled and fought over a ragged bone. The air smelled of tar and alcohol, with the sweet smell of a bonded warehouse somewhere nearby.

"Wait!" Mr Carmichael was curter than I had ever known him, a sure sign that his nerves were also on edge. Walking into the nearest public house, he emerged with two of the ugliest looking men I had ever seen.

"Right lads – a golden boy each if you look after my carriage until I return."

The taller and uglier of the men nodded. "Aye, nae bother, son. We'll take your sovereigns. Naebody will touch the coach when we're here."

I agreed with the man. Old Nick himself would not dare go near the carriage with these two looking after it.

"If it is damaged in any way," Mr Carmichael's voice was edged with steel, "I will hunt you two down and break your legs."

I shivered slightly, wondering again what sort of man sheltered beneath Mr Carmichael's urbane cloak.

"All right then, Matthew and Miss Moffat; follow me." Mr Carmichael walked, long-striding, towards the docks. I had never been in Leith before, so looked around me at the people who filled the streets. At first, I felt very self-conscious in my unfamiliar clothes, but when I saw other women similarly attired, I relaxed a little. As I watched, I wondered at what misery the harsh voices, flounces and brash ribbons concealed. When one group passed close by, and I heard the topic of their conversation, I quickly learned that my education had been sadly lacking in at least one respect, shuddered and edged closer to Matthew. The stink of sharp scent nearly made me choke.

Oh, Mother, I thought, *I am glad you are not here to see your errant daughter.*

The dock gates loomed ahead. Although they were open, a group of uniformed police checked everybody who passed through. We watched as the police stopped a cart, questioning the driver and examining its load of sacks by thrusting a spiked pole into each one.

"You can enter," the sergeant in charge said. A tall man with mutton-chop whiskers, he said something to the three constables that made them laugh.

"Lag a little behind now," Mr Carmichael spoke quietly. "I'll pave the way. Follow in a few moments and be careful of that sergeant."

Despite my nervousness, I could not help admiring Mr Carmichael's calm as he strolled up to the policemen. Looking like a man without a care in the world, he spoke to them for a moment, laughed, and handed each a cheroot from a case he produced.

"What's he doing?" Matthew asked me.

"Making friends," I guessed. "He told us to give him a few minutes and then pass the police." I tried to still the rapid acceleration of my heart. "Are you ready, Matthew?" I patted his arm, feeling the hard swell of muscle.

"Yes." Although Matthew did not attempt to pull away, neither did he reciprocate, much to my disappointment. I felt as if I was pushing all my affection into a sponge that accepted without giving anything back. It was most frustrating.

"Come on, then." Remembering Mr Carmichael's instructions, I wrapped my arm around Matthew, which was not unpleasant, and stepped towards the dock gates. I could feel Matthew trembling under my arm. "It'll be all right," I murmured, "now remember you are a drunken seaman." I shook him. "Come on, Matthew. Sing!"

I began the chorus: "Farewell and adieu, to you Spanish ladies,
Farewell and adieu, you ladies of Spain."

My voice trembled as we neared the police. The sergeant watched us through hard eyes, before gesturing one of his constables forward.

Matthew joined in the song, "For we're under orders to sail for old England. But we hope in a short while to see you again."

"You two!" The constable pointed to us. Still holding Mr Carmichael's cheroot in his hand, he stepped closer. "Come here."

"Come on, Tam," I tried to roughen my voice. "The bluebottle wants to see us."

"What's to do, officer?" Matthew stopped his song in the middle of a line.

"Yes," I tried a drunken giggle, "what's to do, officer?"

The policeman removed a copy of the wanted poster from his pocket, looked at it and Matthew. I saw his face close in puzzlement as he tried to imagine Matthew without the beard, and I realised I had to do something to distract him. Pulling Matthew close, I planted a kiss on his cheek. It was not a hard thing to do, even if Matthew did not respond.

"Come on, Tam," I said. "You've got a ship to catch!" I smiled at the policeman, hoping my charm diverted him from his quarry. "Can we go now, Inspector? I want another minute alone with Tam before he's on the briny ocean."

I was aware of Mr Carmichael watching from 50 feet away with an expression almost of despair on his face.

"What did you say your name was?" A second officer joined the first, both ignoring me as they peered at Matthew.

"He didnae say." I wished that Matthew would speak. "He's a bit quiet sometimes." I tried to shake some life into him. "Come on, officers! He's got a ship to catch before she sails without him!"

The first policeman gave me a less-than-gentle shove. "I didn't ask you, ladybird. I asked your man."

"He's Tam," I prompted. "Tam Neilson."

"Tam Neilson," Matthew sounded hoarse.

"I told you to keep quiet, woman!" The policeman pushed me again, harder than before. "Any more from you and I'll have you in the lock-up, and not for the first time, by the look of you."

"Tam Neilson," Matthew repeated.

"There's no need to attack the woman, Officer." Mr Carmichael stepped forward to defend me, bless him.

"This is not your concern, sir," the policeman touched the brim of his hat to Mr Carmichael. "She's only a common streetwalker. We deal with her type every day."

"Common!" I decided to take the officers' attention away from Matthew. "There's nothing common about me!" I was quite enjoying acting, knowing I was hidden behind my disguise, although a bit nervous about the lock-up, whatever that was. I wondered if I should slap the policeman, decided I might get arrested and settled on a display of huffiness instead. "Common indeed!"

"Get away," the policeman put his picture away and gave me a third shove, "and get your man on his ship." He shook his head to Mr Carmichael, man to man. "He's welcome to her. Women like her are just trouble."

"Thank you, officer." Mr Carmichael nodded and strolled behind us. "Women are always trouble, whatever their rank!"

The supposed humour defused the tension as the police laughed.

"Trouble!" I snorted, grabbed Matthew's arm and dragged him away, for sudden paralysis seemed to have struck him. "Come on, Tam! Where's your ship?"

That was a genuine question for there were many ships moored nearby. I was not in the least knowledgeable about nautical matters and only saw a collection of vessels, with a profusion of masts, spars and furled sails.

Mr Carmichael must have guessed my confusion, for he stopped alongside one vessel, looked at it pointedly, carefully studied the name written across her stern and slowly walked on.

"That's our ship." I had to cling to Matthew, as he nearly dragged me across the ground in his eagerness to get to safety. "Take your time," I hissed. "You're meant to be drunk, remember! And with your girl. The police may still be watching."

I should have known the ship at once, for she was one of the few that boasted steam power. She lay beside the quay with her masts and rigging stark against the darkening sky and her tall funnel emitting the occasional spurt of smoke. Even in the fading light, I could make out her name, painted in white letters across the dark woodwork of her paddle-box. *Heron's Pride.*

Heron again – that was another clue. For some reason, I remembered the heron at the Lover's Pool and smiled. Matthew had regained some composure, so we moved at a more sedate pace towards the ship, as I gave noises of encouragement.

"Nearly there, Matthew, and you'll be safe. Only a few more steps."

Honestly, it was like teaching an infant, but I had to do what had to be done. The poor lamb was trembling. I held him close, watching as Mr Carmichael stopped a dozen paces ahead, ostensibly examining the rigging of a brig while most of his attention was on us. If he was nervous, he hid it well.

Heron's Pride was low in the water, with easy access from the quay to the ship. I took a deep breath, counting the distance. "Only 20 more steps, Matthew," I said. "Just 19, 18 more steps and you are safe."

I had been aware of the man in the shadow of the ship to my right but paid little heed to him as I eased Matthew across the ground. Now, with the ship only 10 steps away, I started. The voice sounded like the crack of doomsday as it shattered all my hopes.

"I know you! Matthew Juner! You are under arrest!"

I heard somebody scream with the shock. It might have been me, or it could have been Matthew, I do not know. I only know that I nearly fainted as Andrew Dewar made a lunge for Matthew, with his big clumsy hand clutching at Matthew's shoulder.

Without thinking, I barged sideways, unbalancing Andrew, pushed Matthew in the opposite direction and ran deeper into the docks. Only then did I see the second man beside Andrew. Not particularly tall, he was as broad as any collier, wore a very smart coat and waistcoat and had the hardest face of any man I had seen. I knew without a doubt that this man was the messenger-at-arms. He had caught up with Matthew at last, when we were within 10 steps of escape.

"The ship!" Matthew nearly screamed. "We'll have to board the ship!"

"Not now," I dragged him into the shadows, looked over my shoulder and saw the messenger helping Andrew to his feet. "If you board her, you'll be trapped there. Come on!" I pulled him behind me, looking for somewhere to hide. Fortunately, the quayside was covered with boxes, packages, sacks and barrels. I saw Andrew recover and lumber after us, hoped he had not recognised me and ran for the deepest shadows I could find. Darting towards the gate, the messenger moved much faster. I could not see Mr Carmichael at all. Had he abandoned us? I could not believe he would do such a thing.

The noise we made had caught the attention of some sailors, who lined the bulwarks of their vessels, watching us, cheering and whistling as if at some sporting event.

"Dirty peelers!" One man jeered at the police. "Chasing poor sailors!"

I wondered if I had helped start a riot, wondered what Father would say and ducked behind a rickety old shack, looking for somewhere better to hide.

"In here, Matthew!" Leith Docks was a confusing place, with its collection of warehouses and huts near to the water, piles of sacks containing I-knew-not-what, lengths of ship's masts and other nautical paraphernalia and a profusion of empty casks and barrels. I ducked behind a pile of empty hogsheads and watched as Andrew sprung his rattle, with the harsh sound attracting policemen from all across the docks.

"It was Juner." I heard Andrew's voice plainly. "He had some doxy with him."

"Where is he now?" The sergeant asked.

"Over that way." When Andrew gestured vaguely in our direction, the police formed a line and marched toward us, some tapping their long staffs against the palm of their hands in a business-like manner.

"Spread out." The sergeant took charge. "Form a line and hunt them down."

I felt Matthew move beside me. "Keep still!" I hissed.

We crouched there, side by side, so close I could feel the warmth from Matthew's body and hear his short, shallow breathing. Reaching across, I took hold of his hand and squeezed, hoping to reassure him. He did not respond.

"Keep searching!" Shouting orders, the messenger boarded *Heron's Pride*, presumably in case we had somehow eluded the police and managed to get on to the ship.

I kept still, feeling Matthew tremble at my side. "They can't see us," I whispered, watching as the police came closer, calling encouragement to each other and occasionally stopping to examine something that caught their interest. With the dark mounting, the police lit bull's eye lanterns, pooling the yellow light before them, creating new shadows as they searched. I felt sick yet excited.

"I see you!" a stocky man on the extreme right shouted, shining his lantern in the opposite direction to where we hid. "Over there!" He ran forward, banged his staff against an empty barrel and swore when a rat scurried out.

"Hey, bluebottle," one of the sailors jeered. "Are you going to arrest that dangerous criminal?" Other sailors responded with jokes far too crude for me to write down.

"Come on, Matthew!"

With the police distracted in trying to kill the rat, Matthew and I crept away, hugging the darkening shadows. I heard the police responding to the sailor's jibes, wondered where Andrew was and tried to get around the flank of the blue line.

I could feel my heart pounding within my breast as we moved. As luck would have it, a haar slid in from the Forth, a thin damp mist that clung damply to everything and helped conceal us.

"Thank you, Lord," I breathed. In the mist, the police voices sounded hollow, as though they spoke in a tunnel.

"Halloa! You there!" I had not seen the second line of policemen until one focused his lantern on us, with the haar diffusing the light. "That's them!"

A second beam of lamp-light joined the first, flicking over us and back, to shine full in my face. Temporarily dazzled, I raised my hand to protect my eyes.

"We've got them! Stand still, you two, or it will go hard on you!"

"They've caught us!" I heard the despair in Matthew's voice, even as I gathered my strength ready to run.

"Not yet, Matthew." Gripping his hand as tightly as I could, I tried to haul him upright. "Come on!"

I heard the thump of boots as the police marched towards us. "Come on, Matthew!"

A second later, the clatter of hooves and grind of wheels drowned out all other sounds as the closed coach raced across the dockside. One moment the police lanterns reflected from the glossy woodwork of the coach, the next they shone on nothing as the coach raced past. It ground to a halt a few feet from us as the driver sawed at the reins.

"Get in!" The voice was sharp, imperious. I looked up, still partially dazzled, if very relieved. The closed coach stood before us with Adam Carmichael on the driving seat, all huddled in a greatcoat, his hat low over his forehead and a yellow mask covering the lower half of his face. When I look back at my life, that moment stands out as one of the highlights. It was if a barrier was crossed or a door to a truth that should have been obvious opened in front of me, yet Mr Carmichael was in no mood to allow me to deliberate on my discovery.

"Get in!" Mr Carmichael repeated. "Hurry!"

Matthew was first in, with me a second later, scrabbling for balance as Matthew banged the door shut and the coach took off with a jerk that knocked me off my feet and on to the seat.

I am unsure if it was my nerves or a sense of relief that made me giggle, but I did. I lay back on the leather seat and laughed, with Matthew staring at me as if I had taken leave of my senses, which perhaps I had.

"Hold on!" That was Mr Carmichael's voice, clear as day through the multiplicity of noises of the docks. It might have been evident to everybody else, but only then did I realise that the highwayman who rescued Matthew from the prison coach had been Mr Carmichael. I had been so intent on helping Matthew, I had not put all the facts together. The closed coach, the yellow mask, the element of daring – why was Mr Carmichael going to so much trouble?

Even as I pondered the question, I heard a terrific clatter, the coach shook, there was an outburst of shouting, some vivid language, and then we picked up speed once more.

"The ship!" Matthew said.

"Forget the ship," I said. At that moment, I could happily have pushed Matthew out of the coach, he seemed so self-obsessed, although I knew his concern was for the colliers and the combination rather than for himself. I began to giggle again, knowing that we had just forced through the dock gates and Mr Carmichael was driving us to destinations unknown. I was aware of Matthew staring at me. I was aware I was acting irrationally, but I did not care. I am sure a madness descended upon me for I was content to allow life to take its course, dragging me along with it. We rattled on, bouncing over the cobbles, turning corners at such acute angles that Matthew and I were thrown around like boats on a stormy sea. I hung on to the strap, watching Matthew as my nerves gradually settled down.

"It will be all right," I said. "Mr Carmichael will see us through." I believed that to be true. I had developed great faith in Mr Carmichael's abilities. I had witnessed them at Balantrodoch Church and now when rescuing Matthew. In fact, I was developing great faith in Mr Carmichael. *My* Mr Carmichael.

I thought of him donning his yellow mask to hold up the prison coach, and I thought of him tearing his shirt to bandage my ankle. I thought of his bright, mockingly humorous eyes and his stern expression when he escorted Mother and me though the mob in Dalkeith. Dear Lord. I sat up with a start. I had come here to help rescue Matthew, not to think about Mr Carmichael's eyes.

"How are you, Matthew?" I asked.

He forced a smile as he clung to the leather strap. "I am very well, Miss Moffat."

"Robyn," I said. "My name is Robyn."

"Robyn." Matthew said.

"I wonder where Mr Carmichael is taking us." We seemed to have been travelling for hours. "Not the New Town house, anyway."

"No, we've gone too far for that," Matthew agreed.

We sat in silence, being jolted around the interior of the coach as I searched desperately for something to say. Matthew appeared content to return to his thoughts.

"When you get to America," I tried to get a response. "What will you do?"

Matthew stared at me before replying. "If I get there, I'll find a labour organisation that will support us."

"You won't be able to return to Scotland now," I said.

"No," Matthew agreed. Honestly, I'd have been as well trying to talk to my horse-chestnut tree for all the conversation I got in that coach.

"How can you help the colliers from so far away?" I asked. "How about your mother?"

"I'll send money," Matthew was happier talking about such matters. "To the combination as well as to Mother. I might send for her later when I get settled."

"You will miss your friends in Midlothian." I put out a hook, wondering if I might get a bite.

Matthew looked at me. "They are work colleagues, Robyn, more than friends. I want to help the entire community, rather than a few individuals."

"Surely, though…" I tried again. "Surely there is somebody you will miss?" *How about me, Matthew? How about me?*

Matthew faced me with his eyes as steady as ever. "I do not think so."

Trying to talk to Matthew was hard work. "Nobody? Not a special friend? Or a sweetheart?"

Matthew shook his head. "No. I have no time for such things."

Well, that settled that then. I wondered why I had spent so much time on this man. I knew the answer, of course – I had spent time on him because he needed help more than anything else. Like Mother, I collected waifs, strays and the afflicted, and Matthew fitted into that category, somewhere. I had looked for an attachment while he had not. Joining Matthew in contemplative silence,

I cast back my mind to all our previous encounters, seeking evidence of any affection.

There was none, and there had never been any. Although Matthew had been as polite as anybody and had shown immense gratitude for my help, at no time had he demonstrated any sign of affection. Once again, I had cast my hat at the wrong man, and any fault was entirely my own.

Slumping on the seat, I stared out the window. The haar had thickened into a fine drizzle, and now that my excitement had burned out, the depressing weather perfectly mirrored my state of mind.

What should I do now?

Chapter Eighteen

"Here we are."

By the time the carriage stopped, I had the beginnings of a headache and was heartily sick of being thrown about like a leaf in a storm. I emerged to a familiar building for we had arrived at Esk House in Inveresk, the house where Hugh Beaton had heard my version of Matthew's story. "Does Hugh's cousin not own this property?"

"He does." Mr Carmichael stood at the carriage door to let us out. Although he looked tired and was spattered with mud kicked up by the horse's hooves, he was as erect as a guardsman.

"Will Hugh's nameless cousin give us sanctuary?" I knew that the hard face of the messenger would haunt my nightmares for a long time to come.

"Yes," Mr Carmichael responded with a smile. "I am Hugh's cousin. This house belongs to me."

"Oh," I helped Matthew out of the carriage. *That explained the intimate conversations.* "I thought you had the house in Edinburgh."

"I have that one also," Mr Carmichael said. "Come away in."

While a willing servant took the horse and carriage to the stable block, Mr Carmichael ushered us into Esk House. On my previous visit, I had been too preoccupied with Mr Beaton to notice details of the house, but now I looked around me. This establishment could not have been more different from Mr Carmichael's townhouse. While exotic furniture and strange objects had filled the Edinburgh address, this house was furnished simply, with good taste. The only pictures were of ships, and when I examined them, I saw they were from the Carmichael Heron Line. Each one had three masts as well as a funnel and paddles; auxiliary steamships, as Mr Carmichael called them.

"What happens now?" Matthew did not spare any time to study the house or the pictures.

"Now we get you away on *Heron's Pride*," Mr Carmichael said steadily. "I don't give up so easily, Mathew," he looked at me, "and I doubt that Miss Moffat will ever give up."

I was not so sure about that. With my head pounding and my realisation that Matthew had no tenderness for me, I rather wondered if I would not be better just returning home.

"How will I get to the ship?" Matthew asked. "She is in Leith unless she's already sailed."

Mr Carmichael checked his watch. "She cast off about 20 minutes ago." His smile lacked its usual humour. "Do you get seasick, Matthew?"

"I don't know. I've never been to sea," Matthew said.

"We'll soon find out," Mr Carmichael said. "Miss Moffat, I am sorry that you won't see the concert tonight."

"I had forgotten all about it," I said truthfully.

"If I am to get Matthew away safely, I'm afraid you will have to stay here alone," Mr Carmichael was all business. "I will take Matthew out on the Forth to meet *Heron's Pride*."

"I'm coming too." I decided without thought. "I was at the start of this escapade and I mean to see it through to the finish."

When Mr Carmichael looked at me, I swear I saw respect in his eyes. "We are going on to the Forth in a small boat, Miss Moffat. It will be cold and very wet."

"Mr Carmichael," I said, "every time I meet you, I get cold and very wet. It may as well be in a boat than in an old church."

"The Forth can get choppy at this time of year," Mr Carmichael warned.

"I'm sure I will survive," I said.

Mr Carmichael shook his head. "I don't like to take a woman out there in a small boat." His voice softened. "But you, Miss Moffat? Yes, I think you can survive anything the world throws at you."

"Where will you get the boat from?" Matthew was not interested in our private conversation.

"I have one in Fisherrow harbour," Mr Carmichael spoke casually as if everybody owned a boat. "She's nothing grand, Matthew."

"Will it get us out to meet *Heron's Pride*?'" Matthew asked.

"She will, although it might be an uncomfortable trip." Mr Carmichael looked at me again, as if trying to warn me not to come.

"When do we leave?" Matthew asked.

"We'll leave as soon as we are ready," Mr Carmichael said. "We'll need warm clothes for you, Miss Moffat."

"Thank you," I could not help as Mr Carmichael arranged things, bringing extra clothes for me, a nautical chart and compass, and a bag full of clothes and other essentials for Matthew, who had dropped his previous bag while the police chased us in Leith.

After an hour or so in Esk House, we left again, with Mr Carmichael insisting that I don so many layers of clothes that I waddled rather than walked. As Fisherrow was only a short distance away, we walked to the harbour, with Matthew hurrying ahead and Mr Carmichael trying to talk to me. However, my mind was in such confusion that I could only reply in monosyllables.

"You are a very determined lady, Miss Moffat."

"Thank you."

"I do not wish you to suffer out there on the Forth, Miss Moffat."

"Nor do I."

"I hope Matthew appreciates all you are doing for him." Mr Carmichael said.

"You are doing much more than I am." I was stung into a reply, realising that I was treating Mr Carmichael as Matthew had treated me in the coach. He deserved better than that.

Mr Carmichael smiled. "Not for Matthew's sake, let me tell you."

"Oh?" The words meant nothing to me. *For whose sake then?*

Mr Carmichael shook his head. "I admire the man's principles, but I don't much like him. Certainly, I don't care for him as much as you do."

I paused, for Mr Carmichael had touched upon the very question which vexed me. "I am not sure I do care for him," I said. "Or not as much as I thought I did."

I felt Mr Carmichael's interest quicken as he moved slightly closer to me. "Yet you still are willing to put yourself in harm's way for him?"

I pondered the question. "I admire what Matthew believes."

Mr Carmichael's smile hid a lot of secrets. "You say you don't care for him, but do you love him? The two ideas are not incompatible."

The question took me by surprise, but before I could reply, we reached the haven of Fisherrow. The name gives the principal occupation away, for Fisherrow was a fishing port rather than a trading port. Fishing was the only industry, so the harbour was lined with creels and fishing nets, oars and the small open boats favoured by Forth fishermen. It smelled of fish and seaweed, while sitting tall in the harbour was a single-masted vessel unlike any of the others.

"That's my boat," Mr Carmichael could not keep the pride from his voice.

"Hurry up!" Matthew glanced behind him.

"She's lovely," I said.

Now, I knew nothing about things nautical but even in the dark, I could see that great pride had gone into building Mr Carmichael's boat. About 30 feet long, she had a sharp prow, a long foredeck and was painted white and yellow, a contrast to the black hulls of the fishing fleet.

"Come on!" Matthew clambered on board at once, setting the boat rocking. I followed, with Mr Carmichael at the tail. He quickly cast off the mooring ropes as he came last, so the little vessel began to bob a short distance from the quay. Mr Carmichael seemed quite a home as he hauled a rope to release a single dark sail. Within seconds, the breeze ruffled the canvas, and we were slowly shifting into the centre of the harbour. The tide was on the ebb, which helped us ease out of the small haven and into the Firth, where the first kick of the waves caught us.

"We're at sea!" I said, waiting for the seasickness I had heard was inevitable.

"Hold on now," Mr Carmichael advised. Sitting at the tiller in the stern, he told me to remain in the middle of the boat, "amidships", as he termed it, while Matthew positioned himself as near to the front, the bow, as he could.

"I can't see anything out there," Matthew peered forward into what seemed pretty formidable waves.

"We're low down," Mr Carmichael busied himself with the tiller, bringing the boat around to meet the oncoming waves. "I know the course *Heron's Pride* will take so I can intercept her before she leaves the shelter of the Firth." He gave a broad grin. "There won't be many ships sailing at night, so we should find her without too much difficulty. Watch for her lights, Matthew."

Clinging to the side of the boat, I did not like to admit my fear as we rose and fell, swooping to the rhythm of the sea. One second we were in the trough of two waves, looking up at masses of dark, spindrift-fringed water, and the next we were high up with the sea beneath us and starlight glittering far above. I could see the lights of land up there, from Edinburgh and the distant shores of Fife.

"The rain must have cleared," I said, stupidly.

"Yes. Are you all right, Miss Moffat?" Mr Carmichael asked.

"Yes." I was not sure if I was terrified or exhilarated. I gave Mr Carmichael my best attempt at a smile, wondering at this new skill he displayed. I did not doubt that he was better at the tiller of the boat than he had been driving the carriage.

"That's the way." Mr Carmichael smiled back before returning his full attention to sailing the boat.

We sailed on, crashing over the waves, with the sea frothing white on both sides, and the sounds much louder than I had anticipated. There was the slap of waves, the hiss of the sea, the sails cracking as the wind shifted and the wooden hull creaking, all of which I tried to identify. I could not judge the passage of time out there on the sea so I do not know how long it was before Matthew pointed wildly ahead. "There's a ship."

Peering in the direction which Matthew indicated, I saw nothing except a few lights bobbing up and down.

"That will be her," Mr Carmichael said. "Hold on now, until we get closer." He adjusted the set of the sail, shifted the tiller slightly, and the boat began to behave even livelier, bouncing on the sea with the bows kicking up white spray that pattered upon us.

"Aye, she's a bit boisterous, Miss Moffat." Mr Carmichael noticed my sudden alarm.

I could not disagree with that. I held on to the bulwark until my knuckles gleamed white. "Will they see us?"

"I doubt it." Mr Carmichael said. "We're low in the water with a dark sail."

"Then how can I get away?" Matthew asked.

"I'll give them a hail," Mr Carmichael said.

"They might not hear you," Matthew was becoming more nervous by the minute.

"Oh, they'll hear me all right," Mr Carmichael promised. 'They'll have a good lookout posted, or I'll want to know the reason why!"

Once again, I sensed the steel behind Mr Carmichael's debonair exterior. I watched him alter the angle of the tiller before he lifted his head. "Ship ahoy!"

I had never heard such a volume of sound come from a human voice before. Mr Carmichael's words echoed across the sea. "*Heron's Pride!*"

"Halloa!" The answering hail came a moment later. "Who is that?"

"Adam Carmichael!" Mr Carmichael bellowed at once. "With a passenger for you."

As we came closer, I saw *Heron's Pride* slow down, with the tall rectangles of her sails reducing as her master ordered them to be furled, one by one.

"Standing by!" That was a different voice, louder, more authoritarian.

"Is that you, Captain Deuchars?"

"It is, Mr Carmichael. I thought you'd missed your chance with that trouble in Leith."

"No – here we come now. Stand by, Captain, and give us some lights for God's sake."

I was amazed at Mr Carmichael's skill as he sailed our small boat alongside the much larger *Heron's Pride*, with the two vessels bouncing madly on the sea and the space between a froth of waves and white water. With both craft rising and falling to different waves, I could not see how Matthew could board *Heron's Pride*.

One by one, a row of lights appeared along the side of the larger vessel, enabling us to make out every detail. *Heron's Pride* was long, flush-decked and lean, with a score of men lining her rails, watching as we bounced crazily on the waves.

"Stand by amidships!" Mr Carmichael steered our little boat until she was close to the centre of *Heron's Pride*. "Hold the tiller," he ordered and, when Matthew remained where he was, I grabbed the vibrating length of rounded wood.

It took Mr Carmichael only a second to lift Matthew's baggage and toss it up to a waiting seaman on the larger ship, and then he took back control of the tiller.

"Well done." His hand rested on my shoulder. "Well done, Miss Moffat."

"I didn't do anything," I savoured these few words until a back surge of the sea pushed us further away from *Heron's Pride*.

"Drop a line!" Mr Carmichael shouted as he struggled to keep our boat level with the larger vessel.

I saw a rope snake down from the stern of *Heron's Pride*. It swung there, a tantalising, dangerous route to safety for Matthew.

Mr Carmichael allowed our boat to lose distance until we were level with the swinging line.

"Grab hold and climb up!" Mr Carmichael roared.

I saw Matthew hesitate. "Thank you!" he shouted. "I am immensely grateful!"

"Go on! I can't hold our position for long."

Just as Matthew reached for the rope, a rogue wave lifted our boat, slamming her against the stern of *Heron's Pride*. Matthew overbalanced, missed his hold and tumbled over the side in a flurry of arms and legs.

"Matthew!" I yelled, made a despairing clutch for him, missed by a yard and nearly joined him in the water.

"Miss Moffat!" Mr Carmichael lunged forward, grabbed the sleeve of my coat and hauled me back inboard but, in doing so, let go of the tiller. The boat veered away from *Heron's Pride*, shipping gallons of cold Forth water as she did so.

"Matthew!" Holding on to the side, I peered at the frothing dark water, hoping to glimpse his head. I did not know if he could even swim.

"Take the tiller!" Mr Carmichael roared. "Keep her head pointing into the waves," and with these words, he stripped off his coat and boots and dived into the churning sea.

"Mr Carmichael!" I screamed. "Be careful!" I watched him disappear beneath the surface with something like shock. It was only at that moment that I realised how much I cared for that man.

For one moment, I stared after Mr Carmichael with my heart racing. When I saw his head emerge from the water, I nearly shouted with relief, until I realised I was on board a madly tossing boat that depended on me to keep it on top of the water rather than underneath.

Now, I had no more idea how to steer a boat than how to fly to the moon, but I had watched Mr Carmichael on our voyage out and tried to emulate his actions. When I gripped the tiller, it seemed to have a life of its own as it kicked and vibrated in my hand. The smooth wood still retained some of the warmth from Mr Carmichael's hand as I pointed the bow of the boat towards the oncoming waves and held on grimly.

I'm all right, I told myself. *Don't let Mr Carmichael down.* I met one wave, stifled my fear and steered to the top of it, had a moment's terrifying vision of white-topped dark waves and then swooped back down again.

When I had a second to spare, I looked around for Mr Carmichael and was shocked to see how far I had drifted from *Heron's Pride*. Without thinking, I altered the tiller and immediately began to close the distance, although the boat heeled alarmingly to the side and shipped gallons of cold water.

Peering through a curtain of spray and spindrift, I saw Mr Carmichael help Matthew on to the end of the rope, with two seamen at the upper end. Matthew clung there for a moment with Mr Carmichael supporting him, and then he began to climb, hand over hand, using his feet to walk up the hull of the ship. I saw him reach the ship's rail, pause for a second, and then willing hands hauled him to safety. He rolled over the rail and did not look back. I have never seen him from that day to this.

"Mr Carmichael!" I wondered if he was also going to board *Heron's Pride* and leave me alone in the crazily tossing small boat. Instead, he took hold of the trailing rope for a long minute, presumably to recover his breath, looked around the surface of the sea, and plunged back in. I was not sure if I was relieved he was not leaving me alone or scared that he might drown out there.

"Mr Carmichael!" I moved the tiller a fraction, trying to steer closer to Mr Carmichael until the boat tipped to the opposite side and water poured in. I think that is the first time that day that I began to panic. With my boat sinking beneath me, *Heron's Pride* sailing away and Mr Carmichael somewhere in the water, I did not know what to do.

I cannot explain what happened next. I can only say what happened. I was staring at the water rapidly filling the boat when a voice sounded. "Take it down."

I started, for there was nobody else in the boat yet the voice was as clear as if I had said it myself. What was more amazing was I had heard those very words in the old church at Balantrodoch.

"Take it down."

"Take what down?" I shouted the question to nobody as the three words reverberated inside my head.

"Take it down."

Take what down? There was nothing to take down except the sail. It must be the sail! Remembering how Mr Carmichael had raised and secured it, I tried to reverse the procedure, fumbling over the unfamiliar knots until they opened. I could not help my gasp as the vast swathe of dark canvas came down with a great thunder and landed in an untidy heap across the boat. Immediately, the boat righted herself, to ride sluggishly on the water, with the canvas sodden all around and bitter-cold water lapping around my knees.

After a moment in which I tried to recover my composure, I looked across the sea for Mr Carmichael, with my heart in my mouth and salt water stinging my eyes. I saw his head a few yards away, with his arms flailing the water, powering him closer.

"Mr Carmichael!" Leaving the tiller, I shifted to the side of the boat and extended my hand as far as I could reach.

"Good girl!" Mr Carmichael grabbed my hand, half hauled himself over the side of the boat and balanced there, panting with exhaustion.

"In you come!" Grabbing hold of Mr Carmichael's shirt, I pulled him in. He lay on the crumpled sail in the bottom of the boat for a few moments, gasping for breath.

"Thank you, Miss Moffat." Struggling to a sitting position, he grinned to me with all the old mockery back in his eyes. "I told you we would end up cold and wet."

"It's your own fault," I said primly, "jumping in the water like that. You could have drowned."

"If I had not, then your friend Matthew certainly would have drowned," Mr Carmichael crawled crab-wise to the opposite side of the boat and began to tidy up the sail.

"I'd rather he drowned than you!" The words were out before I realised it.

"Oh?" Something else had replaced the humour in Mr Carmichael's eyes. "I thought you much preferred him to me."

"No," I said shortly. "I told you I had little feeling for the man."

When Mr Carmichael's gaze fixed on me, his eyes were as intense as I had ever seen. He opened his mouth to speak, closed it again and returned to his task.

I spoke to close the awkward silence. "We'd better get back to land, or you'll die of pneumonia instead." I thought for a second before adding: "To answer your previous question, Mr Carmichael: No. No, I don't love him, and I never did." I think I said that as much for my own benefit as for his. I was saying farewell to Matthew, and where better than in the middle of the Firth of Forth?

"Let's get back to land," Mr Carmichael said. He was strangely quiet as he steered the boat across the Forth, a fact I put down to the effects of cold and exhaustion, for it was bone-numbingly chill out there. I was cold enough under my many layers of clothing, so it must have been worse for Mr Carmichael, soaked through as he was.

My mind was racing but my tongue still as Mr Carmichael steered us back into Fisherrow Harbour and tied up the boat at her previous position. The state of the tide meant the water was lower, so we had to climb rusted ladders to the quay, with Mr Carmichael up first and extending his hand to help me. The fisherfolk were busy, some launching their boats for whatever fishing they planned, with women redding the lines and men talking the archaic language of the sea. They watched us and turned away – we were outside their closed world.

As we climbed stiffly on to the quay, I saw the name of Mr Carmichael's boat for the first time. The name *Robin* was bold in red on a white board, and somebody had painted a fat, red-breasted little robin on her stern. That made me smile, despite my sodden, cold clothes, although I did not mention I had noticed the coincidence.

After toying with the possibility that Mr Carmichael had named his boat after me, I dismissed the idea as ludicrous and walked on. We must have presented a queer picture as we plodded up to the house, with Mr Carmichael splashing with every step and me dressed as much like an Eskimo as a respectable Scottish maiden. Mr Carmichael did not seem to mind, acknowledging each greeting with a wave until he entered Esk House.

Chapter Nineteen

"Build the fires up!" Mr Carmichael shouted cheerfully as we splashed inside his house. "There are two very wet and cold people here!"

Concerned servants scurried around at once, offering free advice and sympathy.

"You'd better get out of these wet things," the plump housekeeper scolded him. "And look at the state of the lady! You should be ashamed of yourself, Mr Carmichael, making her all wet like that!"

"She insisted on going boating," Mr Carmichael said, truthfully. "Now, please light the fire in my study. Bring me dry clothes and something for Miss Moffat here."

"Do you have any women's clothes in the house, Mr Carmichael?" The housekeeper looked at me through kindly eyes.

"No," Mr Carmichael said. "Just bring some of mine – and bring a screen so we can dress in decency."

"I should think so, too," the housekeeper looked from my wet form to Mr Carmichael's dripping body. "Taking the poor wee mite boating at that time of night. I never heard the like!"

"All's fair in love and war, Mrs Mitchell. Even sailing a boat."

"War is it?" Mrs Mitchell studied me frankly. "It must be war because I'd not love a man who made me go out in a boat half the night, Miss Moffat."

"He did not make me, Mrs Mitchell," I said. "If anything, I drove him to it."

"I see." Her smile was subdued but understanding. "I'll ensure the fire is high, and I'll set the screen up myself." She studied me again. "I'll bring some suitable clothes, miss, and not that terrible man's hand-me-downs."

"Thank you," I said, although I must admit a certain twisted disappointment at not wearing Mr Carmichael's clothes.

"This way, Miss Moffat." Mrs Mitchell led me to the study, an oak-panelled room with an Axminster rug over polished floorboards. The servants had divided the room with a solid screen plastered with pictures of ships, with Mr Carmichael at one side and me at the other.

Unable to see Mr Carmichael's half of the study, I examined the portion in which I stood. It was neater than I would have expected from a bachelor, with a roll-top desk, a leather-seated chair, a collection of golf clubs and a bookcase. In my present wet condition, I did not wish to handle the books but read the titles. Mostly business or nautical tomes, there were also books on history and a single volume of *Ivanhoe* by Sir Walter Scott. I smiled at this subtle insight into Mr Carmichael's mind. The wall was bare except for a map of the world and a golfing print showing a handful of men crouching around a ball on a misty day.

"Are you all right, Miss Moffat?" Mr Carmichael sounded quite jovial, despite his long night.

"I am perfectly well, Mr Carmichael," I said. "I think it is you who ought to be careful, wet as you are."

When Mrs Mitchell brought me a small pile of women's clothing and left, closing the door behind her, I was suddenly and unaccountably nervous. I heard the rustle of cloth and guessed that Mr Carmichael was already removing his clothing.

"Mr Carmichael," I said. "Are you all right over there?"

"I am," Mr Carmichael said. He paused for a moment. "If you'd rather I were elsewhere, I can leave the room."

I felt my heartbeat increase. "No," I said. "No. I'd prefer you to stay, please." I found the idea of Mr Carmichael undressing so close to me disturbing, in a strangely pleasant way.

"You may trust me." Mr Carmichael said. "I promise you that you can trust me."

"I know." I began to peel off the many layers of clothing, one at a time. As I watched the pile of clothes grow, I thought of Mr Carmichael doing the same on the other side of the screen, only a few feet away. The same sea had wet us both, and now the same fire warmed and dried us.

"Mr Carmichael," I removed another layer, so I stood in my underthings, with the fire's heat welcome and my heart pounding at what I wished to say.

"Yes, Miss Moffat?"

"Thank you." I said. "Thank you for helping get Matthew to safety."

There was a long pause before Mr Carmichael replied. "It was my pleasure, Miss Moffat."

"Mr Carmichael." I said again.

"Yes, Miss Moffat?"

I phrased my question as delicately as I could. "I have learned that you paid Mr Juner's legal fees. May I ask what compelled you to such generosity?"

Only the crackle of the fire broke the silence of the next few minutes. "I am surprised that Beaton told you that," Mr Carmichael said, eventually.

"He told me nothing," I said. "I found out from quite another source."

"I see. I was trying to help a friend who was interested in Matthew's situation." Mr Carmichael said.

My natural curiosity compelled me to ask the next question, although I already guessed the answer. "Who was your friend, Mr Carmichael, if I may be so bold as to inquire?"

"You, Miss Moffat." Mr Carmichael said, baldly.

"Oh."

I thought of his words as I removed the last vestiges of my clothing. I stood stark naked, appreciating the warmth nearly as much as I savoured Mr Carmichael's company and the delicious knowledge that only a thin screen separated us. I wondered what he would say if I inadvertently knocked over the screen and he saw me as nature intended.

No! I shook my head, shocked that I should ever think such a thing. I was a respectable woman, not some hussy. Yet, still naked, I touched the screen, wondering.

"Miss Moffat." I sensed some tension in Mr Carmichael's voice and stepped back immediately, instinctively covering myself as if he could see through solid wood.

"Yes, Mr Carmichael?"

"How long have we known each other?"

"Since we met at my Horse Chestnut tree," I said. "Nearly three months."

"Three months, and in that time, we have shared a plethora of adventures."

"We have," I agreed. "And I have been wet and cold in each one."

"Wet, cold and miserable." Mr Carmichael said.

I pondered his words for a while. "No," I said. "No, Mr Carmichael. I was never miserable in your company."

"You have no idea how happy your words make me." Mr Carmichael said. "They make my next request very much easier."

"What is that, pray?" There was something very sensual in thus standing unclothed talking to a man, with nothing between us except a thin screen. No, I will qualify that statement. There was something very sensual in thus standing unclothed talking to *Mr Carmichael* with nothing between us except a thin screen. I would not have acted in a like manner with any other man. The very thought makes me shudder with horror, even now.

"I would wish to address you by your Christian name," Mr Carmichael said.

I sighed, although I was unsure if it was with relief or disappointment. 'My Christian name is Robyn," I told him.

"I know. And I am Adam," Mr Carmichael said. "I trust the idea is not objectionable to you, Miss Moffat?"

"It is not," I said.

I began to dress again, listening as Mr Carmichael did the same and wondering how he looked without his clothes. The idea shocked me at first, and then fascinated and finally amused as I wondered anew what Adam would do if I pushed down the screen and smiled to him. The thought made me laugh out loud, so Adam enquired what amused me.

"It was a foolish fancy," I said. "Nothing more. If you ever forget my name, you can read it on your boat, except I spell mine with a Y."

"I named her after you," Adam said. "I will alter the spelling tomorrow."

"Thank you," I felt very humble. "I am honoured."

"If you don't like it, I can call her something else," Adam said.

"Please don't." I said. I started and backed away as Adam placed more coal on the fire.

"Are you decent?" Adam asked.

"Yes." I paused, looking down at myself. Wearing clothes that must have belonged to a maid, I was not elegant, but I was respectable.

"I shall take the screen away," Adam said.

I waited as Adam folded back the screen. Wearing a pair of light fawn trousers and a neat weskit, he smiled across to me.

"I still think you suit a top hat," he said. "Although you enhance anything you wear, Robyn."

"Thank you, kind sir," I dropped in a curtsey.

We looked at each other for what seemed a long time before Adam spoke. "You will eat something before I take you home."

I nodded. "Thank you. Bread and cheese?"

"Cook will find something better than that." Adam seemed reluctant to leave the room. "I trust that you are drier and warmer now?"

"I am, thank you," I said and smiled. "I seem to have a lot to thank you for." I studied Adam as if I had never seen him before.

"You do not need to thank me for anything," Adam opened the door for me. "Come on, Robyn, I'd better get you home."

"Yes," I said, although I had no desire to go home. I wanted to stay there, in that room, and look at Adam.

* * *

I have no recollection what we ate that morning, only that it was excellent and I had a ravenous appetite that pleased Adam's cook.

"I do like to see a woman with a healthy appetite," she approved. "Too many young women nowadays starve themselves to get a wasp-like waist." She shook her head. "What's the point in that, Miss Moffat? I ask you, what's the point in that?"

"I do not know," I said, trying to avoid Adam's eye lest I burst into laughter.

"Exactly so," Cook took my ignorance as support. "Wasps are nasty, stinging things that I swat in the kitchen. Who wants to look like a wasp?"

"Why nobody, to be sure," I cried.

"Exactly so," Cook said again. "Mark me, Miss Moffat; wasps get swatted in my kitchen. Every time. Swatted." She bustled away, a happy buxom woman, the undisputed queen of her domain.

"Mark her, Robyn," Adam repeated softly, "wasps get swatted in her kitchen."

"Every time. I will never be a wasp in her kitchen, Adam," I promised, "and I don't think you should be, either."

"I will try to remember that," Adam said, solemnly.

We left that happy house, with Adam driving the closed carriage and me beside him on the driver's seat. After the adventures of the previous evening, I was tired yet glad to have a pleasant ride through the early winter countryside, with frost sparkling across the fields and the ridge of the Pentlands sharp against the sky.

"I am sorry you did not get to the concert," Adam said as we rolled along the Dalkeith road.

"I am not," I told him. "But I hope that nobody recognised us last night."

"If Andrew had recognised you," Adam said, "he'd have shouted your name, and I was in heavy disguise, hiding behind a yellow mask. Nobody will suspect a respectable ship owner of such blackguard behaviour."

"They might know the coach," I pointed out.

"A dark coach on a dull evening?" Adam shook his head. "There must be fifty such coaches in the area."

I nodded, reassured by Adam's logic. "Adam," I said. "That was you who held up the prison coach, wasn't it?"

Adam flicked the reins as we negotiated the bridge over the Gore Water. "Yes," he said. "That was me."

"You could be hanged for that," I said.

"Only if somebody tells the authorities," Adam said. "Matthew can't do that and you won't."

"You chanced the hangman's noose to help somebody you don't like?" I looked at Adam in wonder.

"I believe I have already told you," Adam said patiently. "I helped him because he was a friend of yours."

I was silent after that, although my mind was churning with a thousand different thoughts. Twice I looked sideways at Adam, and three times I caught him glancing at me. Only when we neared Winter Lodge did we speak again, and a strange shyness had come over us, so we acted like strangers. The bond we had formed the previous night had slackened and I, for one, was sorry for it.

Mother was waiting at the gate, smiling as we arrived. "I'm glad to see you both safe." She looked at me as if to ensure that Adam had not taken any liberties with my person. "You left in a red dress and travelled in a gig and returned wearing blue in a carriage. How strange."

"It was an interesting night, Mother," I said as I climbed the stairs to enter the house.

Then Mother asked the question I had been dreading. "How did you enjoy the concert?"

When Adam answered for us both, my respect for him deepened. "We did not attend the concert, Mrs Moffat."

"Oh?" Mother sounded surprised. She looked at me in sudden alarm.

"No, I took Robyn out in a boat instead." Adam told the truth while leaving out the motive.

"Oh," Mother put a hand to her breast. "That would be nice. Was it nice, Robyn?"

"It was exciting," I said. "Adam's boat is named *Robin*. Is that not a coincidence?"

"Yes, indeed, another strange thing." Ushering us into the drawing-room, Mother rang for some tea while she chattered away about inconsequential household matters. She sat primly on her seat, faced me and said: "And you call each other by your first names now?"

"Yes," I said. "We decided we had known each other long enough."

"That is very informal after only a few weeks," Mother said. "I still call your father, Moffat after 25 years." She shook her head. "You youngsters are changing everything, miners forming combinations, young women calling men by their Christian names, steam trains and strange fashions. Whatever next?"

I waited for Adam to reply, hoping he would make some formal declaration of the feelings I knew he had for me. He remained stubbornly, frustratingly silent on that matter. I glanced at him, trying to convey my desires through my eyes. It did not work.

"You look tired," Robyn' Mother said at last. "I think you need to lie down for a while."

I agreed. After the emotional and physical excitement of the previous evening, waves of tiredness were crashing over me like a Firth of Forth tide. In fact, I could barely keep myself awake. With a brief curtsey to Adam, I withdrew to the welcome sanctuary of my bed, which seemed to sway and surge. The last thing I heard before sleep claimed me was Adam speaking to Father.

"There was no kindness involved, Moffat. It was my duty to the daughter of a friend and business colleague, nothing more," Adam said, and my heart plunged to depths I could not imagine.

My duty. The words seemed to plunge into my heart. After all that we had shared, did I only mean a duty to Adam? After our adventures in Leith Docks, at Balantrodoch and on the Firth of Forth, was I still only a duty? I shook my head in disbelief. No, no, I did not believe that!

No. I told myself. Everything would turn out well. Adam would return the next day to declare his love. I was sure of it. *Please, God, don't let me lose Adam now. Please God, let him return to my side, let him declare his love for me, so that I can declare mine for him. Please, God, let us become man and wife.*

With that thought, I turned over in bed and composed myself to a sleep that was long in coming.

Chapter Twenty

My horse chestnut tree was bare of leaves now, stark and sorrowful as it spread its branches across the slope of Roman Camp Hill. I stood beneath its friendly shadow, looking over the dark Midlothian plain towards the Pentland Ridge and wondered what had happened to my life.

After glimmers of promise, I had found only failure. I had hunted for a husband and found none. I had tested and enquired after every eligible man I knew, and those whom I had not discarded had caught somebody else or had spurned me. I was wounded, unwanted and lost. While Andrew had proved vastly unsuitable, Amy had captured Mr Pringle before I had the opportunity to know him. Mr Beaton was a decent man for whom I could not muster even a spark of love and Matthew, for whom I had entertained high hopes, was a man obsessed with his cause. That had left Adam Carmichael.

Adam. I thought of him: Adam of the humorous eyes that concealed a man of iron and steel. Adam with the resourcefulness to sail a boat well, drive a carriage badly and produce fire on a wet day. Adam, who had helped me, clothed me, fed me and laughed with me, and finally Adam who had vanished from my life, leaving a gaping void filled only by pain and desperate loneliness. I must have written him a score of unanswered letters before I realised I was only causing myself more grief, for the ink on the final notes was smeared with my tears. After writing frantically to both his addresses without response, I had stopped writing, put away my pen and ink and vowed to think of him no more. It was a foolish vow to make, and one I had little chance of fulfilling. I thought of that laughing, terrible man every day of my life.

I sighed deeply, for I retained a great affection for Adam, although I had not seen him since we had shipped Matthew away to America. Every day since then, I had waited, hopefully, for him or a message from him, and every day I had been disappointed. Every day I awaited the arrival of the postman with a letter, even the very shortest of notes, and every day I swallowed my hopes, fought my tears and pretended not to care. My dreams had gradually faded away as I remembered Adam's words about duty once more. That was all I had been to him – his duty compelled him to help me. I was a fool to think anything else.

Duty – that awful word that meant so much to a man. I sighed again before I realised there was somebody else at my tree.

"Miss Moffat." I had not heard Wild Will arrive, although I could see his footsteps in the thin layer of snow that covered the ground.

"Will," I said. I did not curtsey, and he did not bow or touch his forehead. Wild Will did not believe in formal conventions of that sort. If he liked you, Will would speak; if he did not like you, he would not. As in Robert Burns's poem, to Will, the rank was but a guinea stamp and the man – or woman – was the man for a' that.

"You look unhappy." Will was chewing a length of birch bark.

"A little," I agreed.

"Aye." Will lapsed into silence for a while. "Is he worth it?"

"Is who worth what?"

An owl called to our left, the sound eerie in the half-light. Its mate answered a moment later. Will nodded as if he agreed with the owl's sentiments.

"That's a mating pair," Will said. "Is your man worth being unhappy over?" Will did not face me as he spoke but stared over the slowly lightening countryside.

"I don't have a man," I said.

Will's chuckle was surprising. "Yes, you have," he said. "That fellow who helped you push the coach and took Mattie Juner to safety."

"You mean Adam Carmichael." I shook my head. *How the devil did Wild Will know about Adam's participation in the rescue?*

"Is that his name? When you were in the snow, he looked at you like a man looks at his wife." Will touched my shoulder. "You should not let him escape."

"I have not seen him for weeks." I said.

"He's thinking about you," Will said. "Don't despair."

"What makes you say that?" I asked, but Will was already gone, leaving nothing except footprints on the ground.

* * *

He's thinking about you. Don't despair. Will's words resonated inside my mind as I slowly returned down the hill. *He's thinking about you.* Well if he is, I told myself, he's got a queer way of showing it.

Thinking about Adam, I had worked myself into a foul temper before I got home. I snarled at Sims, threatened to slap poor Agnes for no reason and would have kicked the dog if we possessed such an animal.

"Good morning, Robyn." Mother greeted me with a thoughtful smile. "How are you this morning?"

"I am well, thank you, Mother," I responded sharply as I glared at the table.

"I'm glad to hear it." Mother said. "If you act like this when you are well, what would you do if you were unwell? Start a war, or burn the house down, I wouldn't wonder. You may apologise to Sims and poor Agnes as soon as you like."

I grunted in a most unladylike manner, slumped down on my chair, grabbed a slice of toast, dropped it and said a very indelicate word when it landed butter-side down on the floor.

"Ladies don't use that language," Mother said, with more concern than anger in her eyes.

"Now here's a thing." Father ignored our bickering when he spoke from behind his newspaper. "Do you remember that fellow Matthew Juner?"

"I remember him." Mother's look at me was full of meaning.

"He's turned up in America, of all places," Father said. "He's organising funds for his combination from over there."

"Well I never did," Mother said, shaking her head. "Whatever next."

I kept my silence, looking down at my plate in the manner Hugh Beaton had taught me. A hundred emotions coursed through my body as I remembered that eventful evening on the Forth and the false hopes and dreams I had harboured. *He's thinking about you. Don't despair.* Too late, Will; it's too late.

"The house will have a visitor today, Mrs Moffat." Father was unusually talkative this morning.

"Who would that be?" Mother asked.

"Carmichael," Father said. "We have some minor business matters to iron out. When he arrives, have Sims show him right up to my study."

"Yes, Moffat." Mother munched her toast in seeming unconcern, although her gaze was entirely on me.

"It's only business, Mrs Moffat." Father lowered his newspaper half an inch to emphasise his words. "There is nothing to interest you, so you can spare yourself the trouble of listening in the library. That goes for you, too, Robyn."

Mother snorted in indignation. "The idea! As if I had nothing better to do than listen to you."

I tried not to look agitated as I thought of Adam coming to Winter Lodge. I felt a sudden rush of nausea so I could not face even a single bite of toast. Why did he have to return? Could he not allow my pain to dissipate without arriving to waken it again?

"What are you doing today, Robyn?" Mother asked.

"I think I'd like to go for a walk," I said, controlling my voice to hide the renewed hurt.

"Don't stray far," Mother said. "You've already been up to your tree. You'll tire yourself out."

"I'll stay in the grounds," I said, suddenly desperate to walk outside.

Unable to finish my breakfast for thinking about Adam, I dragged on my now sadly battered winter coat and fled outside. I did not wish to meet Adam again, yet I knew my life was incomplete unless his eyes fixed on me, gently mocking yet always watchful. In that state of perplexity, I wandered around our policies, returning the greeting of the gardener with a quick "good morning" and strode away without intention or direction.

Busy after rain, the Winter Burn ran noisily in its bed, with the new growth of spring budding on trees, and the snowdrops already dying back. I picked one of the last survivors, held the tiny white flower to my breast and stifled the tear that prickled my eyes.

He's thinking about you. Don't despair.

After a while, five minutes or five hours, I could not tell which, I heard the slow drumbeat of hooves, hid behind a beech and watched Adam arrive astride Chetak. He looked more weather-beaten than ever, as if he had returned from a long journey rather than merely working in a shipping office in Leith. Straight as Ivanhoe's lance, Mr Carmichael dismounted effortlessly, tossed Chetak's reins to our ever-eager stable lad, and ran light-footed up our front stairs two at a time. I watched as he knocked at the door and swept past Sims with a cheery nod.

"Morning, Sims! I know the way!"

Yes, I said to myself, unable to keep the bitterness from my voice. *Yes, Mr Carmichael, go and do your duty with Father. I am sure the two of you will be very happy together.*

Unable to bear any more, I turned on my heel and walked away, trying to use physical activity to ease the pain in my heart. With no thought as to direction, I strode along unseen paths and found myself at the folly overlooking the Trout Pool. "This is where I hid Matthew," I said, remembering the morning when I had come across him bathing. Even that secret memory could not lift my mood in the slightest.

"And this is where you hid from Adam Carmichael." Wild Will had appeared again, frowning at me from under his shaggy eyebrows.

What the devil are you doing here?

"I'm not hiding, Will!"

"What are you doing, if not hiding?"

I glowered back at Will, angry that he understood me so well.

"Go back home and face yourself," Will said in his rough, quiet voice. "If it's bad news or good news, you will still be yourself afterwards. Nature will always welcome you, even if people let you down."

I wondered what heartache had first driven Will away from human company, or if he had always preferred nature. Even although I knew he was correct, and I was foolish to hide from Adam, I did not find the decision easy. I dithered for a good 15 minutes, peering down the banking to the deep waters of the Trout Pool before I had collected sufficient courage to make a move.

He's thinking about you. Don't despair. Will's words remained, although Will was no longer present. I looked one last time at the Trout Pool and its dark temptation. *Don't despair.*

I took a deep breath and turned away. I had to face reality, whatever it was. Leaving the folly, I made my slow way back to the house, fighting the inclination to turn and run, telling myself I was no coward. I was Robyn Moffat, descended from the ancient Templars, bred from local blood for many centuries. However, even that knowledge did not ease the ache in my heart.

"Where have you been?" Mother ran towards me from the front door. "We've been looking all over for you!"

"Why?" I saw two of the servants hurrying towards me, relief mingled with agitation on their faces.

"Your father wants to speak to you." Mother clutched my sleeve as if I had returned from the dead, rather than walked from my folly.

Honestly, that was the last thing I expected to hear. "Father? Why?"

"I'm sure I don't know," Mother said. "Hurry along now and don't keep him waiting any longer." Mother emphasised her words by a little slap on my arm.

Lifting the hem of my skirt, I hurried into the house, where Sims was in the hall seemingly unruffled by my previous display of bad temper. "Your father requires your presence, Miss Moffat."

"Thank you, Sims. Where is Father, please?"

"Your father is in the withdrawing room, Miss Moffat." Sims was the only person I knew who gave the drawing room its full title.

"Thank you, Sims." Composing myself with a deep breath, I handed my coat to Sims, patted my hair in place, checked the bottom of my dress for mud and pushed open the door, wondering what sort of reception awaited me. I heard Mother patter in behind me, shutting the door so I could not escape.

Father stood with his back to the fire, holding his coat-tails up so he could toast his nether portions. He looked at me without even the vestige of a smile. "Now then, my lady, what's this I've been hearing about you?"

I knew it would be trouble. Adam Carmichael stood a few feet from Father with a frown on his tanned face and his hands behind his back. I avoided looking at him, although my heart raced and the blood rushed to my face. "I don't know what you've heard, Father."

"Don't you, indeed? I've heard you've been up to all sorts of mischief." Father did not move from his spot, and I hoped a red-hot spark from the fire would land on the most prominent part of his trousers.

I lifted my chin, saying nothing. *What the devil had Adam Carmichael told Father? I suppose it was his duty to preach on me. Duty! Damn the man and damn his duty!*

"I've heard about you hiding runaways from the police, going out on the Forth in a small boat and building fires in old churches." Father recited a small catalogue of my sins. "Do you know what you need, lady?"

"No," I replied shortly, as the colour in my face altered from beetroot to scarlet. I could feel my legs trembling and was thankful that my long skirt concealed my reaction from these men.

"You need a damned good man to look after," Father continued.

I felt my heartbeat increase again. "Do I indeed?"

"You do, indeed, Robyn." Father's tone was gentle now. "And I have just the man for you."

"What?" I could hardly believe what I saw as Adam took a step forward and dropped to one knee.

"What?" I felt the tears well up once more, if for an entirely different reason. I believed I was going to faint.

"Miss Moffat. Robyn," Adam looked up without a trace of humour in his eyes. "I have spoken to your father, and he gave me his permission to ask for your hand in marriage."

I stared at him, so overcome with emotion that I was unable to utter a single syllable.

"Well, say something!" Mother urged from behind me.

"Oh, I almost forgot this." Reaching into his inside pocket, Adam produced a small box. "It's a ring," he said helpfully.

I started as I saw the name on the box, written in gold *Mellerio dits Meller*, "That's a French company." I brushed away a tear as I struggled for words.

"They're in Paris." Mother could not help herself. "Mr Carmichael sailed over there especially to have the ring made for you. Well, Robyn! Answer the man!"

"Oh, my Lord." My hands trembled as I opened the box. The ring sat serenely on a bed of red silk. With a delicate gold shank, it was heart-shaped and comprised a single ruby surrounded by sapphires. I stared at it, unable to believe that this was happening to me. "Oh, Adam." I recalled fantasising about such a ring in Balantrodoch church the day of the hunt. "You remembered, but it's too much. You've gone to too much trouble." I no longer tried to hide the tears that ran down the length of my nose and dripped on to the floor.

"Do you like it?" Adam sounded worried as if he thought I might hand it back.

"Yes. Yes," I said. "Oh, yes."

"Well?" I could hear the laughter lingering behind the rasp Mother put in her voice. "Are you going to answer the man or leave him on his knees all day?"

"Answer him?" I stared at my ring. "You've been to Paris? For me?"

"Yes," Adam said as matter-of-fact as if he had walked to Newtonloan Toll.

"That's where you've been," I said. "That's why you didn't come to see me or answer my letters."

"I'll answer them tonight," Adam promised. "I found them in Esk House."

"I sent more to your Edinburgh house." I spoke quietly, still mesmerised by all that was happening to me.

"Robyn," Mother reminded me quietly, "poor Mr Carmichael's still on his knees."

"Yes." I said softly.

"Yes?"

"Yes, I will marry you." I helped Adam to his feet, smiling.

"Good. That's settled then." Father stepped away from the fire. "About time too – anybody could see the two of you were right for each other. A lot of damn fuss about nothing."

"It's hardly nothing, Moffat!" Mother said.

"It is nothing. The two of them should just elope and have done with all this proposing and kneeling nonsense. A blind man with one eye can see they belong together."

"That's not very romantic, Moffat!"

"Come on." Taking Adam by the hand, I led him out of the room. "We'll let those two bicker in peace. They know what they're doing."

We walked away, hand in hand as the servants smiled at us, either openly or behind shielding hands. I led Adam out of the front door and into the grounds, where the first of the daffodils poked their heads out to welcome the oncoming spring.

"You looked nervous when you knelt," I said. "I've never seen you nervous before."

Adam squeezed my hand. "I was not sure you would say yes," he said. "For there have been times that I suspected that you positively disliked me."

I thought for a few more steps, with my feet crunching delightfully on the gravel. "No," I said. "I have never disliked you." I decided to tell the truth. "I did doubt you from time to time when I heard you tell Father that it was your duty to help me." I awaited his response.

"It was my duty." Adam said. "It was also my pleasure, but I was not yet ready to tell your father that. Yes, it's our Christian duty to help those in need," Adam said, "but I would help you, duty or not."

"Thank you," I said. "I wish you had told me that sooner."

"Didn't you understand, you little muffin?" Mr Carmichael shook his head. "I'd do anything for you; rob a bank, send a guilty man abroad, commit regicide, anything."

"Why?" I asked. Although I already guessed the answer, I wanted to hear it for myself.

"Because I love you." My Mr Carmichael said, simply.

"Oh." I looked at him, remembering the kindness with which he had always treated me, and how I had often abused his friendship. "Oh," I repeated. Not every marriage is based on love, and I wanted that simple reassurance.

"I knew you didn't love me," Mr Carmichael said. "Indeed, I thought you didn't even like me a lot of the time, but that did not alter my feelings for you."

"Oh, but I've always liked you," I said, realising a truth that I had striven to hide from myself these past months. "I have liked you since we first met at my tree."

It was Mr Carmichael's turn to look surprised. "You liked me even then?"

"Yes, I've always liked you," I said, looked away and sighed. "No," I said, as I was honest with myself for the first time. "I don't like you. I love you. Even back then I did. I think that is why I did not care when I sent Andrew away."

We were silent for a moment as found I was quite comfortable with being in love with Mr Carmichael.

"You are a muffin," Adam said. "I was ready to propose to you the instant I saw you walking up the hill towards me." Taking off his tall hat, he placed it on my head, then promptly knocked it off as he took me in his arms for the soundest kiss I had ever known.

* * *

I stood once more at the Church at Balantrodoch, where I had sheltered that day of the wet hunt. I remembered Father's words:

"When you eventually choose your man," he had said, *"remember what happened in the old church at Balantrodoch. According to the legends, the old spirits guide their descendants."*

Father had been correct. The old spirits did guide me, but not only with the words of the men I had not seen. They had pointed my way with the natural creatures of the countryside, with the robin that was my name and the heron that was the bird on Adam Carmichael's crest. Now I was back at Balantrodoch, and the church was once again being used for its proper purpose. My heart was hammering until I was sure it would burst from my breast and proclaim my joy to the world.

"Are you certain now?" Father was frowning to hide his affection. "It's not too late to change your mind."

"I'm certain," I said.

"Aye," Father said. "I see that you are. Let's not keep these good people waiting."

When I took his arm, he squeezed my hand with his elbow and stepped into the ruins of my church.

Adam was waiting for me as Father escorted me up the aisle to the altar. I walked as in a dream, nearly unable to separate reality from a fairy tale. I seemed to be looking down on myself from above, as if I were not really there, as though it were somebody else making this momentous, fabulous journey. I could not believe life could be so perfect, yet here I was, and my future stood waiting for me, tall, weather-battered and all my own.

Although I had invited Andrew, I had not expected him to attend, and he had made his excuses and remained away. I did not miss him. Hugh Beaton, however, was present. Round-shouldered but still half-a-head taller than anybody else there, he managed a quiet nod before returning his gaze to his feet. Amy gave me a big smile and waved her fingers while managing to cling to Derek Pringle. She mouthed, "Well done," to me as I passed her. I smiled back and walked on with my feet clicking on the worn slabs. Mother was at the front of the congregation, trying not to cry. I wanted to hug her. I wanted to thank her for 22 years of unrelenting love but settled for a smile and a tear instead. She would understand – Mother always understood.

And then we reached the makeshift altar where Adam and the minister waited; I saw Wild Will's face at the glassless window. He remained outside the church, where he was at home, and I knew he would always be welcome in our house or our grounds, at any time of year, day or night. He nodded, once, and was gone, until the next time we needed each other.

I stood beside Adam, heard the minister's words and made the correct responses, trying to be audible and knowing that every single person in the congregation, even Amy, wished us well. I was part of an "us" now, or would be very soon; that fact only struck me during the ceremony. Never again would I be alone, unless by choice.

When it was Adam's turn to speak, his voice boomed out as though he was roaring orders to the maintopmast. Nobody who attended this wedding would be in any doubt that Adam was my husband, now and for always.

"I do!" Adam said, and we had completed the contract. I was married, Adam was married, we were married.

When the minister said the final words and Adam took me gently in his arms to administer our second-ever kiss and our first as a married couple, I sensed movement beyond the gathered congregation. It was only a shifting shadow against the brilliant colours of the dresses and sombre hues of the men, yet I immediately knew what it was. The old Templar knights were watching over one of their descendants, and everything would be all right. When Adam released me, I looked towards the corner of the church. There was nothing to be seen, yet I knew somebody was there.

"Robyn?" Adam had noticed my glance.

"It's our church," I said.

"Always, you muffin."

We did not leave Balantrodoch until the last of the guests had filed out to the marquees outside to enjoy Father's hospitality. Or eat him out of house and home, as he put it.

Looking around the empty church, I placed Adam's hat on my head, smiled, threw some bread crumbs on to the slabs, and walked away, leaving the heron and the robin side by side under the fragment of roof and the ghosts to their eternal vigil. My hunt was complete, and we had our lives to live.

Historical Note

Although this book is fiction, much of the history is based on fact. 1842 was a disturbed year throughout Great Britain with the miners' strike causing consternation and Chartists demonstrating for increased suffrage.

The collier's meeting in Dalkeith was much as described in the book. Roman Camp Hill still squats above the one-time mining villages of Midlothian, although the Buccleuch Hunt no longer persecutes foxes. Balantrodoch Church, more commonly called Temple Church, is perhaps better known now than it was in Robyn's time, while the ghosts of the old Knights Templar may well linger among the ancient stones.

Helen Susan Swift

Dear reader,

We hope you enjoyed reading *To Hunt A Husband*. Please take a moment to leave a review, even if it's a short one. Your opinion is important to us.

Discover more books by Helen Susan Swift at https://www.nextchapter.pub/authors/helen-susan-swift

Want to know when one of our books is free or discounted? Join the newsletter at http://eepurl.com/bqqB3H

Best regards,

Helen Susan Swift and the Next Chapter Team

Lightning Source UK Ltd.
Milton Keynes UK
UKHW012028300720
367452UK00005BA/168